Charlotte Grimshaw was born in New Zealand and currently lives in Auckland with her husband and two children. After graduating from Auckland University she practised as a shipping lawyer and then as a criminal lawyer, working for the defence in criminal trials, before leaving the law to write full time. *Guilt* is her second novel. Her first novel, *Provocation*, is also published by Abacus.

Guilt

Charlotte Grimshaw

An *Abacus* Book

First published in Great Britain in 2000 by Abacus

The author gratefully acknowledges
the assistance provided by Creative New Zealand.

A CIP catalogue record for this book
is available from the British Library.

ISBN 0 349 11196 0

Typeset in Erhardt by M Rules
Printed and bound in Great Britain by
Clays Ltd, St Ives plc

Abacus
A Division of
Little, Brown and Company (UK)
Brettenham House
Lancaster Place
London WC2E 7EN

For Louis

1.

1987

'Smoke?'

Maria tried giving up cigarettes all the time, she sometimes went without for weeks or days at a stretch. But after a long spell of non-smoking, of prohibition, early in the evening say, outside the dairy after the empty day, after the rain and the cold and the long walk home, after the purchase of newspaper and tin of soup and loaf of bread the old urge would come back, sending her back to the shop, digging in her wallet for dollars, hurrying out again with the packet to walk the last yards home, contentedly, because there could be nuclear war tomorrow (nucular, people would say, with earnest stupidity), and anyway you could get hit by a bus, and cigarettes were a luxury, bad for you, expensive, crisply packaged, and life seemed badly packaged sometimes, so darkly sodden and brown. Cigarettes are an old friend, she thought, whom nobody likes and nobody approves of, one day you make a stand, you give them up for good, for health, for life! But after a while . . . It's no good.

She walked with her shopping under the dripping trees, through the winter dark of the garden streets, while beside her the cars crawled slowly in their lanes over the reflections in the slicked black road. Arguing it out in her mind, idly. You can't give up a friend out of fear for your life. That would be weak, it would be low. Make friends with cigarettes and you'll love them for ever . . . By the time she reached the gate she would have unwrapped the packet and luxuriously smoked one as she walked, wet faced, facing into the drifting rain.

Now she rolled over on the bed and peered at Leon, whose head was obscured as usual by clouds of smoke, the red point of the cigarette glowing as he dragged without taking it out of his mouth. He wore a tight red and blue jersey, striped. Dark blue trousers, buckled black boots, a black belt, with studs. His hair was spiky, brittle blond, his ears were decorated with rings and studs. A metal band on the tip of one ear was connected by a fine silver chain with a stud in the lobe. His hair was cut short at the back, longer at the front.

He gave her his typical look through the smoke, mouth turned up one side in a dangerous smile, eyes full of cynical humour, dark shadows under the eyes, a powerful look. His nose was long and patrician, his mouth was small and neat. Taken all at once he was handsome, tall (six feet three), graceful in his movements, and (evidence in the eyes, in the lines of the power-packed smile) anarchic, criminal, wild and unreliable. Make friends with Leon and you needed to smoke. You were reaching for one sooner or later, for your nerves.

'Smoke?' Leon said. He was stripping the bed. Briskly, 'I'm taking this.'

'How are you going to do that?'

The minibar lay open, ransacked. She sat up and extracted a miniature of gin, rummaged, found no corresponding little bottle of tonic, found Coca-Cola, mixed herself a gin and Coke, stirring it with her finger.

'That's disgusting.' He laughed and coughed. She sipped, made a face, gargled, laughed too and tipped it into a plant pot.

'Fuckingis.'

Leon gathered up the huge double duvet and rolled it into a sausage. The bed was wide, puffed, stuffed, bigger than king-sized. The duvet was crisp and laundered and new, patterned in grey, pink and white, the corporate colours of hotel, law firm, bank.

Leon pushed a white towelling bathrobe, also rolled up, into the middle of the sausage, then, working efficiently with his capable hands, he tied the whole thing up with the belt of the robe.

'Very discreet.' Maria watched, amused on the bed, smoking.

He hoisted the bundle on his back and went to the window. 'Not here,' he whispered. 'Round the side of the building.' He opened the door and peered out into the plush silence of the hotel corridor.

'Whoops,' he said, ducking neatly in again. He turned around and looked at her through the smoke, widening his eyes, one tooth slightly crooked and resting on his lower lip, his face lit up with the usual savage comedy. He flared his nostrils and hissed at her, 'Security.'

Flattening himself against the door. Bent double under the huge bundle on his back. That Leon. Why does he do it, why is he driven so? She got up off the bed and tiptoed over to stand beside him at the door as he reeled around under his bulging knapsack. That Leon. She pushed the bundle away from her face. Why must he always steal the biggest thing in the room? Leon down at Central Police, at the counter grille, checking in unexpectedly, some item of furniture or weighty appliance having been forcibly extracted from about his person and now defying the attempts of the sergeant to insert it into a plastic evidence bag . . . 'It was there, Officer,' he would say, surreptitiously stuffing cigarettes and lighter into his socks for the long wait in the cells, the big cops crowding around him, half hostile, half entertained. 'Just because it was there.'

Maria elbowed him out of the way and tried to listen through the door. No sound in the padded corridor. Somewhere out there the Samoan security guards munched and prowled, lounging weightily in the stairwells and halls, dawdling good-humouredly among the fairy-lit trees in the foyer – those churchy, muscular patriarchs, they looked as if they could take your limp little white hand in theirs, and crush your fingers into soup.

An altercation was taking place out in the street. There were voices raised, a woman arguing, then the sound of smashing glass. Leon turned quickly with his load, knocking Maria over, she fell over the end of the bed and clambered up again. Snorting with laughter and pushing one another they fumbled over to the window and looked down on to the forecourt at the front of the hotel.

A taxi driver had emerged from his cab to have it out with a fare. The woman was arguing loudly, beginning to shout, while the cab driver stood stiffly, answering inaudibly and holding his arm in front of him as if to ward her off. The more she raged and swayed the more stiff and immobile he became.

'Pay you? *Pay* you?' she chanted and spat, poking her finger into his chest, 'I sh'ld call la *pleece*!'

The resolute cabbie spoke quietly, his arm still raised in front of him. The woman hesitated, staggered and swayed. 'On ler way? Las fugn *good* . . .' She began to grope around in her handbag.

At the window above, in the orange light from the streetlight with the shadow streams of raindrops running down his face, Leon raised an eyebrow and grinned jaggedly, like a Jack-o'-lantern.

Two bulky security guards were advancing now across the fore-court, taking their time, closing in. Going over on her high heels the woman began to wail brokenly, 'My purse . . . Been insulted, been robbed', scrabbling in her flapping handbag while they sauntered towards her, coldly taking her in. They stopped to confer with the taxi driver who had relaxed now, leaning against his car with his hands in his pockets watching her reel and curse and tip her hand-bag upside down, and shake it furiously.

Dragging her hands through her tangled hair the woman turned on them, pointing her finger and shrieking, 'Robbedmearrest-himfuckenrobber.' Spinning and lurching in her ruined dress while the men lounged against the taxi and watched with the practised indifference of three vets round a cow with the staggers.

Another guard ambled up and had a few words, handing round a packet of cigarettes. They weren't going near her, she'd scratch your eyes out, or throw up on your clothes. Calmly they chatted and waited for the police.

'Let's go,' Leon whispered. Together they gathered everything up, opened the door and slipped out into the corridor. The jaunty muzak tinkled over their heads, somewhere out of sight a door closed and they heard the electronic ping of the lift.

'Fire escape,' Leon commanded, leading the way. Maria followed, bent over with silent mirth now at the sight of him toiling along low to the wall under his load of stolen goods. Somehow he had forced a hotel towel into his pocket, and a large ashtray into his pants. Maria tasted sickly gin and Coke on her breath. She thought of the plundered minibar and wondered just how drunk she actually was. Drunk enough to go ahead of Leon, to check that the lift had arrived and gone again down to the lobby, to wave Leon on past the lifts, along another plush and silent corridor and into the carpeted shaft of the stairwell. Drunk enough to follow the details of Leon's cunning plan, those details being roughly as follows: he to lurk with large bundle at first-floor window of stairwell, she to descend to ground level, exit the building through the foyer and station herself in the bushes outside to watch. He to lower bundle down into bushes when coast appeared to be clear . . . At this point they collapsed together on the landing in another wave of hilarity. In answer to her earlier question Maria decided Very Drunk, and quite probably Off Her Face.

Now she stood fidgeting and shivering and fending sticks and twigs away from her face, in the bushes. She was across the road from the side of the building, wedged between two concrete tubs filled with large smelly cabbagey flowers. The road behind the hotel was deserted, the asphalt shone with puddles and the rain had thinned to a mist, drifting and blowing around the streetlights. Faintly, from the front of the building, she could hear the drunken woman shouting and crying and arguing with herself, and a sharp wind shivered the trees. No sound from inside.

Then a creak and a thump and the first-floor window opened, and Leon's head emerged. He hissed at her, looking around. She waved the all-clear and he began to bundle the folds of the huge quilt out on to the edge of the sill, lowering it down the side of the building. In the deep shadows between the tubs Maria watched and waited and fidgeted about, tense with hilarious fear.

With about eight feet of the quilt hanging down the wall they both heard voices. Leon stopped lowering and poked his head out of the window. Maria craned around to look, wincing as a sharp twig twanged into her ear.

Around the side of the building came two of the big security guards, walking close together, taking turns to talk into a mobile phone. Leon promptly disappeared inside the window. The two men stopped and talked for a moment and looked about them, one fiddling with the phone and the other lighting a cigarette, while some five feet above their heads the end of the duvet flapped and stirred thickly in the wind. Maria saw Leon's head emerge over the sill. He made a wild gesture at her with his free hand, struggling with the cumbersome folds of cloth, trying to pull the duvet up again. She was crouched low in the dank crevice, clenched fist in her mouth. Don't let go, she whispered. Don't look up!

The two men didn't look up. They began to move off slowly, talking in their deep voices. They walked around the side of the building again and disappeared towards the foyer.

Maria waved at the window. Leon heaved the whole lot over the ledge and into the hedge below. Then he disappeared. Bobbed up again and lobbed a smaller item after the big one. Disappeared again and re-emerged a minute later around the side of the building, having exited nonchalantly through the front entrance.

She fought her way out from between the tubs, stretching and rubbing her arms. After a lot of fumbling and difficulty involving the destruction of a section of the hedge, and a couple of false alarms which sent them off up the street feigning a casual night-time stroll, they extracted the goods, shouldered them up and made off through the whirling rain towards the suburbs, dying of laughter all the way.

They stopped at the all-night diner on Customs Street to inspect their spoils and smoke cigarettes and drink instant coffee out of Styrofoam cups. Leon's eyes were bloodshot, the circles under his eyes were darker than ever, faintly purple like bruises. They shared a sea dog with onion and a squirt of sickly mayonnaise. They leaned against one another and Maria felt all the alcohol they'd drunk swilling around with the onions and processed crab and mayonnaise, an enjoyable burning sensation in the pit of her stomach. There was a mirror behind them and they admired the sight of themselves in the harsh neon light.

'Look at me. Tragic. A wreck.' Maria took a hairbrush and a tube of lipstick out of her bag.

Leon leaned towards the mirror and rearranged his hair, the strands so glutinous with hair gel that he simply picked stray hairs up and bent them back into shape. He gave his characteristic grunt of amusement. 'I look better in the dark,' he observed elegantly, squinting into the glass.

Later they stood at her street corner saying goodbye. He had wound the duvet up tighter and tied it with his belt to walk her home. He had a couple of miles to walk to get back to his house across town. It was 3 a.m., the rain was heavier again now, no longer just mist, but big heavy drops.

'Let me take the quilt. Then it won't get wetter. You won't have to walk through town with it.'

He took it off and slung it over her shoulder. She bent over with the weight of it, staggered around reeling and laughing.

'Smoke?'

'Just give me a couple, for later.'

He put four cigarettes into her jacket pocket, then stood with his arm around her for a moment while they talked. Those security guards. Monsters. Two inches from their heads. Leon laughed and shifted around on his feet, never still, always swaying and fidgeting with his characteristic lurching grace.

Then they said goodbye again and she turned and walked off under the burden, under the pohutukawa trees lining the long dark road, and turned into her gate, number 10A Ashton Road.

She let herself into the silent house. Smelled old carpet in the hall. Groping her way into the kitchen, smelt damp and decay in the sink, old bread, old food. Old shoes in the sitting room, an old wallpaper smell, old paint, dried glue. In the bathroom, fresh smells. Fresh mould, fresh shit. The house was not really this bad, she told herself. During the day it was cheerful enough, liveable in, filled with busy life. But during the night, in the pitch darkness when there was nothing but the smells . . . During the night the house was reduced to the bare sum of its collected odours. Of damp, principally, and mould, and shit.

She washed her face and cleaned her teeth in the bathroom, then, feeling hungry, went to the kitchen and inspected the situation with regard to bread. There was none. A strong smell, but no bread. The same applied to bananas, peanut butter, milk and cheese. The overpowering scent of these comestibles filled the room, yet not a trace of any of them could be found in actual form in the dark nooks and recesses around the kitchen bench.

Maria found a dry tea bag and tiredly made a cup of black tea. She turned off the kitchen light and groped her way back to her bedroom. She turned on the light.

She knew immediately that someone had been in the room. Books had been moved. The television was turned to a different angle. The straight line of her pairs of shoes had been kicked into disarray. There was even a hollow in the bed where someone had sat.

And watched television. And idly picked up books, and tripped over her shoes on the way out. And – she bent down and examined her bedcover – dropped crumbs all over the bed.

Maria felt the hairs rise on top of her head. She went to the French windows and checked the latch. It was loosely locked. The little window over the bed was locked fast. Quickly she went out to the hallway and turned on the outside light. The French doors opened on to a small verandah level with the lawn, which was surrounded by a low, white wooden wall. The lawn was sodden out there, covered with little sticks and leaves blown from the trees. When she turned on the electric light she could see that the verandah was covered with muddy footprints. There was a long scrape of mud where a foot had skidded down the wall.

She turned back into the bedroom. On the floor under the table lay a white paper bag from the shop up the road, unmistakably marked with the muddy imprint of a boot.

Maria shivered and sat down on the bed. Her alarm clock ticked in the silence, the fridge whirred faintly in the kitchen. Water gurgled in the guttering and the wind rustled in the trees. Maria lay down on the bed fully clothed and closed her eyes.

'He's been here,' she whispered to herself, with infinite pleasure.

A mile away Leon stopped under a shop verandah to shelter from the bucketing rain. He buttoned his coat and pulled the collar up around his chin, hunching his shoulders, craning up at the sky. He could see the rain blown almost horizontal by the wind over the motorway bridge, and above the bridge the city lights had turned the clouds a sickly orange. The gutters ran with water, oily rainbows shone in the puddles. He looked up and down the empty street. Nothing but wooden shop fronts, plastic bread crates piled up outside the dairy, the morning papers tied up with plastic twine. Nothing but the desolate street in the pre-dawn rain, nothing but the rain and the wind and the regular squeak squeak of a hinge somewhere up above him in the rickety house above the shop.

While he leaned against the shop window and smoked a cigarette and waited for the rain to ease it got heavier. He waited longer and it got heavier still. Huge drops danced on the round lid of an oil drum marking roadworks across the street. He looked at his watch.

Just after four. He shoved his hands into his pockets and shouldered out into the downpour, moving in a slow jog across the motorway bridge and down the street towards Grafton Bridge.

Water began to trickle down the back of his neck. His face was drenched, drips ran into his eyes and he could smell hair gel and hairspray running out of his hair and into the side of his mouth.

Ahead of him the mass of trees hung over the road. He stopped to look at them, admiring the weird effect of the rainy light, the black cloud behind the trees and the leaves glowing a sullen underwater green, the branches waving in the wind as if they were underwater weed, as if the rain had flooded everything and he was walking along a trench at the bottom of a deep freshwater pond.

He turned on to the bridge and the cool drops blew in his face and he felt exhilarated by the water and the green and the loneliness of the wet dawn. He crossed Grafton Bridge, over the tangled bush in the gully down there and the orange lights lining the black lanes of the empty motorway.

He passed the hospital with its high windows and white walls and turned into Domain Drive, and now he felt as if he could walk for hours, roaming like an animal, breathing in the rain, swimming through the air. He ambled through the darkness under dripping trees, past the duck-pond spot-lit with red and green lights, over the pavements split by giant tree roots. It was getting lighter now, and the occasional car rushed past him on the road with a gust of air and a spray of muddy road water.

By the time he reached Seaview Road his exhilaration had faded and become a dreamy satisfying weariness. He was completely drenched and beginning to feel cold and his fingers were stiff and numb. He turned into the drive, feeling in his pocket for his keys. Today was Sunday, he thought with satisfaction. Suddenly he was looking forward to getting into bed.

He unlocked the door and walked in, detecting the scent of hair gel again, and hairspray, and the old ash of thousands of cigarettes. On the inside of the door was the large picture of a pig which he had spray-painted there in an idle moment a couple of months ago. The light was on in his bedroom.

Leon's room was painted in several shades of blue. Decorations hung about the walls and ceiling – chains, mirrors, telephone cords, photographs, a large wooden figure of a man painted by Leon. His studded belts hung around the mirror. There were patterns stencilled on the walls with spray paint, and telephones of many different shapes and sizes stuck to the walls.

By the side of the bed was his chest of drawers, painted pale blue, and on top of it his belongings scattered in chaotic disorder: cans of hairspray, pots of gel, cans of spray paint, felt pens, highlighters, ballpoint pens, telephone parts, a set of screwdrivers, wires, an anglepoise lamp, several overflowing ashtrays, packets of Rothmans cigarettes. One cordless phone, one dial phone, painted blue and red and yellow. One slim-line push-button phone bearing the sign, 'Porter'.

His clothes hung on a piece of wood strung on two chains and suspended from the ceiling. Underneath his boots and shoes, more telephones, and a number of large ornamental plants in silver pots. A television, painted pink and silver, rested on a black table at the end of the bed.

By the bed stood a stereo on the top of which the words were scribbled in glowing pen, 'I'm not involved and I know absolutely NOTHING'.

Leon took off his sodden clothes and headed for the shower. He stood in it for a long time enjoying the heat on his chilled body. Then he padded into the kitchen and looked around for something to eat. He made himself an omelette with a lot of onion and tomato, and toast and a pot of coffee, and a capful of vodka to go with the omelette. Then had a couple of cigarettes, and more toast, and the last of the vodka in the bottle.

He combed his hair in the heavily decorated mirror with its photos and chains and telephone cords. Photos of Leon in nightclubs. Photos of Leon on the ferry to Waiheke. Leon doing his hair on the beach, Leon holding up a dead fish he'd found on the sand. Leon and Maria on Rangitoto Island with a cask of wine, Maria about to fall into the sea. Maria with her mouth open, laughing, about to scream.

It was light outside now and the birds were beginning to sing. (Those fucking birds. He was always threatening to shoot the self-righteous tui that tootled and clucked outside his window every morning at 6 a.m.) He felt in his wet trousers for his wallet and keys and laid them on the blue chest of drawers. He took the hotel key out of his boot and hid it behind a piece of loose wallpaper above his bed.

Anything else to put away or hide? All in order, he thought, drawing the curtain on the watery dawn, and sank down into a vodka-warmed sleep, dreaming of swimming and telephones while the pompous tui puffed itself up on the branch outside in preparation for the morning chorus.

Leon slept peacefully among his things. His things that he carried home in the night. Telephones in particular, all models and makes, all shapes and sizes, the latest slinkiest and dinkiest models. Telephones most of all. He stole them and brought them home, tinkered with them, wired them up, unwired them. Often his room resembled a Telecom workshop or communications centre with all the wiring and cords and little switchboards spread over the floor and bed.

When he discovered a new model of phone he had to have it, and when he got it he brought it home and wired it up for himself. He painted his phones, drew on them, decorated them. He stuck mirrors on them, shells, glitter. He took parts off one model and stuck them on another to make monster and hybrid phones. He was an artist, a telephone artist, and he spent an inordinate amount of time thinking up ways to steal new models of this most favourite appliance.

While he was working on the theft of phones other items often caught his eye. Pot plants, for example. He favoured large corporate plants, rubber plants from hotel foyers, immense bushes and flowering shrubs from commercial shows and displays. In addition, anything else that he could find that was crisp, shiny, desirable, anything on offer in empty arcades, public buildings, carparks, lobbies and parks.

Leon was the nimble figure at 1 a.m., shadowy in the deep shadows around the band rotunda, patiently unscrewing the hanging basket with its colourful burst of pansies. He was the spry culprit behind the memorial greenhouses, abducting the cupids and carrying off the ornamental fish.

These prizes he carried home on foot through the dark and dripping suburban streets. Tall, gracefully lurching, cigarette in mouth, face set patiently to the task, ever ready to crash bodily through hedge or bush at the sign of approaching headlights or guard dogs or angry neighbours' strong-beam torch.

He carried his things home, not to sell, but to keep for himself, to stock his shelves and decorate his house. He painted some things and took some things apart and arranged them around himself, and his flat was an Aladdin's cave of stolen booty, to his intense and busy satisfaction.

And the hotel key, hidden now in the fold of wallpaper just above Leon's head? To go back. Leon and Maria drinking cocktails in the bar of the Hyatt Hotel. Leon throwing money on the bar (he always pays).

Many cocktails into the evening, lounging on the puffed and creaking hotel leather, observing that the reception desk is devoid of attendants, that the barman has disappeared out the back and that the foyer is largely empty, Leon takes it into his head to saunter over to the reception desk and slip into the area behind it. Surveying the rows of boxes and shelves his eye lights on a box labelled 'Emergency Porter', and in a moment he has opened the box and slipped the thin bronze key into his pocket.

When the staff return Leon is lounging as louche as a cat on his fat chair, smiling mildly, and tapping his fingers on the rim of his empty glass.

And imagine the amusement and delight of Leon and Maria when they discover that the innocuous looking little key is a skeleton, capable of opening every room in the hotel!

2.

A morning mist hung over the low brick walls and drenched lawns along Connick Street. The wooden houses stood at crooked angles in their scratched and peeling coats of paint, all odd shapes, odd sizes and colours, all configurations of lean-to and sun porch and glassed-in verandah. The warped fences and sagging hedges meandered along the house fronts; here and there a fence had collapsed and lay ruined on the pavement. A whole window with pane and frame intact lay abandoned on one of the grass verges. Long grass grew on the lawns and pushed through the paving stones of the concrete paths, everywhere there was a pungent smell of wet plants, wet onion grass and the sour smell of the milk-weed growing thickly over the corrugated iron fences and wooden garden sheds.

At number 365 a dead wheelbarrow lay on the lawn half covered by the weeds. On the front porch an old bathtub grandly rotted. Bottles stood in a row on the brick wall, the glass mottled and milky, bluish with mould. An old fringed bath-mat hung heavily on the rotary clothes-line, strung up with broken plastic pegs, the wire of the clothes-line sagging under its sodden weight. Wooden steps, once painted green, now bare wood with flecks of green paint sprinkled here and there, led up to the front door.

Number 365 was a large, dilapidated, wooden bungalow with big windows, wide hallways, high ceilings, and echoing draughty rooms. There were five bedrooms, all occupied by one or more shabby and transient tenant. There was a cavernous living room which lay on the south side of the house in the shade of a gigantic pohutukawa tree, a room so completely sheltered from sunlight that a green twilight sometimes at noon was the only alternative to the naked electric lightbulb which usually illuminated its clammy interior.

The large kitchen at the back of the house looked over the back garden, a sloping area fenced with corrugated iron, containing an old blackened garden incinerator and a jungle of towering weeds. The garden in turn backed on to a dank gully full of bush where nobody went except the cats and a couple of the tenants, who ventured down there occasionally to hide their drugs.

An ash-grey cat came creeping across the front lawn, climbed the steps and leapt on to the wall of the porch. Nosing along the wall it found the open window and slipped silently under the blind. All the curtains and blinds were tightly shut. The residents of Connick Street were asleep, it being seven o'clock in the morning, and a Sunday. All along the street the doors were locked and the cars were parked, windscreens blinded with mist and water. Occasionally deep inside a locked interior a door slammed or a lavatory flushed, up on the main road there was the odd drone of a car. But no one was about. The trees dripped in the foggy silence and the blades of grass on the dewy lawn were little daggers, made of glass.

Marcus Klein felt the cat land beside him and step daintily over his legs. He was used to being woken by it, by its pedestrian progress over his body. He had found it as a thin, ungainly, tottering kitten trapped inside an old tyre in the garden – it had probably been the runt of the litter and left for dead – and it had rejected the attentions of the other tenants and attached itself to Marcus. He had been charmed by its trust, and had put a saucer down for it in his room. He called it the Silken Annihilator. Under Marcus's care it had grown sleek, lithe, agile and silent.

Marcus leaned over to push the Annihilator off and felt fire run up his arm from his hand to his shoulder. The suddenness and sharpness of the pain, the unexpectedness of it, was terrifying. He fell back in the freezing sheets and, still fighting his way out of heavy sleep, thought at first that the cat must have attacked him.

He was hit with another searing wave of pain and managed to understand, through his bewilderment, that he must lie still and wait for the wave to pass. But the agony intensified, it throbbed and pulsed so extremely that a whimper of panic escaped him, and he felt his eyes fill with tears.

He shut them to calm his confusion, breathing in, breathing out and with the deep breaths he felt himself revolving sickeningly, his body falling dizzily away. He was nauseous and opened his eyes. Steady. He must not vomit. If he threw up the necessary movement, the convulsion, would kill him. He stared at the ceiling and lay rigidly still while the Annihilator prowled somewhere near the end of the bed and a slow painful minute went by. *No idea.* He had no idea what had happened. Something terrible had happened to his left arm, that much was clear. But what? When?

Flat on his back, frightened, shocked by the waves of pain, Marcus lay and waited for memory. He waited, quite confidently at first, for understanding to come to him. But the seconds went by and absolutely nothing came into his head. There was no memory. Last night was a black hole. There was nothing in his mind but pain and confusion and the terrible heat in his arm. And something else he was becoming aware of. His legs and body were freezing cold.

Now, as he lay and waited for the knowledge that so terrifyingly wouldn't come, he began to be afraid that the Annihilator would leap on him, as it often did, and knead his body insistently with its claws, wanting him to wake up, wanting attention and breakfast.

He listened, but the animal had stopped prowling and sniffing around, and gone sinisterly quiet. The thought of it leaping at him from an unexpected direction, his involuntary explosion of frightened movement and the volcano of pain which would ensue, was too much to contemplate and he began to move experimentally until he had managed to lever himself half upright and half push the quilt off his body.

He wiped his forehead with the back of his right hand, staring hard at the ceiling for a moment while a surge of heat shot up his left arm and concentrated itself boilingly around his left shoulder.

Inching forward, he got himself upright and lifted his arm away from the sheet. The arm felt heavy and alien, twice its normal size. Wincing, he bent his head, every movement causing him excruciating torture, and inspected the damage.

Around the thumb and forefinger of his left hand were four deep grey-white craters, each circle overlaid with a tight canopy of translucent skin, the bubbles of flesh bulging with fluid. The skin around the blisters was red and raw, and stiff, as if it would soon peel away. A trail of fiery skin ran up his forearm past his elbow to his upper inside arm, where a sprinkling of similarly agonising blisters blazed a path into the scorched wasteland of his armpit. He leaned down and sniffed. That smell, you couldn't mistake it. Burnt hair.

He heaved a tearful and frightened sigh. The room smelt bad. The air was bad. Burnt wool, old hangovers, old socks, the smell of damp carpet. Last night's smells, after all that hard living, the farts of someone very old or dying, someone disgustingly unwell. He leaned his head against the wall, surveying the room without moving, eyes swivelling dimly in his head. Burnt hair . . . Jesus! In quick reflex, putting his right hand up to his head, feeling all over, no no, relax, he wasn't *bald*. Just in agony now with the sudden movement. Perhaps a cigarette, to clear the air . . . But he had no strength. Nothing left at all.

A charred blanket lay by the door, and a plastic watering can on its side, and some blackened items of clothing were strewn about. An anorak and shirt, clearly burnt and sodden, had been hung on the back of the chair, by someone. By her, he supposed. He moved again, and let out a little whisper of pain. *Her.* Chrissie. Where? He looked at the other side of the bed, her side when she stayed, the side with the hollow in it that she liked, the side with the bedside table and the tacky jewellery box and that rubbery pot plant she watered with the watering can and joked that she talked to, her side.

He peered down. No little pile of ashes down there? He lifted the covers, jumped back with a quack of fright but it was only the cat peering balefully out at him. It hissed at him and he dropped the quilt back over it.

And she wasn't on the floor anywhere. He twisted and turned gingerly to look. No blackened corpse. Safe to assume then that *she* hadn't gone on fire. Self-pity washed over him, his head ached. He felt so cold, utterly freezing. Where *was* she? The Annihilator settled itself next to his body and he pulled the quilt up around his chin. The sheets were soaking. Had she been here last night? He struggled again to remember what had happened. Was she there as usual when he came rollicking in? Sitting up in bed in her skimpy T-shirt reading magazines and chattering and trying to make tough jokes, keeping up with his cynicism (he was famous for his cynicism), his hard humour, his world-weary banter. Or big-eyed and serious, frowning over some weighty issue or social injustice, her indignation trailing off at the last border post between the end of her vocabulary and outer space. Chrissie, with her beautiful face and her compact charisma, was always the perfect essence of herself, nothing less or more, nothing spare or untidy or superfluous about her, she was impervious, jaunty, cute. He had a pornographic fantasy – after-nuclear war, Chrissie emerging from the rubble in scanty possum skins, a gladwrap miniskirt, theatrical dirt marks daubed on each cheek. Fucking her in the ruins. Lawless and wordless in the waste-land. His Chrissie: she was immutable.

But she hadn't been there when he got home. (Had she?) She wasn't there when he got home and he'd lain down in his clothes and the room had rocked and swayed and his insides had sloshed and shifted as if his body were a spirit level filled with heavy fluid and the bed was a ship running up the wave and down the swell, and his blood ran slowly slowly, from his head to his feet to his head, until the wave turned him upside down and he fell, and floated away. Normal. The usual Saturday night.

So she wasn't there (or was she?) and he must have gone to sleep alone. A line of cobweb ran from the top of the wardrobe to the opposite wall, an impossibly long rope, floating slightly in the stir of the air. He followed the wavering strand with his eye. She wasn't there and he had been alone.

But wait. Had she come in later, after he'd got home? Marcus closed his eyes in miserable frustration. Something had happened (obviously) and it had to do with Chrissie. Yes, he was sure of that. So where had she gone? And why had she gone? He moaned softly. Would she, was she capable . . .? She'd never been violent, not really. But she was reckless. Heedless.

Another thing: to have got so drunk and stoned that he didn't remember a thing, that was not good. Oh, this is *not good*, Marcus whispered to himself.

He thought of something else. Carefully he reached his good arm down and felt around under the mattress, and he felt the lump there – his manuscript, untouched, safe on the unburnt side: his novel. A couple of hundred pages, typed on his manual typewriter – he worked on it laboriously, late at night, when no one was around.

His searching and lyrical depiction of Auckland life. Low life, in particular. He called it *The Hard Men* . . .

He raised his eyes towards the ceiling. Imagine if his manuscript had gone up in flames. He must get it Xeroxed, and store a copy somewhere else. This wooden house, after all, full of zombies and junkies, all smoking and burning and cooking things late at night when they could hardly stand up: this place could go up at any moment.

He fell back. His head thumped painfully now and the Annihilator was purring and kneading with its claws, scratching his leg. Marcus cast his eye over at the watering can on the floor, searched for a dry patch in the clammy sheets. Obviously there was someone somewhere he would have to thank. Whoever it was who had put him out.

Marcus waited for more long seconds. No one came. He concentrated on not panicking as another wave of nausea gripped him. He tried to think back. Yesterday, he remembered, he'd made the mistake of having lunch with his parents. The house in Meadowbank with its stone floor kitchen, tinkling Vivaldi, crisp chardonnay, the *London Review of Books* on the glass coffee table below the African mask and the batik pattern on the wall. Blinding rain drumming on the blue plastic cover of the spa pool outside, melancholy of the white sky over the gully.

He'd stood listening to his parents' friends, a woman with painted claws and a necklace of shells, spectacles like yellow windscreens, talking of Labour-think-tank-the-PM, and her husband, an architect who thumped the table and pronounced the latest figures unthinkable, and laughed a gusty haw haw, and played with the unforgivable leather bracelet on his freckly wrist. Marcus, in moody silence, stared out the window at the aquarium of the garden where the green ferns flipped and swam in the wind, flashing their silver underbellies, grey network of ponga bones.

'In ten years' time . . .'

'Waste of young talent . . .'

'Unthinkable.'

He had turned quickly, defensively, but they were absorbed, the woman had her hand on his father's arm, the architect played absently with his neck scarf, Marcus's mother hovered with the raised bottle of wine. She looked up at him, her round face flushed;

for a moment he thought she looked at him with sympathy, with mother love. He looked blank, and she took hold of the bottle and said in her ironic drawl, 'Let's go through and eat. Mar?' She gestured briskly. Tough midget in thick specs, long wool skirt, little helmet of left-wing hair. Make yourself useful. Take this. Carry that. She ordered him about, had him uncorking, fetching plates and glasses – my hopeless son (she liked to confide, rolling her eyes, talking behind her hand) will he ever come right? Just a phase they told me at first, it's been the same for years, since he was about sixteen. He was full of promise, pretty bright. Excelled at school. One day we came home and he was sitting on the floor playing some album, and how did the chorus go? 'Slut, Slut, Dirty Bitch.' (From then on, it was all downhill . . .)

'Unthinkable,' the architect roared, playing with his bracelet, eyeing the young man with twinkling sympathy. We were all young once, but were we so aggressive? Ah no. Ours were gentler, *groovier* days . . .

Marcus hadn't brought Chrissie with him. He could swim in this stream, he could relax and be as obnoxious as he liked, freeze his mother off, drink chardonnay by the gallon, be brutally rude to the old man. But Chrissie would start drowning straight away. It would irritate him, make him uneasy. She would be polite. She would even be charming. She would get into conversations about rape, domestic violence, the peril of the rainforest. She would be fresh-faced and sweet and smile radiantly at the old man, the old man pleased and awkward, plying her with wine. She would sit on the wicker chair with her hands on her knees, glancing sideways at Marcus occasionally, checking his face. And he would see his mother watching her like a cat sizing up a mouse.

Afterwards he would have to hustle Chrissie out of the house, push her into the car, drive like a maniac and be terrifyingly rude to her for three days, until she'd coax him back with some mollifying action like shaving off all her hair or getting a tattoo.

She had a small tattoo on her buttock – a Chinese symbol. Thinking about it would have given him a hard-on normally, but in the circumstances he put it out of his mind and concentrated on the question of whether it would be more painful to get out of bed and get help, or just to lie there and not move.

Chrissie had a minute tattoo on her buttock, she was small, with tidy little legs. She was a beautiful shape, in fact. She was five feet three inches tall with a tough pretty face, sharpish teeth, fine even skin. Hair unfashionably shaven off at the moment, with just some curling wisps at the back of her neck. Silver rings, three or four in each ear, three big chunky ones on her fingers. Graduate of Western Springs College, with pass grades in aromatherapy, good deeds and witchcraft, she left school at sixteen and became a waitress, and lived with her mother sometimes and sometimes with some boyfriend or other. Her father lived in Australia and owned pasta restaurants, he was rich but malevolent she said, they didn't talk to him any more. She said once she thought her father was a criminal. Mafia connections, perhaps, protection rackets or drugs. When she talked about her father she conjured up a brutal Italian rapist with tight curls and gold rings on his gigantic hands. There was something implausible about this portrayal, something about her round-eyed delivery of it, the hesitations and sighs, the sudden rushes of enthusiasm with each newly stacked embellishment, that reminded Marcus of a small child laboriously constructing a tower out of blocks.

Anyway, her surname was da Silva, which was Spanish as far as he knew. Not Italian. Marcus wondered whether she really knew her father at all. He wanted to use Chrissie's description of her father nevertheless, in his writing – Marcus always thought, always received information, as a writer. He had thought of himself as a writer since he was a child, although nobody knew this, yet. His parents didn't know it. They thought he was a wastrel and a bum (which, strictly speaking, currently, he was). Chrissie didn't know it. She was blithely, innocently uninterested in books and reading. She liked astrology and *The Woman's Monthly* (Hollywood section) and fashion magazines and TV. She wanted to go to tech and study design because she could draw and was good with her hands, she'd enrol one day when the time was right, when she'd saved up some money and was in the mood. In the mornings she sang in the shower in the bathroom next door and came back into his bedroom in her black underpants, her legs were brown even in winter, she looked like a gymnast, picking her skinny way through the wreckage of his room.

One evening when he was playing poker out there under the lightbulb with the hard men she came in wearing big shorts tied up with a sort of rip-cord and a tiny top and she leaned over sweetly and kissed him goodnight. She could do that to him there and trip off out of the room and it was all right, the hard men watching her skip off to bed, off you go girl, good as gold, with your gorgeous little legs. She fitted in at Connick Street, she was respected and liked. She was cheerful and striving, she liked to get stoned, she had girl-friends she said that she loved.

Marcus opened his eyes and tried to locate the wavering strand of cobweb but a pale light was shining through the edge of the blind and whitening the room and it was gone. Last night . . .

Last night was obscured behind clouds of hours, difficulty, pain. Driving away from his parents' house, stopping at the lights at the intersection in the early evening rain, riding the clutch on the low hill and the sky up there a non-sky at a non-time of day, it wasn't afternoon it wasn't late, he wasn't sober and he wasn't drunk. Tearing off from the lights, roaring down through the suburbs, the big old car swinging along with its creaks and echoes and groans, the gap of time between the turning of the steering wheel and the car's reluctant response.

Chrissie had wrecked the steering, driving too fast around the corner outside the morgue in Park Road, skidding on an oil slick and smashing into some parked cars. It happened in slow motion, she said. Time slowed as she spun and spun, crying what's going to happen now?

After hitting the parked cars she tried to flee, panicking, and smashed up a couple more. Residents of the street came out and pursued her. Strong men held her down until the authorities arrived. She sat on the grass verge with her head spinning, looking out through the legs of the surrounding guards. Seeing how small she was the police gently extracted her from the clutches of the mob, took her to the station and gave her cups of tea. And after that the shit went on and on for months and months, insurance claims, her court appearance, every time they got up in the morning there was some new consequence of that day. He thought of her spinning in the careering car, *what's going to happen now?*

He had driven to Connick Street, dropped off the car and gone to

the pub. Where? The Three Lamps. There was a band, and the
hard men were at the bar, and he proceeded to get smashed. He
remembered eating a meal in there, sitting in the stained wood nooks
with the fan-shaped lamps and the giggly waitress who was about
fifteen and couldn't handle the customers at all, who was hilariously disorganised and inept, bringing them the wrong food three
times and then the wrong drinks and generally making herself the
life and soul, get on there girl, yur, with your nice big ones.

So that had been that, until twelve o'clock. Then they'd spilled
out on to the street and walked and walked, not in the direction of
home, but down College Hill through town to the streets down by
the wharves. He remembered staggering past the Downtown
building, arm in arm with someone, singing, the pavement seeming to lurch and quake and throw him off balance, whoever it was
beside him pulling him up before he fell flat on his face. Cold air
off the sea as they came out by the wharves, sudden clearing of his
head, the lights of Devonport across the harbour, the black water
still and calm around the docks. The moored ships lit up with
orange lights, the water calm but moving, always moving, as if live
things were writhing deep down under the oily rubbish and the
mud.

Crossing Quay Street he caught the toe of his shoe in the old
tram track and stood helplessly stuck watching cars line up at the
lights ready to charge and mow him down, until hands seized hold
of him and pulled him across to stand in the queue outside Quays
nightclub. Standing sobering up a little as the Maori doorman,
twenty stone and six feet three, extracted a rowdy customer from the
queue by the hood of his purple jacket, carried him across the pavement and punched him down into the middle of a pile of bin-bags.
The customer lying inert in the rubbish, oblivious to his girlfriend's
hysterical screams. The big doorman smoothing his shaven head,
returning to his place and glaring down the length of the queue
with a comically pop-eyed squint as the customers shuffled their
feet and looked down, high spirits suitably subdued.

But the doorman let Marcus in, surprisingly. He had expected
the big arm to go up to block his way, even that he would be swept
into the air and smashed in the face, and deposited unconscious
with the other corpse in the rubbish pile by the gutter. He looked up

at the huge face of the doorman as he passed – impossibly fat jowls, the great head closely shaved, moustache over Maori upper lip curved like the side of a violin, the big sad brown eyes. A bluebird tattooed on the top of one hand, between the index finger and thumb. Obese arms. Obese *fists.*

After they had let him in he couldn't remember much except that Maria had been there with that faggot friend of hers, and that she had tried to get him to go somewhere, to some bar or hotel – she said something about a key. But he hadn't been able to understand what she was talking about and the next thing he knew she was shouting some instructions at him over the music and telling him that she was going to leave, and she was going off with a wave past the doorman who stared after her with his ferociously bug-eyed glare.

Left alone at a table Marcus watched the black lights flickering on the dance floor and the lasers sweeping around the walls, red beams whirling with liquid light, illuminations of flying dust, flying skin and sweat and hair. Where was she going? A hundred heads nodded and swayed on the dance floor in time to the beat. The music was so loud he could feel his body vibrating. You couldn't talk to anybody – everybody packed in together, moving together, everybody speechlessly alone.

Out on the street an ambulance was drawing away with a melancholy whoop. He looked the other way. The bin-bags had been cleared and the street was empty. Maria had gone home, he supposed, and wondered whether he should follow her. She might have some wine at her place, and they could talk.

He searched for his wallet and found some cash. Around the corner from Quays he fell into a taxi and instructed the driver to take him to her house in Ashton Road, her mean little street shaded by lines of pohutukawa trees and chilled by the five-mile shadow of Mount Eden. As they drove past the prison he looked away so that he wouldn't see the dreary walls and the bottomless courtyards, the windows covered with mesh and slats of wood. Once recently the news reported serious trouble in the prison, footage showed the inmates setting fire to toilet paper and pushing it out between the slats. You couldn't see their faces, just the streams of burning paper, and the big brown hands. He never looked at the jail. He never looked at the back of ambulances, either.

The lights were off in Maria's room. He paid the taxi driver and got out anyway. She would be in bed. She would get up and twitch back the curtain, peer out and whisper, 'Is that you?', the nervous laugh trapped inside her voice, heroically suppressed. When Maria was trying to keep her cool the side of her upper lip would quiver suddenly and she would put her hand quickly up to her mouth, looking to see if he had noticed.

Last week he was sitting on the bed with her and felt the bed suddenly begin to shake. When he turned to look at her she was shaking with laughter, not just chuckling, but consumed with mirth, or hysteria. Shoulders heaving, eyes screwed shut, tiny snorts and explosions and shrieks coming out from under her hands. She wouldn't tell him what the joke was, and he had no idea what was so funny, unless it was that terrible fart he'd unleashed the moment before. He stared at her disapprovingly, eyebrows raised. It was unnerving the way he could make her laugh. He had only to lift a finger. The smallest joke and she was off, shaking and mopping her brow and wiping away the tears.

So, as far as he could make out she was generally pleased to see him. She would unhook the French doors and invite him in. She would even disappear off into the kitchen and rustle him up a musty piece of cheese on toast and a palely orange cup of tea.

He would sit on the bed in his big leather jacket and his ripped jeans, eating up the food while she watched. Her room was neat and bright. The walls were freshly painted. Her shelves were stacked with books. There were colourful pictures on the walls. The room seemed like a haven, some nights. Aesthetic. Orderly. A secret place. He found his way there, out of the chaos of his nights. When she opened the door he felt the guilty pleasure of cheating, not just on Chrissie, but on his life. It felt like coming home when she let him in. But home was soft. He lived hard. In the morning the urge to escape would come to him, sharply.

Always he could feel Maria watching him. Sometimes she was in a bad mood, turning and twisting her hands and making unfunny jokes, and he would sense tension and unhappiness somewhere near the surface of her mood. If she had been at the pub she would throw herself around the room in a restless way, sitting down on the heater, getting up again, pacing around the bed. But she was more relaxed after a few drinks, her jokes were funnier and she could look him calmly in the eye. She always had a scrutinising look, but when she had been drinking she could look at him without watching him. Without looking as if she were scanning the bar code of his face for all data so far unscanned, the close inspection making him nervous, causing him to block her out immediately by looking away. If she had had some wine she would look straight at him and smile without any lip-quivering or hysterics and he would give her his characteristic grin (all irony and pointy teeth), grab her by the arm or leg and briskly manhandle her into the sack.

He liked getting her into bed. When they were a bit drunk they threw themselves at one another without thinking about it. When they weren't drunk they did the same things in bed, but Maria stone-cold sober could be unnerving. He could feel her thinking. It made him feel awkward. The silences were loud. She lay in bed with him thinking about him, and knowing all about him, and drawing her own ungovernable conclusions.

She changed all the time. With a bit of a hangover in the mornings she would be uncomplicatedly affectionate and loving. They would make toast and huddle up under the covers and she would barely bother to look at him through her dim and reddened eyes. She would hug him and wriggle around in the warmth under the covers and kiss him when he left. On a work morning, on the other hand, after a cup of tea and an early night, she was all thin arms and twisting fingers, all strange sharp remarks or sudden snorts of mocking laughter. He wondered on those cold mornings whether she went back into her room after he had gone, threw herself on to the bed and . . . What? Storms of weeping? Oceans of tears? Or a million hysterical laughs. Who knew.

His bedroom back at Connick Street was a riot of sex. He and Chrissie were all over each other every minute, she was irresistible with her tattoo and her bristly little head, and her rip-cord shorts. So why couldn't he resist all these visits to Maria's? He couldn't give Maria up. He would find himself at her house without having planned on going round. The urge to see her came to him, and it felt like the acknowledgement of a weakness, because it was loneliness that drew him there, the need for her company, for all the information of her personality coming at him. And the sensation of being reacted *to*.

Maria was subtle, nervous and acute, she registered everything – shook with mirth, trembled with nerves, flashed with scorn, winced with pain – Maria was a riot of data. She was a telephone switchboard in permanent danger of meltdown, overloaded by the incoming, the outgoing. She understood all his witticisms, although didn't respond in kind – she was either laughing too hard, or she muffed her lines, her face contorted with trying to keep it straight, she'd turn away and take a quivering breath, and sigh – she understood too much. She understood *him* too much. It was why he had to push her away. He would go home to be alone again, with Chrissie.

But last night. Opening the door of the taxi at three o'clock in the morning, falling out on to the grass verge by the rubbish bags under the pohutukawa tree, the taxi already paid off and droning away into the rainy night. An owl hooting and jeering at him from the trees, crickets chirping and bleeping in the jungle of wet foliage at her gate. Picking himself up, trudging up the path with his hands in the pockets of his jacket, climbing over the wall on to the porch, rapping on the window pane. And there she would be, alone in her lonely bed. Lying in there and *thinking*. Whispering out into the blackness. 'Is that *you?*'

He felt his face with his good hand. Last night the night had attacked him. Going through her gate, a sharp twig growing out of the shaggy hedge caught his ear and raked a cruel track across his face. Blinded, he staggered into a low dry-stone wall and cracked both his shins on the porous rocks. The crickets sang their delight at his fall, the owl gave a high-pitched whoop.

He hopped and cursed his way across the lawn and climbed the wooden wall of the small balcony outside her room. As he was climbing up a splinter embedded itself in the tender flesh under one of his thumb nails, and in the dance of pain that followed he slipped on the moss-covered planks of the deck and hit his head on the wall. Blind, infuriated, sucking his thumb, he pounded on the French door. Inside all was dark and silent. Rain blew slanting in under the eaves, drenching the back of his jacket. He banged again, shivering in the freezing wind. There was no answer and so, filled with a certain amount of self-righteous indignation at the treatment being meted out, he had proceeded to attack the rusty old lock on the door and woundedly smash his way in.

Then he had waited around for a couple of hours. Even sneaked into the kitchen and riffled the bread bin for the last few bits of bread. In her room he watched television, lying on her bed. He propped himself up on her pillows, and draped the bedspread half over himself, still wearing his damp and muddy boots.

A melancholy feeling came over him. He began to get up every few minutes and look out of the window along the street. Where was she after all, out there in the night, when she should be at home with him.

He got up and wandered around the room, going through the books on her desk. Textbook on contract. Criminal law. Textbook on torts. Whatever torts were. His mother had wanted him to study law. My son the lawyer. She'd never got over it, the way he'd just left school and refused to go to university.

'You're throwing everything away!' she'd screamed at him, waving copies of his primary school IQ tests, his glowing reports: Marcus's project on recycling a revelation! Marcus a pleasure to teach! Such political insight from a six-year-old! Clearly a favourable home environment, such a head start for a child . . .

'You bloody fool!' his mother snapped, all those years ago when he was sixteen, and had woken up different all of a sudden, as if a nihilistic vampire had flown in and bitten him during the night. She didn't understand him, she wept bitterly and wrung her hands. She couldn't see why he needed to get away. He couldn't tell her that the claustrophobia she induced in him was so extreme that sometimes he felt physically sick. Mornings. Meal times. Evenings. Weekend evenings most of all. Inside with his parents in the evening, in the weekend, inside the big, comfortable, orderly house with its rules, its locked doors, the relentless Vivaldi plinking softly at the edges of the room, he endured agonies of deprivation. He was deprived, above all, he felt, of life. Out there beyond the cushiony glow of the room, life was salty, hard and savage, life was putting up its derisive fists and jeering at him, and sniggering, and pointing at his balls. And as he winced and paced and snarled and smoked, his parents stared at him coldly, or pleadingly, hurt and angry and indignant, full of the protest so often made it no longer needed to be, I give you *all this*, and you throw it in my face.

'You don't know how lucky you are,' his mother angrily said. 'You don't even know you're *alive*.'

There were a few novels strewn around Maria's desk. *Bleak House*. *Little Dorrit*. Big fly-blown old doorstoppers with yellowing pages. *Portrait of a Lady*. He lit a cigarette, exhaled and pushed them on to the floor. There was a letter on the table from one of Maria's old friends who'd gone to live in London last year. He settled down on the bed and began to read it, snorting cruelly at the misspellings, the corny enthusiasms, the careful strings of mixed metaphors and split infinitives, yur, who was this dumb chick? You had to laugh. All my biggest love, Serena. And still Maria didn't show.

Finally he had thrown the letter on the floor and mooched angrily out into the hall to ring for a cab to take him . . . not home, no. He'd gone looking to get stoned. Very stoned. Hadn't he.

Now Marcus raised his frail and pounding head and moved slightly in the chilly sheets. He could hear sounds in the kitchen, the creak of the floorboards, the bang as someone slammed the kettle down on to the metal bench top. Low rumbling of masculine voices, punctuated by the usual hacking hoiks and coughs. The odd wry hungover laugh or groan. The hard men had arisen. They'd be out there now wringing the last tea bag into a couple of broken cups and bearing the steaming brews proudly to their girlfriends who would be lying with searing hangovers in the stinky bombsites of their rooms. Then it would be back to bed until the afternoon.

Marcus called out to them, softly. He wondered how long he had been awake. The pain was more bearable now that he had lain without moving for a long time. His arm felt huge and heavy and pulsed with a regular throbbing heat. But the worst pain now was in his armpit. He called out again and the movement of his diaphragm ignited the fire under his arm. 'Mike? Mike?'

The cat stretched and scratched. Someone opened the kitchen window and spat out noisily into the gully. That would be Mike, or possibly Mike.

'Mike? Is that *you*?'

The kitchen window slammed. He heard a loud laugh and called out again, louder this time, his voice rising into squeaky despair, and then he heard slow footsteps coming down the hall. The door opened and Mike's face appeared round the door – stubble of blond hair, blunt good-natured face, bright blue eyes reddened by a hundred ruinous hangovers.

'Yeah, mate?' he said absently, and then his eyes began to widen as he looked around the room, vacant amazement slackening his features and dropping his bristly jaw. 'Fuck! What's been happening in here?'

Marcus squeezed his prickling eyes shut. *Oh*. It was going to be *all right*. Alone in there for a moment he had suddenly imagined that they knew. That he was dying in here and they didn't care, even that they'd done it to him – set him on fire – themselves, for a laugh. That the world had gone mad . . .

He opened his eyes. Mike's face was a sunbeam, a lamp, of warmth and horror and concern as he stared wonderingly around the room, his mind working feverishly to understand what had occurred.

'There's been a *fire*,' Mike suddenly announced. He went to the door and bawled down the hall. 'Mike! Everybody. Get up!'

Mike walked gingerly over the blackened floor, picking up the burnt blanket and fingering the scorched clothes on the back of the chair. He picked up the watering can.

'Somebody's . . .? Who put it out? Did you?'

His eyes closed again, Marcus tinily shook his head. No idea. Someone put it out and went away.

'Without any of us *noticing* anything?'

'Heavy night for all,' Marcus whispered through immobile lips. Mike was searching around the floor. Looking behind the base of the pot plant and under the bed. Sneaking a look round the back of the armchair.

He coughed. 'Er . . . and . . .?'

'She's not here. I've looked.'

'Christ, that's all right then.' Mike brightened. 'Where is she then? She was here last night.'

'*Was* she?'

'I can't remember when. She must have waited for you and then gone. Anyway, aren't you going to get up? The bed's all wet. Are you hurt?'

Marcus signalled at his arm with his eyes. Mike came close and gently moved away the covers. Then he was up and bawling for everybody again, and they all came into the room, Mike and Branko and Darlene, and Brendelia and Jaycene, the girls all screaming at the sight of the room and his wounds, Brendelia in the hallway sobbing for an ambulance, Darlene carefully holding his hand and saying, 'Does it hurt, does it hurt?'

Branko walked about swaying and shaking his head and muttering into his hands. Marcus watched him as he sniffed around the room like an angular dog. Branko was tall, dark and paranoid, he was obsessed with war and death, and walked the streets in the mild Auckland winter wearing a cap with furry earmuffs, as if he expected to be breaking the ice on his taps in the morning and shovelling through six feet of snow. He leaned over Marcus with a look of sepulchral satisfaction. Not even safe in our beds. Briskly and cursorily he inspected Marcus's chest and arm, nodding to himself, as if he were at home with charred and blackened bodies, the death toll in the morning after the terror of the night.

'He's Croatian,' Darlene would whisper by way of explanation when Branko was being particularly eccentric and arcane, although no one really knew whether he had been in the area during the war.

The ambulance came, whooping and screaming along the silent street.

'Stand back,' Brendelia shouted at no one in particular, ushering the two ambulance officers into the hall. Two muscular guys with moustaches and big competent hands, smelling strongly of antiseptic, entered the room and inspected it in a neutral way: what people get up to you wouldn't believe, the way people are killing themselves all over the suburbs, every day.

'Hello,' said the biggest one to Marcus, 'you'll be fine. My name's Dave.'

'Oh, that's all right then,' Marcus whispered, jaunty with relief.

Then they were counting one two three and lifting him on to a stretcher and covering him with a bright red blanket so that he was overwhelmed with gratitude and embarrassment, the hard men marching along beside the stretcher, Brendelia shrieking along in front as they drove him around the dead bathtub, under the clothesline, along the line of the bright green hedge and through the gate, out on the street where there was nothing above him but the great cloud banks and the pale dot of the sun behind the cloud, intense at the centre and fading into outward rings, as if someone had thrown a flaming arrow into the liquid surface of the sky.

In the back of the ambulance Dave was tweaking gently at his sleeve and Marcus screamed suddenly through his teeth.

'Give him pain relief!' Brendelia had forced her way into the ambulance and loomed over him, her necklaces and chains tickling his cheek. He stared into the fat folds of breast bulging from her black bra. He moaned. He could hear the hard men's stereo in the car behind when they slowed at intersections, respectfully lowered to about a thousand decibels. He moaned again. He loved them all. They took care of him, and he in turn would take care of them. For ever. How he loved them. And they were all in his novel, of course. His hard men. And their chicks. Down to the smallest detail.

Dave had pushed Brendelia aside and was doing something else to his arm and Marcus's eyes blurred suddenly as he turned his head, his vision froze like a still photograph of something in motion, sounds boomed and then whispered in his ears and he could hear Dave talking far away. He opened his eyes again and saw rows of windows and felt cold air on his cheeks. Then he was inside a corridor in a sudden blaze of neon light and he closed his eyes and felt everything begin to spin.

Before he went out again he saw the shape of her face above him in the darkness, leaning over him with the light behind her so that he saw the roundness of her cheek and the line of her neck where it curved to meet her shoulder, and the wisps of shaven hair, and he put out his hands to hold her arms, to stop her falling into him, but a bright light was being shone in his eyes and a voice was speaking his name and the room turned upside down again, and she was gone.

Far far away he could hear Brendelia, crying. 'Someone will have to find her . . . find her . . . Find *Chrissie*.'

3.

From somewhere a long way off metal and wood squeaked and banged, squeaked and banged, but Maria was curled in a ball under the duvet dreaming about Marcus. A circular track of muddy boot-prints marked his warpath around the bed. Her novels lay on the floor where he had left them, and the floor was strewn here and there with crumbs.

She was sleeping late, sleeping on and on, knowing that she was sleeping. The early morning had been silently fogged with water and dew, now a wind had got up and was whistling in the leaves of the hedge, blowing away the mist, worrying its way around the wooden house, rattling the windows and hissing through the chinks in the unlined walls.

In Maria's room the crumbs drifted across the floor and formed a tiny dune against the wall and the curtain billowed out suddenly as the wind caught hold of the unlocked French door and yanked it open wide. Maria opened her eyes and saw black branches moving against the white sky. Then the half-open red curtain filled like a sail and spread out horizontally as the wind flew into the room and the hinge of the French door squawked and the door frame flew back and crashed into the wall of the house.

She sat up in the sudden riot of her room as the curtain danced and throttled itself and the letter from London swooped in an updraught over the bed and spiralled wildly around the walls. The edge of a poster began to tear off the wall and out in the hallway a cupboard door slammed shut.

Maria sat in bed coldly watching the wind. Let it wreck the room, look, the whole corner of the poster was flapping loose, the letter from London torn and sticking to the mirror now, the cold air tearing down the hall and into the musty kitchen to drive the sad smells away. In the garden the rotary clothes-line turned with terrible effort, old metal grinding on old metal with the sound of agony in its constricted iron throat. The dead bare twigs at the top of the pohutukawa waved tiny stiff good-byes at the racing clouds.

Maria got up to shut the door. She saw her flatmate Ernest coming up the path with a bag of shopping and the paper, his face screwed up against the wind. She got back into bed and he came into the hall and poked his head around her bedroom door. His hair was slicked neatly down to his head, unruffled by the wind. He was slant-eyed, bespectacled and clever, with pasty cheeks and freckles on his nose, and nicotine-stained teeth. Ernest was a journalist, he covered petty crime and traffic. He wanted to be a political editor, but he was just starting out, and had to spend his time at inquests, courts and police stations.

'You know what they say about Auckland. If you don't like the weather . . .'

'Wait ten minutes.'

He squinted happily at her. He was feeling domestic.

'Want some omelette or something?'

'No thanks.'

Maria got dressed and lay on the bed thinking about Marcus. She had left the door unlocked last night after she went to bed in the hope that he might come back. She had known that he would have called a taxi and gone home to Connick Street, but still she'd hoped that he would come. She imagined him sitting on the end of the bed, watching her TV, turning to her mockingly and asking, as the images warped and fizzed, 'Was this the first TV ever made?'

He had broad hands, strong arms, a long-nosed angular face and pale blue eyes. Thin mouth and pointy teeth. He wore ripped-up jeans, big boots with the laces loose. He owned a cat called the Silken Annihilator . . .

Ernest called out but Maria ignored him and lay staring at the ceiling. Marcus. He was hard, ironic and contemptuous, and he was blackly humorous as well. He was sharp and caustic but he was good-natured with his friends. He seemed to get on well with all those losers he lived with. They certainly loved him. He was the despair of his parents' life and had thrown his advantages away, out of principle, he told Maria, because he didn't want to be a middle-class shit and to be claustrophobically pampered and spoilt.

And anyway, he was going to be a writer. He was writing a novel about Auckland, he said. A searching, hard-hitting work about people who lived in the real world. How could he do that unless he carried out the proper research? According to him, by going to university and studying law Maria was embracing all the weak and bad things he'd left behind. She knew that he thought of her as a *sheep* following a conventional and unoriginal path. She knew he thought these things about her and she loved him for that too. She thought of herself as pragmatic, and of him as extraordinarily naive.

She had a feeling about life that he didn't have. That if you flirted with life it would *rape* you. She felt she had known this for a long time. You had to take life seriously, or you'd end up in a dark alley, so to speak, with your pants around your knees. So she hadn't followed his example and dropped out. She didn't listen to him, even though he was the most intelligent person she knew. Instinctively she had kept control, kept her own propensity for chaos and crime in check, enough to stagger home from nights out with Leon and hunker down to her essays.

She had another idea which sounded ridiculously prim, but which she liked: that everything she did in Auckland would be for the sake of self-improvement. So she worked hard, ate well, exercised, read a lot. Also smoked a lot, because that kept her interesting and trim, also drank a lot, because that kept her amused.

This week she would start her new job at Quinn St John, the large glossy, commercial law firm occupying ten floors of mirror building in the downtown area. She was to work in the property department. They had hired her after an interview at the university, before which she had taken two Codral tablets in the hope that they would make her fanciable and smooth. Do not operate machinery after taking, the packet said. May cause drowsiness. They sounded strong. They were the only pills she could find in the bathroom. She was ill with nerves.

The interview was conducted by two of the firm's partners, a mild old man in pin-stripe grey and a little woman in a big-shouldered dress.

'I've always wanted to be a lawyer,' Maria found herself saying to the woman who seemed to find this wide-eyed naivety amusing, who seemed to find everything Maria said amusing, probably because it was, Maria supposed, since she was a wreck by this stage and was astonishing herself with her own surreal fluency. Later she learned that she had been 'lucid', 'confident', and 'with impressive general knowledge'. They had hired her. She had remained astonished and delighted for a week.

She had phoned her mother with the news of the new job. The phone was answered after many rings and she heard the effort in her mother's voice, the struggle to adjust the tongue to talking again, after so many hours and days. Maria's mother spent her life holed up in a small concrete flat in Tauranga. You always knew when she'd be home – straight after work at the bookshop she would walk quickly back to her solitary meal and her doorstopper paperback classic. No one had read more heavy literature than Maria's mother. Except long-term prisoners, hermits, cloistered nuns. Celine Wallis had lived like that since Maria's father had died in a car crash when Maria was one year old.

Living with her mother back then, Maria had been aware of her own dangerously disruptive store of energy. Even as a small child she had felt as if Celine would crumple up if Maria's voice – or her thoughts – were too forceful or loud. And Maria did seethe and burn and nearly die with feeling, and occasionally scream the place down. At any disturbance in the atmosphere, if she sensed any unpleasantness or aggression in the air, Celine would race into her room and compulsively pick up a book. She read enough to know everything about the whole world, yet the real world confounded her and sent her scurrying for cover. She was otherworldly, undercover, defiantly defeated, and when they argued, which was often, while Maria ranted and stormed and threw things outside the locked door of Celine's room, Celine would sit on the other side of the door with her hands over her ears, frantically immersed in *Bleak House* or *The Man Who Loved Children*.

When Maria became a teenager she had forged out into the world (she sometimes thought now) with a burning desire to crash into life, to come up against it and feel its heavy, decisive force. For a time she had seemed destined to acquire a criminal record, so fascinated was she with the authoritarian, masculine power of cops. Those big humourless studs of the open road in their mirror shades and Crimplene slacks, grimly pursuing the fleeing Honda along the country lanes. (The little Honda was Celine's car – much borrowed and abused by Maria – so that poor blameless Celine, venturing nervously out to the supermarket, would find herself whooped at and chased, pulled over and menaced by the law, and Maria wondered guiltily sometimes, whether she had intensified her mother's agoraphobia herself, by rendering Celine's licence plate so notorious, so red-hot, in the police computer.)

In those years Maria incurred a dangerous number of traffic convictions just because it amused and titillated her to be pursued, taken in hand, roughly addressed. Stop me, arrest me, before I . . . Attention seeking, you'd call it now. And she did so love to flirt.

Maria's eye fell on the edge of the stolen duvet, which she had hastily shoved under the bed last night before going to sleep. Stolen property. Life would have to change now. She would have to behave herself, she would have to be more careful. She would get up and take the quilt over to Leon's house. She reached down and pulled it out. It really was a magnificent quilt, huge and luxuriously thick, and she wished she could give it to Marcus. She had slept in Marcus's room in Connick Street a couple of times and it was cold and dank over there, the windows didn't fit properly in their casings, and there was nothing to warm the room except a heater the size of a toaster. She had woken with the Silken Annihilator pacing up and down her legs, to the sight of the wind blowing the leaves of the pot plant beside the bed, and of a map of mould on the ceiling in the shape of Australia. After nine o'clock or so the reprobates of the house had come blundering into Marcus's room and gathered in a huddle around the bed, causing Marcus to rouse himself and light a cigarette and hold forth in companiable grunts on the subject of stereos and nightclubs and drugs.

After his friends had wandered out again and he was standing in his underpants scraping tinned meat into a saucer for the cat, Marcus had become, quite suddenly, articulate again, and told Maria that the Connick Streeters would all feature (in disguised form of course) in his novel. Maria had wondered at the quick change in his manner. Clearly he saved the deepest vernacular, the grunt-speak, for his flatmates. With *her* his speech became quite clear and direct, his sentences lengthened and became intelligent and self-mocking. Watching him with his flatmates that morning she formed, to her own private amusement, the image of him as an explorer or an anthropologist, squatting down, spreading his hands over the cooking fire, trading beads and talking fluently in the language of the tribe.

She wondered about his novel and what it was going to be like. He kept the manuscript under his mattress, he told her, and worked on it at nights. It was called *The Hard Men*, and he had been working on it – putting his heart and soul into it – for four months. Despite the unmistakable twinge she felt on being told the title of his work, a twinge of amusement, was it, or at least of reservation, Maria still sighed with fond admiration as she imagined him bent over his typewriter late at night, his scarf wrapped tightly around his neck, his feet on the one-bar heater, his head full of observation, irony, insight.

'How do you do it?' she would gush. 'I wouldn't have the patience. Just sitting there writing hour after hour.'

'I have short coffee breaks,' he sternly replied.

There was a smash from the kitchen, interrupting her thoughts. Ernest's struggles with hand-eye co-ordination regularly turned the kitchen into a bombsite of splatterings and shards. He loved to cook and to bring home exotic herbs and fancy ingredients, which ended up splashed across the stove and the wall behind it, or rotting wetly in the back of the fridge.

Maria got up and went to inspect the kitchen. The dishes were piled into a precarious tower in the sink. A noodle hung from the door of one of the cupboards and the stove top had been dyed green. Apart from that she thought the place strangely tidy, until she entered the bathroom and reeled gaggingly out of it again.

Ernest was innocently eating his concoction in the living room, wearing his dark glasses and watching *Star Trek* on TV. He would probably lie there all day, cerebrally, chain-smoking.

'Are you going to clean up?'

He smiled sweetly and vaguely over the tops of his shades.

'At least the bathroom . . . It's nauseating . . . Can't you . . .?'

But Ernest's mind was far away as the TV rattled on, Warp factor six Mr Sulu, he's dead Jim. Starship out.

Maria rang Marcus but there was no reply. 'Burglar!' she imagined herself saying. 'I should have called the police.' Or, 'You could have kept your boots off my bed!' She could never calm down when she talked to him. Always trying to be the life and soul. She would say something that seemed thigh-slappingly funny to her and hear the suppressed shriek in her own voice and the silence on the other end as he breathed patiently into the phone. Then he'd say, 'Mike's made my breakfast.'

'What is it?' she'd say, hanging on.

'Vegetarian bacon.'

'Is it green?' And she'd be heehawing with laughter about this until she realised that he had hung up long seconds before.

Now she listened to the phone ringing in the empty house at Connick Street. She wondered how they could all be out of the house on a Sunday morning. Mass overdose? Busted by the drug squad? More likely the phone had been cut off.

She got dressed, loaded the duvet into her car and drove towards Remuera, wondering what was happening at Connick Street. They certainly took a lot of drugs over there. They did everything, the smoking and snorting and inhaling and popping, with all the accompanying melodrama. There was always someone over there whirling around the room and hitting the wall or lying glazed on the vinyl sofa.

Neither she nor Leon ever took any drugs, another reason why Marcus found her unacceptably respectable and straight. Leon was too busy drinking to bother himself with other substances. For her part, Maria thought (secretly) that there was something unforgivably humourless about heavy drug abuse. Crowded around under the lightbulb in the back room at Connick Street they were as single-mindedly and religiously solemn about their activities as Christians or triathletes. Mike, for example, last week, surfacing bulging-eyed out of the acrid fumes and announcing 'This is interesting shit', the assembled Connick Streeters nodding reverently while Maria drank wine in the corner and smirked into the gloom.

Also secretly, Maria was wary of taking something that could wield unpredictable and destructive power over her brain. Marcus's friends never really knew what they were taking, or how effective it would be.

So Maria was just an old-fashioned girl, with a moderate-to-heavy intake of alcohol and cigarettes. Leon, too, was a model of order in this respect. He stuck to vodka and crime. Liberal amounts of both.

Leon was in his garden, sitting on a canvas chair and combing his hair in front of a mirror he had propped in the branches of a small tree. He frowned with intense concentration and picked a can of hairspray up off the grass, carefully parting the brittle hair and spraying it into shape.

Maria carried the duvet down the path on her shoulders and draped it over the lemon tree. He grinned at her in the mirror. The wind was roaring in the trees above the house but down in the garden the air was mild and still. Leon's father's corgi lay fatly at his feet on the grass. He finished his hair, lit a cigarette and poked the dog with his foot. 'She's gone all quiet because I threatened to kill her.'

'Poor Fifi.'

'Mimi, not Fifi. I'm baby-sitting her. She gets hormonal and starts to shriek. I told her I'd throw her down the stairs.'

'I'm hungry.' Maria prodded the dog absent-mindedly.

While working on his hair Leon was also watching Mrs Camcook in the garden beyond the hedge. She was a red, boiled, glaring little woman, on her knees at the edge of her flowerbed, glancing up at Leon and stabbing the earth with vicious enthusiasm, as if the flayed soil had been transformed in her imagination into the vulnerable flesh of Leon's chest. Mrs Camcook and her husband hated Leon with the virulence typical of heavy suburban warfare. Leon was unsuitable, and he looked funny, and he lowered the tone. And then there was his behaviour. Mrs Camcook regularly called the police when Leon played his stereo too loud or burned things in the back garden in the middle of the night. He called her Mrs Camcook because she and her husband activated their Camcook anti-theft device when they left town, which switched their house lights on and off at set times of the day and night, this device being advertised on TV to the tune of a merry jingle: 'You're always at home with a Camcook.' But Leon knew that when the lights started going on and off regularly next door he could nip over and help himself to the contents of the Camcook wine cellar or their rows of carefully cultivated pot plants.

They went inside. Maria spread the stolen duvet out on Leon's bed. Leon's bedroom was in its usual state of chaos, smelling of paint and glue and hot plastic, and the floor was strewn with pieces of telephone and parts of an electronic sign, which Leon was planning to install in the window at the front door.

'What's it going to say?'

'Something simple, unpretentious. I thought perhaps Fuck Off Fuck Off Fuck Off.' He yawned. 'Any other ideas?'

By the side of the bed was the old dial phone painted red and blue and yellow and beside that a small push-button phone with its own receiver removed and a huge heavy old receiver glued on to it instead, as if the slim little phone had experienced some monstrous swelling or growth. Maria ran her hands over the top of Leon's chest of drawers. Rows of spray paint, coils of telephone wire, empty Rothmans packets, hairspray and glue. A piece of hardboard leaning against the wall painted to resemble a massive circuit board, with silver phone parts glued at the junctions of the wires.

Maria played with the bits of phone. She sat and watched as Leon wired parts of the electronic sign together. His right hand was large and capable but the left one, although it was usable, was deformed, with only three fingers and a tiny misshapen thumb. He had been born with the deformity, and born naturally left-handed, so that he had to use the deformed hand to write. He always hid his left hand and never talked about it and when he sat on a chair he would hide the hand between his knees.

One night in the pub Maria said to him, 'Let me see your hands.' He refused but he didn't mind, she could tell, he just laughed and told her no. They had known each other for so many years now she could say anything to him, she told him that he drank too much, that his legs would go with the drink like old Mr Riggs's up the road, she told him not to drink every night, she told him about her quarrels and fights, she told him all her jokes. He laughed at her. He was twenty-five now. Two years older than Maria.

When they had first gone out together and he had walked her home she had expected him to kiss her or to try to persuade her to invite him home to bed. He was half Czech – his parents had emigrated after the war – he was tall and striking, with his earrings and his blond hair. He would put his arm around her, he would hug her, he would give her half his packet of cigarettes. Then he would stride off down Brighton Road shouting in a high voice 'Bye!', sounding like a character out of his favourite film, *Cat on a Hot Tin Roof*.

She often stayed over at his house and slept in his bed but they never had sex, and after she had got to know him she thought of him as gay and wondered why she had ever thought of him in any other way. He was as camp, after all, as it was possible to be. But he didn't have a gay life, it seemed, because he had her, and for a long time now they'd done everything together. For the time being they were one another's man. Once there was a power cut in town while they were shopping and he held her by the hand in the dark crowded arcade and when the bags got too heavy he switched the load to his right hand and put the deformed hand into hers.

Soon after they had first met, years ago, he invited her for a weekend away. They hired a car and drove down to Wellington, found a fancy hotel and immersed themselves in room-serviced debauchery. At 4 a.m. Leon was in the hotel pool in all his clothes drinking vodka and eating a steak sandwich, at 5 a.m. they were in the car, weaving their way down a one-way street the wrong way, Maria laughing so much her body hurt, Leon peering manfully ahead, vodka bottle between his knees. Then the scream of sirens, the high-speed reverse. An attempt to escape into the hills, in reverse. On a dark stretch of road he stopped the car. 'Meet you later,' he said and she got out. And then the car was surrounded. Maria hiding, watched as Leon was led away. For him getting arrested was half the fun.

Afterwards Maria took a taxi from the scene, winding down while the taxi wove its way down out of the hills, downtown to where she waited for him to be booked and brought back to her out of the cells, tall and rakishly blond among the uniform blues, his fingers covered in ink, making jokes, benevolently. That Leon, what a star. He was the Antistar, emerging from the iron stage door with its bars and grilles.

And then, and always after that (she was hooked straight away), Maria had the taxi waiting and they drove on through the dark, back to the hotel where they lay in bed and laughed and watched the morning news. Maria woke in the early afternoon and saw him sleeping, the big shoulders, the graceful lines of his face. How many convictions did he have? A long list, although nothing worth a jail sentence, yet. Just endless fines, reparations, compensations – a string of minor convictions, caught from playing with the law. Who but Leon would make crime into drama? Who but Leon would turn crime into art? He decorated his house with crime, he made his sculptures out of stolen goods. For Maria he made live TV with a million frights, a million terrible laughs.

'*There's ink all over your hands.*' He lay on his back that morning, in Wellington, in the grey hotel light. Violet shadows under his eyes. Fingerprints, thumbprints and a mugshot too. They must have been surprised at the station when they picked up his left hand to push it on to the black ink pad, not knowing where to put each print on the form with its ten boxes: twice four for fingers and twice one for thumbs.

They went away again. 'What shall we do?' Maria would say, arriving at his house in the weekend, in those years when she was a student, when she had endless free days and Leon, it seemed, had endless money and ideas. And he would consider for a moment, delicately, shading his eyes with his hand: 'Perhaps we should *go away*?' Leon blazed his way through small towns in the rental car, outraging all as he went. In a drab North Island town Maria, walking ahead of him among the stoical, monosyllabic inhabitants, looked back and saw how exotic he was, how much taller, wilder, more elegantly and hilariously alive.

Once, at Waiheke Island, Leon was arrested for swearing by a local constable with too much time on his hands, who imprisoned Leon in a tiny concrete shed in his vegetable garden while he waited for the police launch Deodar, and the water police, called out in force, marched Leon on to their boat and handcuffed him (so he told Maria later) to a pole while they transported him across the Gulf. Maria went home by ferry and met him outside the station, and they wandered merrily home through the dark streets. He didn't have to do much to get into trouble, Maria reflected. All those cops, for a simple expletive that the police used themselves all the time. But Leon attracted that sort of attention – small-town cops followed him around, waiting for him to come out with an absent-minded 'fuck' or 'cunt' as he rummaged in his bag for another can of beer. As soon as they laid eyes on him they knew they had at least one bit of police business that day. They couldn't resist him, and he couldn't resist them. What they wanted he gave, and more. What he wanted . . . And the townspeople, he made their day, as they stood talking in one of Leon's aftermaths, big arms folded, scandalised, shaking their heads, or big-eyed and excited, sketching diagrams in the air: he came from over there, and they cut him off there, and as soon as I saw him – and I said to Reg I said – as soon as I saw him I knew.

'One day,' Leon said, smiling his luminous smile under the glass bottles and buoys and nets that festooned his favourite Auckland pub, the terrible Schooner, a mock ship in Victoria Street, 'one day, they'll kick us off the planet.'

Coming back from the toilets, unscathed, unmugged – the trip to the Schooner toilets a dangerous excursion, the toilets being a wilderness of unsupervised violence – standing under the crooked handwritten sign that read 'Toliets', Maria saw him looking over to check that she had emerged, saw the extraordinary face smiling across the gloom and felt (oh alcoholic sentimentality but it was true, it was *true*) such love for him that she blurted out, 'What can Czechoslovakia be like? Is everybody there like *you*?'

That night at midnight an obese behemoth took mysterious offence and approached the table, resting his bunched, tattooed fists on the back of Maria's chair, growling and looming and threatening until Leon, seeing no way out, rose with a certain willowy dignity and smashed his fist, his good fist, into the blunt, pitted face. In the astonished silence that followed Leon collared Maria and dragged her out into the rainy street where they took refuge crammed together in a phone booth while the maddened Schooneran, bursting out into the street after them, roared and menaced and ran this way and that searching for them, before passing noisily on down the road and into the night.

At Lake Rotoiti in winter Maria felt so peppy with fresh air that she went swimming in the lake in her underwear while Leon sat on the wharf, drinking and smoking and remonstrating: 'Jane Fondle! Olivia Neutron-Bomb!'

They slept together in the motel bed and in the morning Maria

woke with bronchitis that had been brewing but was now intensified by her cold immersion in the lake, and Leon rose, as fresh
as usual after last night's debauch, sallied forth in the rental car
and returned two hours later with a new dent in the car, two
parking tickets, newspapers, Sausage McMuffins, burgers,
lemons, honey, Coldrex, rum, and tins of toheroa soup which he
boiled on the motel element and served to Maria with lemon, in
a large vase.

Later that day Maria slept in the back seat of the car and woke
alone in a car park in Rotorua, her face stuck to the cold vinyl, her
vision blurred, a strange smell of metal in her mouth and nose
and throat. Pulling herself up, coughing, she looked out of the
window, across a shadowy concrete expanse, saw parked cars,
ramps, pillars, the metal doors of a lift. Maria opened the door and
made for the lift. She located the button. She pressed. With a ping
it arrived. She entered and encountered, simultaneously, four
tourists – tight cluster of elderly American affluence: height, girth,
tartan, pressed tans and fawns, crisp bright-whites – and her own
image in the mirrored wall of the lift. Skewed and mangled during
her sleep in the car Maria's sunglasses ran on an angle from left
jowl to right temple. Her hair on the same lines – flat to her head
on the left and on the right a veritable palm tree of hair, resisting all
attempts to smooth and subdue. The lift rose, Maria lurched and
swayed, the bunched Yanks stared fixedly ahead, willing away this
unsavoury intruder. The lift played a carefree plinking riff. Maria
coughed outrageously in the tight space. Turning towards the
tourists with a flourish of her hand, intending, by way of apology,
some light, throwaway pleasantry, Maria exploded into another
bronchial roar. The Americans shifted unhappily, pressed closer
together and held their breaths. Surprised by the force of the
cough Maria sat down with a crack on a tartan suitcase. The lift
slowed and the Americans pressed forward. Wordlessly, his face
creased with pleading outrage, one of the tanned old golfers tugged
at his tartan case. Realising what he wanted, Maria graciously rose,
and the American stepped backwards, grasping the buckled handle
of the case. The lift door opened to a hotel foyer, marble floor,
artificial trees, baggage trolleys. In the lift the Americans were
grappling with their cases and bags, and Maria was tangled in the

straps of a fawn sports bag, and one of the pot plants in the foyer – an imposing tree of the *pinus* variety – was moving suddenly across the lobby towards them, and now Leon and the pot plant burst into the lift. 'Get back,' he commanded, rapidly pressing the buttons, and as the lift door closed there were shouts in the foyer and a uniformed bell-boy ran towards the lift, just missing it before it closed and began its downward plunge. '*Hey*,' protested one of the elderly Americans, before Leon turned on him with one hand inside his jacket. The tourists shrank back. 'Look at this,' Leon said to Maria. He reached into his jacket again. The old Americans moaned. He fumbled for a minute and pulled out a long, black telephone receiver, with red buttons.

'Hey,' Maria said appreciatively. 'I've never seen one like that before.'

'Exactly. Look at the base. It's cordless too.'

'It's beautiful.'

They fiddled with it, their heads together. 'See this button, it's got some sort of speaker mode, maybe an intercom . . .'

The lift pinged and the doors opened to the car park. They stepped out into the shadows. Behind them in the lift the Americans silently reached for the buttons. Still talking, Leon and Maria walked to the car, forced the pot plant into the back seat, got in, and headed for the road and the motorway north.

Now in Leon's house, in Leon's room, Maria felt herself falling asleep on the bed while he worked silently on the wiring of his sign. Pictures drifted into her head from the edges of sleep. Leon standing on the roof of Brooklyn Flats and hurling a television down on to the car park below, smash! What else are televisions for? Leon sleeping on the beach at five o'clock in the morning with his head on a wine cask as the sun rises over the hazy sea.

Or Leon and Maria wading in the fishpond behind the greenhouses where the wedding couples go to be photographed, ankle deep in the cold water in the grey light of a rainy dawn, the white sky breaking up into humidity and drifting down on to their heads and the white gloves of the arum lilies raised in pale applause.

In her sleep she saw the shadow of her hand over the red wash of her eyelids, sun rising over the black curve of a hill. She saw the shape of Marcus's back as he lay beside her on his side, asleep. She felt the solid weight of him in the bed and the heat of his body on her stomach, on her legs. But Leon whispered close to her ear, 'Hey . . . I have to go to work.'

She jumped awake and sat up. He was kneeling next to the bed, screwdriver in his hand.

'I have to go in to work this afternoon. For a couple of hours.'

She said without thinking, 'Marcus came over last night. I missed him.'

Leon rolled his eyes and stood up. He shrugged and smiled thinly. 'Him. The way he stomps about . . . as if he's had his brain removed.'

She got up off the bed. 'No, he's really clever. It's just that he's gone into rebellion, and got lost . . . Or, he has an idea about life . . .'

She went on in a rush while he looked down at her and laughed the way he always did when she was in earnest. Folding his arms while he listened to her talk, his savage grin turning his face into a mask.

'It's not funny.'

'It's sick.'

'I'm serious.'

Leon unhooked a jacket from the chain wardrobe. He took out a packet of Rothmans and gave her half.

'I love him actually.'

'Ugh.' Leon writhed. Then he looked out the window and said quickly, 'Where are you going now? Do you want to come to work with me?'

He had the work van and they drove across town to the big commercial barn in Ponsonby where Leon had the mezzanine floor workroom and huge work table to himself now that he was called a graphics manager and made more money than the workers down on the showroom floor. They made commercial displays for trade fairs and conferences, sometimes for television advertisements and films. Up in his workroom under the skylight Leon turned into a carpenter, wielding drills and cutters and saws, ordering his assistant Carol around through a mouthful of nails. Carol was a youth whose real name was Burnett, and who trailed about after Leon shaking his head and laughing in a long-suffering way.

Downstairs in the boardroom Leon conducted meetings with his bosses in the long afternoons when they would send Carol out for wine and plan logistics for the next project and Leon would become shrewd and businesslike, dragging on his cigarette and turning the pages of the budget or the ground plan while his bosses nodded thinly in the brown light under the tinted windows and whispered in the papery quiet, and took notes.

The place was empty now, on Sunday afternoon. Only three or four people at work. Maria sat on a stool in the workroom with a cup of coffee. She picked up the phone and dialled Marcus's number, listening to it ring and ring. She was about to hang up when the phone was answered. A woman's cautious hello. Maria sat up straight on her stool, tipped over the coffee, went into her usual flap.

'Oh there *is* someone there, I couldn't believe you'd all be out on a Sunday . . .'

But there was dead silence on the other end, the usual patient stoicism of the Connick Streeters as Maria gruesomely joked and jollied along.

'Heavy night over there was it, suppose you were all in a *coma* when I rang?' Maria felt herself making faces into the receiver with the strain, her casually shameful 'Is Marcus there?' sinking like a stone into the embarrassing pool of silence. Seconds passed until Maria lost her nerve and rapped out sharply, 'What's the problem? Is he dead?'

'I don't know,' the voice said in a derisive tone that brought Maria up short.

'Who is this?' she said.

'Who's *this*?'

'Is that you Brendelia?'

'Is that you Brendelia?'

'Can I speak to Marcus, please?'

'Can I speak to Marcus, please?'

'Oh, fuck this!' Maria grappled flusteredly with the phone cord as it snaked around her hand.

'No,' said the voice. 'Fuck *you*.'

And hung up. Maria's chin sank on to her chest. She thrust the phone on to the work table. Where were Leon and Carol? Were they in the room? She looked sideways. They were, of course, they

they were right there, Leon at the end of the desk cutting squares of black tile, Carol scratching his raw face and playing with a scalpel. Both watching her as she swivelled the stool around and stared out the window willing away the shameful, hurting prickle of tears.

Leon tossed her the cigarettes. She took one mechanically and glanced over at them. 'What a bastard,' she said heavily.

'What did he say?'

'Nothing. It wasn't him. It was some woman.'

'Oh.'

'Oh never mind,' she said. 'Forget about it. Forget about him.'

'Yeah, fuck him,' Leon said happily, attempting a southern drawl. 'He was trash.'

Maria wandered around the warehouse while Leon worked. She was frustrated and restless, picking up bits and pieces of stuff, drinking several cups of coffee. She decided to drive over to Connick Street and find out what was going on, got her bag and halfway out the door, then decided it was a bad idea, she would look a fool going over there uninvited.

She couldn't decide who it was she had talked to on the phone. It was Chrissie, she supposed. But it wasn't like Chrissie. The voice was flat and hard, and so caustic. Surely Chrissie's voice was lighter, more girlish, more dumb?

Maria recalled herself chatting jokily into the phone (that twinkly, tolerant tone she assumed, like a Girl Guide leader – you young people, can't tell me anything new) and cringed and stabbed a hole through her Styrofoam cup with her finger, spraying hot coffee on to the front of her shirt. Carol looked up from his work bench and smirked at her and then turned red, and looked unhappily away.

Anyway Chrissie was supposed to be gone. She was supposed to have left Marcus weeks ago because he was unkind to her. He was always cloistered with the hard men while they conducted drug-taking experiments, or labouring over his novel, always irritable and preoccupied and not talking. That was what Maria had understood. But how did she actually know this? Marcus never told her anything specific, just that Chrissie had gone away, woundedly, to live with her mother in a tiny house somewhere in the western suburbs, where she and her mother watched the soaps and dreamed of making a world trip one day, if they ever won the lottery. Marcus said to Maria one night as they walked towards his house, 'Do you know what they dream about? Do you know what they go on and on about? Having enough money to go to Disneyland.'

He kicked the gate hard with his foot, and Maria chuckled in superior agreement, ridiculous! Later she had laughingly mentioned Disneyland and his face had creased satisfyingly as if he were in pain.

That morning after she'd stayed he was less sarcastic than usual and lay on the couch in the living room with his head on her lap. He had a hacking cough, he said he felt sick. He thought he had TB or whooping cough, he was pale and gloomy and said he was ready to die. Maria had sat there in the green twilight for an hour or two looking down at his creased forehead and the wiry blond of his hair. For a long time she sat there in the gloom perfectly still, saying nothing at all, perfectly content.

And there was no sign of Chrissie when Maria stayed over, no feminine things by the side of the bed. Just an ugly plant in a pot, and some bits and pieces of cheap junk on the bedside table. But how often did Maria stay with Marcus? Hardly ever. It was usually Marcus who came knocking at *her* window, late at night. For all she knew he could have had Chrissie waiting over at his house while he climbed in the window at Maria's.

Maria sighed. She last saw Chrissie a month ago, walking along Queen Street with one of her girlfriends, between shifts at work and heading for McDonald's probably, or Burger King. Tripping along on her perfect little legs, with her fragile face under the neatly shaven head. Giggling her way towards a burger or 'furter or a packet of chippie creams, in a plastic nook. In neonland. Somewhere in the mirrored malls.

Maria stopped pacing. She felt as if things were occurring that she should know about, as if she were shut out of some essential knowledge. She waited impatiently on the mezzanine floor until Leon came to find her. He tried to cheer her up on the way home.

'You'll be a good lawyer. You're completely corrupt.'

'Thanks. Did I ever tell you I know a woman called Christal da Silva?'

He rolled his eyes. 'You've told me that.'

'Oh. Sorry. It's just . . . Marcus . . .'

Ignoring her, Leon pulled over in Ashton Road. Today he had reacted to any mention of Marcus with impatience, amused contempt. Last week in the Schooner Maria had got on to the subject of Marcus – she had ideas about him, she would run on about him, forgetting herself: in her mind he represented a particular phenomenon, he was an oddity, someone, somehow at odds with himself . . . Coming out of her monologue she realised that Leon had been silent throughout, watching her, his eyes mocking and amused, but tolerant too, affectionate and resigned. She changed the subject. Leon had such a quality – was it personal, was it *Czechoslovakian?* – of ancient suffering turned to knowledge. She would be earnest, she would be chipmunkishly solemn, and he would smoke and sip and sit back with his teasing smile, and she would sense his infinite subtlety. Sometimes there might have been a flash of pain in the blue eyes. But Leon was tough. Leon moved on his own wild plain, beyond her, beyond the pale.

He gave her half his packet of cigarettes, revved the accelerator and roared off up the road, shouting good-bye over the noise of the engine. She hurried up the path and unlocked the door. The hallway was full of smoke. Clouds of it drifting and billowing greyly around her as she opened the living room door and peered into the gloom. The TV in the far corner played syrupy orchestral music, and a school of purple and yellow tropical fish rippled across the screen: *Treasures of the Pacific*. Ernest liked to watch nature programmes on Sundays, they made him feel fresh. Christ. Maria coughed and flapped, 'Can't you open a window?'

On the couch Ernest moved slightly and made a snorting noise, he was asleep, or unconscious. Maria crossed the room, pulled up the blinds and flung the windows open, the smoke pouring out of the room and flying up to join the clouds racing fast towards the top of the suburb, as if the extinct crater of Mount Eden had become a mouth sucking in the sky in a long, angry breath.

Maria stood over Ernest and shook his shoulder. He turned and moaned, pushing her away. She went into the kitchen and set about clearing the disaster he had created in the couple of hours she had been away. He had been blending again, some egg or milkshake mixture. Since he had broken the lid of the blender (dropped it then stood on it) he tended to use any item that came to hand to keep the maelstrom of liquid inside the jug of the machine. His sleeve for example, or his hand. An old pair of underpants. Clearly there had been an explosion of matter near the windows. A problem with the overfull rubbish bag, and so on.

Maria restored order with a certain amount of grim satisfaction. It was a discipline to be thorough. She needed order. Her own room was usually spotless and tidy. She liked cleaning. Sometimes she would come home from being out with Leon, and drunkenly reorder her drawers and tidy her room. Then she would wake in the morning in her spotless cell, with the books lined neatly on the shelves and the tidy desk with her notes and folders carefully set out, the door shut firmly against Ernest's good-natured chaos. In this way life retained shape and purpose. The events of the night were kept in their rightful place, in the night. You had to take life seriously . . .

In this way Maria moved purposefully forward, reading text-books, writing essays, taking exams. Leon was purposeful too during the day, moving through his hours at work. His colleagues had no idea what he got up to after hours. Or if they did they didn't care. They were non-conformists themselves, although successful. One day he'd be permanent down there in the brown boardroom, maybe driving a Rolls-Royce like his boss, why not.

Maria went into her room which had been knocked out of shape in the night by Marcus and in the morning by the wind. She tidied everything and dusted and vacuumed. She felt better and made a cup of coffee in the renewed kitchen while Ernest lay, still uncon-scious, on the couch. She stood over him drinking her coffee, looking down at his pale grey face, the spectacles pushed crookedly up on to his forehead. You could never be angry with Ernest, with his enthusiasm, his bad driving, his struggles with hand-eye co-ordination. He was brought up on a commune in the Far North. He had left when he turned sixteen, his mother weeping after him at the carved kauri gate. No wonder he was addicted to television – he had never watched one until he was a teenager. No wonder he had never learned how to flush the lavatory. He had lived a life of long-drop toilets, bare feet, reading by candlelight.

Maria sat primly in her orderly room. Perhaps she would ring Marcus tomorrow, perhaps not. She would ring Leon definitely. She could rely on him. Her last friend – she always thought of Leon, for some reason, as her *last* friend; she supposed it was because he was her best friend, the one who would be left when all others were gone.

Maria had a few girlfriends, like fat, dishonest, guilty Serena who got fired from every job she took on, and freckly Pepi who was vegetarian and who yearned vainly – she was as bumbling and grace-less as a toddler – for a career in creative dance. They were good friends, but when she was with them Maria couldn't shrug off the feeling that they were, ineluctably, a weaker drug, and she would find herself at the end of an evening with a powerful craving for Leon. Extremist that he was, he had the effect of making the people around him seem flavourless and pallid.

Maria hummed and sang as she dusted her shelves. She often wondered about her own destructive tendencies. Clearly she had an antisocial nature. Serena and Pepi, for example, would sit in a bar and joke and laugh and make lively conversation. They would have a nice night out. And then they would go home. For Leon, on the other hand, especially in the first year she'd known him, the evening would have only just begun. He would head out of the bar, stroll down the road and set fire to a phone booth, just as he was passing. Or blow up a car. Or do a little smash and grab, one brick through the window and there was a nice new stereo or TV. And from the first time they'd met, years ago, when she was a disorderly and excitable fifteen-year-old newly arrived in Auckland to stay with her aunt, Maria was with him, watching in the shadows, beside her-self with fascination and glee.

There was nothing violent, and nothing dully businesslike, about Leon's crime. There wasn't really a profit motive, although he kept the trophies that he stole. It was a performance. It was dangerous, it was rebellion, but it was comedy above all. He would roll his eyes in mock desperation, he would spin and hurl a brick with a flourish. As the sirens wailed he would tiptoe theatrically away into the shadows, laden down with his goods, often escaping by a whisker, by the skin of his teeth. Maria was the assistant but more importantly the audi-ence (hiding behind something usually, to escape detection) and the more she laughed, the wilder his routines became. She once read a Woody Allen interview in which he described Diane Keaton as 'behaviourally funny'. That was Leon, she'd thought immediately. Behaviourally funny, crashing drunkenly through the streets in his striking clothes, gorgeous under his spiked blond hair, the wild comic intensity burning in his eyes.

She described Leon's exploits to Marcus. 'You sound like a folie à deux,' Marcus said once, rather priggishly, and she supposed he was probably right.

And the price for Leon's theatre, the entrance fee, was the risk – at any moment player and audience could be bailed up, thrown into the police van and taken to Central Police, to be booked for an appearance in another show, the District Court. Leon probably appeared there because he liked to get caught on some occasions to vary the play. Usually he went home alone but sometimes he went home with the cops: it partly depended, Maria thought, on whether he felt that the action called for an arrest. (And try explaining this to the tut-tutting magistrates, the baffled police, the harassed and irritated duty solicitors – I did it because it was in the script.)

It might have amused him too, as added spice, the extra adrenaline needed to survive in the terrible concrete warren of cells under Central Police. He would emerge alert, wild-eyed, briskly waving good-bye. 'Sorry I can't stay longer,' he would say mockingly as he was leaving.

What did it cost him, his performance art? It was his whole life, and so he lived hard. He was beautiful, with dark shadows under his eyes, and a throaty smoker's laugh, and the air of someone forever in extremis, because only the extreme would do, because it had to be all or nothing, because chaos was the force that kept him right up against the line of life, and touching it.

Maria walked up the road to buy herself a Chinese takeaway and sat on the bench in the takeaway bar waiting for the food to be cooked. She watched some little boys play-fighting and shouting at the bus stop.

There was nearly a fight last night, she remembered suddenly, in the queue at Quays nightclub. A rowdy youth in a purple jacket with a hood kept spitting at her feet and Maria, who hated spitting, who couldn't step over a phlegmy hoik on the street without retching, turned on him in the queue and told him angrily to stop, to *quit it*, and glared at him, into his little eyes. His face was mean and craggy and he was muscular and stocky, built like a barrel. A nose-breaker, arm-twister and head-butter, for sure. A woman-hitter, unmistakably.

But as she and the man in the purple hood had squared off, Leon, who had been watching silently, had taken Maria by the arm and walked with her to the head of the queue, the man following behind them taunting and jeering, and as they had reached the solid mass of the Maori doorman's bulk, his huge arm had miraculously gone up and he had let them through.

She had looked back as they were whisked inside into the crowd and the doorman was frowning after her with his huge sad brown eyes, and then he turned away to face the crowd outside.

She never did see the man in the purple hood after that. It seemed that he had never made it through the door.

4.

Marcus Klein was ready for discharge on Wednesday morning, two days after he had been brought in. He was given forms to be filled out for the out-patients' clinic and told to report back in a couple of days. They gave him a prescription for the painkillers he had been taking, little pills that did something strange to the roof of his mouth and made the edges of everything seem sepia brown. The tablets were brought around on a tea trolley by a crafty Samoan nurse who leaned over the bed and asked insinuatingly, 'You wan some trugs, eh?'

He was stiff all over, with an ache of pain somewhere behind the sepia confusion of the pills, and his arm seemed to him to be leaden and heavy, and to smell very strange. He felt he was in no fit state to leave, he could have lain there for another week in the sterile calm behind the white sheets of the hospital blinds, hiding, tended to by his Island temptress and the soothing contents of her trolley.

The thought of his room at Connick Street filled him with depression and dread and when his friends came swinging in on Monday, bringing with them the disorder of their street boots and clothes, their smells, their warm smiles and their claustrophobic sympathy, he had to stop himself turning his face to the wall and shouting at them to go away.

He lay with his cheek on the white pillow case, staring as the green hospital stripe seemed to waver on the white linen and turn brown.

'He's stoned,' Brendelia whispered tenderly, leaning over him and brushing her chest across his ear. The ear burned and itched. He turned over. Brendelia's face loomed in front of him so that he

could smell her thick make-up and see the loose flesh of her face
quiver slightly as she purred at him and straightened his pillows.

He lay under the overpowering shelf of the Brendelian breasts.
She wasn't very old, only in her early twenties, but fat and a big
bosom and that heavy face, the flaps of the cheeks like the jowls of a
beige bulldog, had turned her stolidly maternal before her time.
She cooed at Marcus, heaving him around, apparently trying to
tuck him in. She liked to treat Marcus as if he were a little boy.

With Mike she was tenderly strict and ordered her cup of tea in
the mornings like a benevolent madam, sending him staggering
along the corridor, pale with exhaustion and pride after a stormy
night on board the gigantic barge of her thighs. Marcus stared up at
her and wished that she would just go away.

She wasn't with them, of course. He had heard them coming
along the corridor, they never went anywhere without creating a
commotion.

Darlene, who was darkly silent in the background as usual, had
brought Marcus some green grapes. When Mike and Mike were
leaning out of the window to smoke, Marcus tried to draw Darlene
closer, in the hope that she would tell him something without him
having to ask.

Darlene wore her tight-fitting black work uniform – she
worked as a greeter in a restaurant in a big hotel, emerging from
a stained wood booth at the front of the restaurant to escort the
diners, who eyed her slender stockinged legs and tried to joke
with her and received absolutely no response. Opinions on her
were divided, Branko had told Marcus, one manager wanted to
fire her for being too cold, the other liked her style, it subdued the
diners so much that they ate without complaining and left a large
guilty tip.

She washed the grapes for Marcus in the hospital sink and
dropped them on to the sheet in front of his nose. He watched a procession of tiny half-drowned insects decamping from the stem and
trudging off down the sheet.

'I'm supposed to leave here in a couple of hours, after they've
come and had a last look at my arm.'

'It smells funny in here.'

'So how's my bedroom?'

'Just the same.'

'Does it look very bad?'

She shrugged and began to turn away. He reached out for her arm and said, 'Wait . . . Has anyone . . .'

Darlene stood looking at him steadily out of the green slits of her eyes and he hated her suddenly, he could see she knew what he wanted to know and that she wouldn't tell him – she'd never break out of a lifelong habit of constipated meanness to help him . . . the bitch.

Marcus felt his forehead, he was sweating. He struggled around in the sheets. He'd get her fired from work. He'd tell Branko to get rid of her, tell Branko to tie her to a tree and shoot her. She was standing over the bed twisting her hand around her thin brown wrist. Then she leaned over him and said quickly, 'You want to know where Chrissie is. All I know is . . .'

Marcus struggled to sit up but there was a shuffle of feet outside and the swish of the heavy swing doors and the doctor swept in, flanked by a senior nurse on one side and Marcus's sly trolley-maiden on the other and followed by ten medical students squelching respectfully along behind in white coats and soft-soled shoes.

The senior nurse swiftly ejected the Connick Streeters, with a clip around the ear for Mike for smoking and a deaf ear to the argumentative submissions of Brendelia and they all went happily protesting off down the hall, leaving Marcus to shrink under the collective gaze of the peppy old tyrant and his subdued disciples.

'Ready for you, Mr Goodfellow.' The nurse pummelled Marcus into position while the doctor took a brisk look at the clipboard on the end of the bed and tossed it over at his students.

'Good good, no problems, no problems . . . no problems?', this last a question, directed at Marcus.

The students looked expectantly down at him, a collection of clean-cut intelligent faces, spectacles, orderly collars, tidy casual clothes under the white coats, expressions ranging from attentive to anxiously bored (he was not an interesting case).

'No problems?' The doctor leaned over and shouted down at him. Then he leaned over at the students and said jovially, 'Smoking in bed.'

Marcus cleared his throat and replied with a creaking attempt at dignity, 'No problems, apart from the huge *burn* on my arm.'

The students looked at him curiously, some of them with faint hostility. But the doctor laughed and invited them to gather round and watch as the dressings were taken off and Marcus felt that he was experiencing terrible pain somewhere beyond the brown cloud of the pills.

'No need for a graft. Right as rain in no time, good as gold. Just look in at the clinic in two days' time.' He rotated Marcus's wrist gently as he spoke and Marcus replied in humiliated grunts, playing dumb, the poor ignoramus who smoked in bed. The shiny faced students looked on, neutral except for one clever-looking chubby blonde girl who smiled at him with sympathy as if she had a weakness for the poor and the uneducated and the weak.

They wrapped his arm up again, shutting in the faint smell of burnt flesh that had sickened him so much when he had woken up three days ago, alone, not knowing what had happened. *He still didn't know . . .*

But they were saying something to him, they were leaving, scribbling on their clipboards as they went. The doctor paused at the door with the students clustered around him, hesitated, then said, looking curious and serious and faintly mocking all at once, 'By the way, Marcus, how *is* your wonderful mother.'

'Oh fine, no problems at all,' Marcus whispered and fell back on to the pillow and the students filed out, the chubby girl surprised, the eyes of the others full of derision, he could see it, derision and scorn.

The swing door swished shut. Ah, humiliation. His eyes burned, as if they would have filled with tears if they weren't so dry and hot and brown with shame. The doctor *had* looked familiar: some old tennis partner of his mother's no doubt, one of those limber old stick-men she had over for lunch on Sundays. Marcus lay and burned in the sweaty sheets. What he wanted now was to find her, find that Chrissie and fuck her to pieces. Then bash her up, then fuck her again until all the pain and the itch of his shame was gone. He would pick her up by the ear when he found her and throw her screaming into bed. How could she have done this to him? Her, with her round mouth and her skinny legs and her cartoon-round eyes. He was going to find her and he was going to sort her out. And then. Then he was going to leave her.

'Did I tell you that I caught fire?'

He waited for it, the silence then the long indrawn squawk of Maria's giggle. He enjoyed hearing it.

'But what do you mean?' she said.

'I caught fire.'

He lay on his bed, flicking his ash into the plant pot. While he'd been away the Connick Streeters had lovingly fixed up his room. Stripped the bed, washed everything, turned the mattress over, vacuumed and washed the carpet (and who knew where they'd borrowed the vacuum cleaner from). The hard men had tenderly helped him from the taxi, supported him up the path to the door.

'I've dusted,' Brendelia informed him with indignant pride before he turned her out of the room, feigning weakness. They had carried the mattress out on to the verandah Brendelia said, and draped it on top of the old bath to air. Now the mattress emitted no smell of smoke but was cold and lumpy and probably fireproof on account of being so exceedingly damp, and the hollow where Chrissie used to lie was gone and replaced on his side by the lump of bedspring that formed the reverse of the hollow.

He wriggled his shoulder blades and listened to the sound of Maria's voice. What was she telling him, something about her new job, an orientation course? 'The firm's so big,' she said, 'it's like a factory.'

'What do you have to wear?'

'Wear? Just corporate style clothes, you know, woman's equivalent of suit and tie.' She laughed, an apologetic sound. 'Not your style.'

Not his style. Not Chrissie's style. Shaven hair, trim curves of her small brown legs, in rip-cord shorts. He pictured Maria in a suit. Pinstripes. Stockings. Suddenly he said, 'Why don't you come over?'

'I can't. I'm only on the lunch-break, we're having salmon pastries,' and she launched into a description of the lunch and the boardroom and the other recruits on the orientation course at Quinn St John, talking on in her nervous way, her account full of ironies and absurdities and all the other ingredients desperately chucked into the stew of her talk.

He was disappointed. He wanted her to come over straight away. He listened to her, enjoying the sound of her voice. She was nervous, as usual. Super-articulate. He wanted her to sit by his bed and tell him things. He was in such pain.

He felt the tremendous effort going on on the other end of the phone, the battle she fought every time she called. She'd forgotten what he'd said, she hadn't taken him seriously.

'Did I tell you I caught fire?' He said it again, to stop her talking.

She hesitated. 'Do you mean, really?' She snorted uncertainly again.

'I went on fire in bed.' He could hear her fumbling with the phone. She wasn't meant to be using it, she'd said, she was supposed to be mingling with the other recruits. She'd sneaked away . . .

'Were you smoking in bed?' she asked carefully now.

'I usually do.'

'And you set yourself on fire?'

'Probably.'

'Are you hurt?' This with a suppressed shriek of laughter into the phone. He moved the receiver an inch away from his ear and said, 'I've been in hospital,' and then lay back and listened with satisfaction to the chaos of her response. 'I had no idea you'd find it so droll,' he said politely, and of course – and it really was unnerving – that mild observation set her off all over again.

Maria filled in the wrong part of a form, then embarrassedly scrib bled it out. She looked over the table but there were no other forms with which to make a fresh attempt, and she handed up the crumpled effort to Ms Klara Leather, orientation instructor for the current module, Office Systems.

The new recruits of Quinn St John were learning how to request property searches and to make up trust cheques and how to ask for documents to be typed up and items to be copied and how to open files and close files and to itemise costs and disbursements and how to order cases out of the database, all of which required the filling in of forms and the ticking of boxes, the keeping of carbon copies, the filing of forms in the correct trays to the correct secretaries who sat in little wooden nooks silently typing in the tinted corporate light.

When they had arrived that morning the recruits were directed to a boardroom in the air-conditioned hush on the twentieth floor, seated around a large table and told to introduce themselves to the group. Themselves and their interests. Ms Leather watched each floundering victim closely and made secretive ticks and notes on her clipboard.

Having got through this embarrassment, and having had to go first, 'My name is Maria Wallis, born in Tauranga, studied at Auckland University [which was true], interests: skiing, jogging, aerobics, cycling,' which was all lies of course, but which, judging by the clean-cut appearance of her fellow recruits, in their case would probably be true, Maria retreated back into her seat and stared at the grey sky hanging heavy with moisture around the tops of the buildings outside. She imagined herself telling Marcus about it: 'I've never been skiing in my life.'

As she expected, Maria's pretend sporting interests were the narrowest of the group, she appeared quite a sloth compared to the triathletes, water-skiers, captains of first elevens, netballers, marathon runners. Ms Leather smiled coldly and took notes.

There were twelve of them, all to be orientated, then sent to work as law clerks in the various teams – banking and finance, corporate and commercial, litigation. Maria was to go to commercial property. 'Welcome to Quinn St John,' smiled the icy Ms Leather. 'We're confident you'll all do well.'

They practised with forms and files, then took a tour through the labyrinth of the firm, ten floors of offices, dim reception areas, the glass coffee tables piled with slippery brochures, bright modern paintings on the walls, the tiny click of keyboards, the silent conference rooms overlooking a landscape of roof and duct and lift shaft.

Maria looked down and saw the canopies on the buildings far below, grey and tan and blowing hard in the easterly wind, mute-buttoned, no sound up there in the glass tower but the far-away roar of the canned air circulating in the pipes. A green crane like a gaunt stick-insect slowly winching a load across the skyline and the tiny cars racing far away up the slope of the harbour bridge. In the distance the harbour was turquoise under heavy cloud, speckled with white caps.

In the dry air of the library the spidery librarian showed them how to extract cases out of the legal web and in the word-processing rooms the chubby Sherryns and Deslies waved friendly greetings at the recruits and clicked away under pictures of cute monkeys and furry kittens and postcards that said 'Don't ask, I'm going real fast' and 'Secretaries are human too'.

Then back to the boardroom for a role play, during which Ms Leather took the part of a terrifyingly dissatisfied client, and finally adjournment for the catered lunch of low-fat salmon pastries, coffee and fruit, during which Maria mingled with the group long enough to learn that Ms Leather was in training for an 'Iron Woman' event which involved jogging around the perimeter of the North Island. Not to be outdone the ruddy-cheeked recruits chimed in, modestly revealing themselves to be in training for various gruelling sporting events. When Ms Leather raised the possibility of water-skiing to Rangitoto to raise money for charity and looked keenly around the assembled party, Maria mentioned the Ladies to no one in particular and edged slowly out of the room.

She whispered into the telephone to Marcus, 'They're all paratroopers. Or incredible liars.'

She glanced up along the padded corridor but it was empty and quiet. She had found her way into the top reception area near the lift. The phone had been too tempting, on her way back from the Ladies she had quickly dialled his number. I'll hang up if it's not him she thought, and he had answered. It was the first time she had called since last Sunday, when the venomous voice had confused and baffled her and hung up the phone. She didn't mention the voice but talked on, entertaining him with details of her current ordeal. Trying to tone herself down but she couldn't help it, she was so happy to be talking to him again after so long, and he was so funny in his deadpan way, it was hard not to just break down and . . . But what was he saying to her now, something about being on fire?

'I'll come and see you at six,' she said after listening to him properly at last, and it was only after she had put down the phone and hurried back to the group that she realised she was meeting Leon at six o'clock, in a bar on the roof of the Clayton International Hotel. 'Can I put Leon off?' she thought, looking at Ms Leather, who was up the front now armed with a whiteboard and a pen, drawing diagrams and pointing with a long plastic pointer.

His whole arm burnt, from his hand to his armpit, he could have been killed. Two days in hospital. Not avoiding her but hurt, in pain, bewildered with painkillers. How reckless he was, how self-destructive.

'You could have killed yourself,' she'd scolded, and he had modestly agreed. And how keenly observant he was, about the doctor, and the medical students, and the sultry nurse. She would go straight to Connick Street in a taxi, take some luxuries, some magazines. But Leon . . . Leon would be waiting.

One of the firm's partners had joined Ms Leather now to talk to them about filing documents in court. Maria watched as the partner slouched across the room in his rumpled suit, shirt hanging out the back of his trousers, his shoes dragging along the floor as if they were sticking to the carpet when he lifted his feet. While Ms Leather introduced him he stood looking at the floor, shifting from foot to foot and darting glances out at the group from under his floppy brown fringe.

Maria flicked towards the relevant pages in the book of precedents on the table as the partner, named apparently Mr Giles Speer, riffled through the Xeroxed pages, lost control of the book, grabbed for it as it fell and succeeded in catching one of the pages only, so that it tore in half and the book fell in disarray to the floor. Scrabbling for it, he backed into Ms Leather's whiteboard, causing it to fold up and collapse with a decisive bang. The group shifted and tittered.

'Don't panic,' murmured Ms Leather, rolling her eyes and smiling with sealed lips. Giles Speer picked the board up, glancing sideways at her from under his hair. Shifting and fidgeting and smiling at them all he began to explain filing procedures for court, and as he talked he pushed the hair out of his eyes and rocked on his heels and reached around and tried in vain to tuck the back of his shirt into his trousers. He had a roundish face and a nose peeling with sunburn. Maria watched him talk, noting his awkwardness, his untidy suit, his schoolboy hair. Pretty unsmooth, she thought to herself, and liked him for it.

But she needed the phone again, because she couldn't possibly meet Leon now that she knew that Marcus was lying there all burnt. What to do? Please sir I want to use the . . . Just like school.

She sat listening and looking out the window while the wind stirred the water lying on the flat concrete roofs and the pedestrians were little whirlwinds of coloured cloth far below, blowing along the windy canyons of the streets.

Half an hour later they were allowed to get up, and Ms Leather announced that they were to have a tour of the District Court. They assembled outside the boardroom and rode silently down in the mirrored lift to walk the short distance to the courthouse. There they were to make a quick tour of the courtrooms and offices, led by Ms Leather and one of the court clerks. They were given a talk by a registrar, and shown into the courts where the civil matters were heard.

On their way out again they passed the criminal courts, outside which the day's criminals sat in sullen rows. Maria looked along the line of blotched and beaten and tattooed faces. She saw broken teeth, wraparound sunglasses, faces hopelessly obese, or impossibly thin. The criminal lawyers hurried through the halls shouting pleasantries at one another without stopping to talk.

Ms Leather hurried the recruits past the criminal courts, since Quinn St John was a commercial firm, but Maria lingered, mainly because she was hoping to find a phone. She watched a running child pursued up the corridor by its mother, captured, swept up into the air and heavily slapped, the great hand on the tiny leg, the desolate wail, the tiny face over the large shoulder, borne bumping away up the hall. A woman shouted furiously at someone and raced into the toilets with her hand over her mouth as if she were about to be sick. An elderly couple argued drunkenly, feebly pushing one another and stumbling against the walls. Young men sat staring straight ahead with their arms folded, their legs wide apart in black jeans, black hair short on top and long at the back, eyes hidden behind black sunglasses.

Maria hurried up the hall pretending to look for someone, looking into the faces that were set into the attitude of stubborn neutrality necessary for enduring long waits, crippling fines, the heavy imposition of heavy time. She couldn't tell whether they were looking at her or whether they were even awake behind the sunglasses. She walked on up the line until she stopped and said loudly without thinking, 'Oh, it's *you*.' The line of eyeless faces turned slightly and looked in her direction, in silence.

'You're the doorman,' she said, already feeling ridiculous and beginning to back away.

He lounged on the seat in front of her, his massive arms folded. She was about to say something non-committal and hurry off when he stood up and offered her his enormous hand. She shook it with relief and the eyeless heads turned slowly away. She said, 'Sorry, I just . . . I go to Quays quite often . . .'

'I remember you,' he said. 'What *nyou* here for?'

Maria glanced up the hall at the disappearing figure of Ms Leather. 'I'm actually doing a tour . . . of the court.'

'A tour.' He repeated it, amused.

'Yes, well . . . I . . .' She looked down at the bird tattooed on his hand and laughed. Then the door of the courtroom opened, and a thin policeman emerged, and consulted a list of names.

'Wiremu-McDonalds-Ihaka!' he shrieked out in a jerky nasal voice. 'Ihaka-W-M!'

The doorman from Quays clicked his tongue cowboy-style, and winked. 'What's your name?' he said. She told him.

'Ma-ri-a,' he repeated, imitating the cop. 'Got to go, Maria,' and he winked again and sauntered towards the policeman.

'Wiremu Ihaka?'

'Yo.' Looming insolently over the cop, every movement of his large body conveying derision and insult.

The policeman pushed open the swing door. He ushered the doorman in ahead, took a firm hold of his clipboard, glared at the blank row of faces along the wall and stalked into the courtroom, pulling the door shut behind him.

Maria was leaving when the policeman came out of the court-room again. As he passed she stepped politely into his path and asked, 'What's going on in that court?'

The cop stopped and glared suspiciously at her out of round and close-together eyes. 'The charge? Perverting the course of justice.'

'Oh, really?'

He looked curiously at her, but a sergeant leaned out of a nearby room and called to him and he turned and marched off, whistling, as if to ward off further affront.

Maria looked down the corridor but the party had vanished, and she hurried after them. Ms Leather had herded the recruits into a circle outside the front doors of the courthouse, and as Maria tried to infiltrate the group without being noticed she was telling them that they were expected upstairs in the Quinn St John drinks room, for an informal meeting with partners and members of staff.

'But I can't,' Maria thought, glancing up towards the roof of the Clayton Hotel. She would have to think of an excuse for not going. In the foyer of Quinn St John she sidled up to Ms Leather armed with a hastily invented lie about an appointment, which thin false-hood Ms Leather received in stony silence. Maria offered more, into the void. 'Dental. One of those things. Tooth just falling to bits.'

She realised that she was looking to the right and scratching the tip of her nose with her finger, actions which, as Ms Leather had just taught them in Office Communication/Body Language, signalled clearly to her audience that she was telling a lie. Maria hurried off out of the building as the other recruits waited for the lift up to the drinks room, aware that Ms Leather was staring narrowly after her and making notes on her clipboard with her ballpoint pen.

Maria entered the tinkling rock garden of the hotel foyer and skated towards the lifts. She rode up through the thin glass tower and walked up the artificial grass slope to the outdoor roof area where the bar tables were grouped under umbrellas around the pool. Up there tourists in sports clothes and sunglasses lay sprawled on deckchairs in jet-lagged comas, ignoring the view, ignoring the small swimming pool, the water in the pool heavy green and blown into little waves by the wind. The sky hanging over the city of rooftops was grey and low with rain.

A solitary waiter played with the cutlery at a long buffet table by the bar while the white canopy over his head flapped and tore at its strings. Suddenly the waiter leapt and danced, clutching his hands at the air as napkins blew up and whirled around in the wind, and were whisked up by an updraught and snatched down by a down-draught to settle on the surface of the pool, where they spread and floated fan-like across the surface and were retrieved by the waiter who scooped them up with a long-handled net.

Leon sat on the far side of the pool, with his feet up on a low wall, staring out over the roofs. Standing up and greeting her now, with his sunglasses sitting low on his long graceful nose and the crooked

tooth resting on his lower lip, and his gold earrings, he looked like a
pirate, or the jack in a card pack. Or the joker. Colourful, handsome – the wild card. He was already working his way through a
bottle of wine and she sat down ready to tell him about the orientation course and the recruits and Ms Leather.

The white wine burned cold into the lining of her stomach and
made her feel light and she felt a surge of childish gratitude that she
was employed, in a law firm, that she would have a shiny office, that
she would be a lawyer as she had always wanted.

Leon listened and laughed. He bought another bottle of wine
and they drank it and watched the afternoon sky, the clouds moving
grey light over the city and over the green sea far away, shadows
moving over mirror buildings, tiny movement of cranes. Behind
them the tourists slept in the silence while the warm wind blew
over them, rippling their tracksuits, rippling the turquoise pool,
and the waiter sat on a deckchair of his own, playing with the handle
of his long net. Soon tiny drops of humidity began to drift down,
speckling the surface of the pool, causing the tourists to stretch and
grumble and shake themselves.

Leon stood up near the low fence at the edge of the roof and held
out his hand to feel the raindrops. Maria watched him swaying at the
edge of the roof.

'Careful,' she said.

She went to the Ladies. She sat on the lavatory and put her head
down on her knees and felt drunk suddenly, felt as if the marble floor
were falling away. Suddenly she remembered Marcus, and that he
was hurt, and that she had to see him. She hadn't told Leon about
Marcus going on fire in bed, since Leon never really wanted to hear
about Marcus. *Did I tell you I caught fire?* Maria sat in the cubicle
and laughed into her knees remembering the things Marcus said.

She went back to the table and Leon began to wave the waiter
over. 'More wine?' he called thickly. 'Why not?'

Maria said abruptly, 'No.'

He hesitated. 'What's wrong.'

She spread out her hands and told him about Marcus: Marcus
lying in his bed of pain, drugged, with painkillers, attended to by
that crew of inebriated louts. The questionable nursing capabilities
of the hard men and their chicks.

Leon snorted dismissively and waved at the waiter.

'He'll keep,' he said.

'I have to go,' Maria said firmly.

Leon marched over and gave the waiter an order. Then he came back and stood in front of her near the fence at the edge of the roof. He eyed her over the tops of his dark glasses and waved his finger at her. He swayed suddenly and she jumped up out of her seat and said angrily, 'Be careful. You'll fall off.'

'We've been in the boardroom all day. Celebrating a big deal. Drinking a crate of wine.'

He stepped away from the wall. The waiter brought over another bottle of wine and Leon took out a roll of bills, peeled off a couple and thrust them at him, grandly instructing him to keep the change.

Leon offered her the bottle and she shook her head impatiently. He tipped it up and drank out of it, then turned away from her and began walking along the low wall.

'Will you please stop playing around on the edge of the roof,' Maria said loudly. He turned and swayed and drank from the bottle again.

'You're giving me a heart attack.'

'Stay here a while,' he said. He pushed his sunglasses on to the top of his head, staring at her with his intense gaze, dark circles under his eyes, the wickedly crooked tooth making the suspicion of a laugh on his lower lip. She stared at him, distractedly admiring the way he looked. He swigged again and offered her the bottle. She took a swig and said complainingly, 'I want to go. I can't explain, I have to go. Nothing can stop me.'

She looked sideways and he was laughing at her, holding the bottle in his big right hand, keeping the left hand hidden under his arm. He swigged and teetered again near the low, unsafe wall.

'Come and see me off,' she pleaded.

'Nothing can stop me,' he mocked, but he came away from the edge and put his arm around her. 'Take these.' He took half of the cigarettes out of his packet and gave them to her. 'Do you want some money?' He felt around in his pocket for the roll of bills.

'No, no, I'm a worker now. I get paid.'

She fended him off and said goodbye quickly, and walked off towards the steps without looking back.

'Nothing can stop me,' he called after her in a high voice.

Now she was hurrying. Tapping her feet in the lift. Trotting out of the foyer, trying to find a taxi in the crowded street. Hailing in vain, finding a taxi rank, falling into the cab with the urgent instruction 'Connick Street,' listening to the staccato small-talk of the friendly driver, one Very Speedy Wong Chiu (according to his name tag) of Kurtesy Kabs. Very Speedy drove, indeed, at great speed, she noted, and very skilfully, despite his having to peer through a curtain of swinging knick-knacks. A tinkling fringe of lanterns, charms and necklaces dangled from the ceiling of the car, and a forest of ornaments decorated the dashboard and swung from the rear-view mirror.

'I'm going to see a sick friend,' she told him happily as they careered along, causing him to turn on an obliging burst of tootings and overtakings. They pulled up and Maria paid, nodding and smiling and signalling her thanks, and hustled along to Marcus's gate.

He would be expecting her. Waiting for her to come, waiting to hear her footsteps on the stairs. His pale face, creased with pain . . .

She knocked on the door and waited. There was no reply so she hurried up on to the verandah to where Marcus's bedroom window was open, and lifted the blind to peer in. He was lying on the bed on his back with his eyes closed, snoring slightly. Carefully she climbed through the window and stood over him, watching him sleep. Then she tiptoed around the room with her finger on her lips and examined the cardboard box which held his bottles of pills.

The room had been cleaned up, and there was only a small scorched area near the bed, and a brown tinge to the bottom of the curtains. There was a strong smell of damp, as if the room had been scrubbed and washed, and not properly aired. She bent down to inspect his bandaged arm. She sniffed. What was that smell, surely not burnt flesh? But how awful. She touched his shoulder and he rolled over and flung out his arm, hitting her hard on the arm with the back of his hand.

She jumped back in shock. She sat down on the chair, staring. His face was immobile, his breathing was deep. But of course, he was still asleep. She had probably hurt him. She must be more careful.

With great care, occasionally rubbing her tingling arm, Maria retidied the tidy room. Furtively, checking to see that he was still asleep, she dusted his sills and used the leftover water in the plastic jug to water his parched pot plant. Holding her breath she straightened the cover on his bed; emboldened when he remained inert she made an attempt to fluff up his pillows but withdrew hastily when he rolled over, propped himself up on his good arm and regarded her with a look of deepest malevolence.

Marcus felt every part of himself flinching as he raised his body and looked around the room. He said through clenched teeth, 'When I'm asleep it doesn't hurt.'

She apologised, she hoped she hadn't woken him up, she'd just been sitting here, just hanging out here, she'd felt like checking out this burn thing, thought he was probably having her on.

He looked at her with something closely resembling disgust.

'I've only just come in,' she said, making a little rush across the carpet to take something out of her handbag, tripping over the plant pot and falling into the chair. She fixed her eyes on a point on the wall and tittered falsely.

'No you haven't,' he said nastily. She stared at him, round eyes, round mouth opening and closing, like a fish.

He said, 'You've been in here for ages. Ever since I woke up in agony with you groping my arm. Ever since you blundered through the window like a herd of elephants.'

Her cheeks went scarlet. She stared fixedly at the sills. He struggled around on the bed, furious, he couldn't stop himself. He had wanted her to come around, he had waited and waited until he had fallen into a sick, heavy sleep. Now he was savaging her. She had touched his shoulder, and he had woken with sudden fear. It was the pain, the pain. He felt like an animal about to die, lashing out, as if his mouth was full of blood and all his flesh was torn away and she just sat there on the chair with red cheeks, and a fringe of flattened hair, her nose all sweaty from her little exertions, giving her nervous little laugh.

'I'm in pain,' he rasped at her. 'Can't you understand? It's *agony*.' He picked up a mug from the bedside table and feebly threw it on to the floor. She rubbed her eyes with the back of her hand and peered at him from under her fringe, her expression appalled, embarrassed, miserable. Her eyes strayed again towards the sills. He felt momentarily sorry for her. Dusting. The stupid bitch. He was angry again. The bed was damp, the pain was wrapped around his arm like a hot blanket. He had been waiting for Mike to get him some sleeping pills, but there hadn't been anyone in the house for hours.

'Have you got any tea?' she was asking, defiant and upset.

He sank down on to his back, muttering. 'I don't bloody know.'

She went out to the kitchen and came back with a couple of mugs of weak tea which they drank together in silence. Then she said in a high, polite voice, 'I'd better go.' She put the mug carefully down on the bedside table and stood up, torches of humiliation flaring in her cheeks. 'I think I'll go out through the door.' Giving her fake laugh, glancing at the window through which she had entered.

'Wait.' He was sorry. He wanted her to forgive him. Everything was alien and frightening. He had lost his equilibrium. He wanted her to stay.

She stood stiffly and waited. He reached out and took hold of her arm. He tried to pull her down on to the bed. She resisted, he pulled harder and she fell protesting on to the bed beside him. He put his arms around her and felt the heat from her flaming face. 'You look really stupid all red like that,' he said. 'Like a traffic light.'

He felt her wince and pull away. 'Don't go,' he whispered and held her very tight.

Then he made a valiant attempt to fuck her but by the time he'd got all his clothes off and manhandled her out of hers he was nearly weeping with the pain in his arm and he had to call a halt. They lay there for a while without moving.

'The spirit is willing,' he said politely. She gave a tiny snort of laughter and lit a cigarette for him. But she was unusually silent. He could feel her unhappiness. She lit a cigarette for herself and said in a tough, flat voice, 'It's very damp in this bed.'

He pulled her on to his good arm and they lay there cosily, and he felt better suddenly, as if it didn't matter. It didn't matter that his arm was on fire. It didn't matter that he was dying. That he couldn't work on his manuscript. That he probably couldn't have sex ever again. That when he had heard Maria climbing through the window his sleeping self had started up out of the depths of unconsciousness, flooded with adrenaline, with panic, with the words running wildly through his head – Her. It's her. Chrissie.

Maria hurtled in a taxi through the night full of rain, leaving Connick Street behind. 'See you some time,' she had called to him, slamming the door shut, as if she didn't care at all, but thought to herself, that was awful. Awful. Filled with embarrassment and pain she pressed her red cheek against the cold window of the cab.

The shadow taxi slid across fences and walls. Maria travelled past dead backyards, past ragged hedges, through the desert of gas station supermarket grey underpass. The skyline jagged with pain, pain raining on the streaming streets. Maria travelling across town at the speed of pain found the lights on in the windows of Leon's tiny house. My last friend, she always called him. My last friend.

5.

Maria knocked and heard footsteps in the hall. She said to the door, 'It's me,' and then leaned against the door jamb and waited. There was a short silence.

'Let me in,' she called.

A deep voice behind the door said, 'Who?'

'Maria.' She hesitated. 'Is that you?'

The door opened a crack and a face bearing a strong resemblance to Leon's, particularly around the eyes and nose and mouth, peered at her through the crack in the door. The same calculating, goblin-ish stare, surveying her knowingly from head to toe, the same barely suppressed amusement at the data being received. She stepped backwards, tripping over the doormat. 'Is he here?'

The face widened into a jagged Leon-shaped smile. 'The goon is in the shower,' Leon's father whispered out at her, 'no doubt recovering from the *shenanigans* of the *night*.'

Vic Pavel opened the door and let her in. He took her wet jacket and ushered her down the tiny hall, asking in his heavy Czech accent how she was, and how her new job was, and what she wanted with the goon so late on a rainy night when all good people should be in bed.

She sat down in the kitchen which was warm and bright and smelled strongly of garlic. Old Vic had been cooking something elaborate and the stove was crowded with saucepans and heavy casserole dishes. Leon shouted out from the bathroom, 'Who's that, Father?'

The old man growled through the bathroom door, 'Your nice girlfriend. Better hurry up.' Maria watched him as he made her a cup of coffee.

Vic Pavel was very like Leon, even though Leon was thin and the old man was broad and heavy. They had the same wide blue eyes, the same nose, the same handsome and wickedly laughing mouth. He gave her coffee and asked her 'Cake?', raising his eyebrows comically and reaching over to bang with his fist on the bathroom door.

The bathroom door swung open and she could see Leon frowning with concentration into the mirror as he combed his hair. He squirted in some hair potion, combed it through and came out to the kitchen.

'What happened to Marcus?' he asked her innocently.

Maria stirred her coffee, looked at the ceiling and said casually, 'Nothing. I just wanted to come over.'

'Nothing could stop you?'

'Don't laugh at me. Don't be evil.'

Leon looked pleased. 'Father came over to cook some stews. The kitchen will reek of garlic for a week.'

'It smells great.' Maria leaned back in her chair and the old man offered to heat her up some soup. He clanked around at the stove while Leon smoked contentedly and laughed at her and Maria drank coffee and ignored him laughing, and Vic sensed a gap in the conversation and embarked on a long monologue on the subject of his insomnia, for which he had hit on a solution – he had decided not to go to bed at all.

'I lie there, it's so boring,' he said, flapping his hands over the rising steam. 'Suddenly I wonder why I'm lying there night after night, waiting for sleep. Why bother? I'll be awake all night tonight. I'll be doing my gardening around four.'

'I could rig you up some spotlights,' Leon said. The old man laughed. He put two bowls on the table. The soup was rich and full, more solid than liquid. Maria and Leon ate two bowls each and then smoked and drank a shot of vodka and Maria sat about while Leon and the old man conferred about some plumbing question under the sink.

When Leon had bought the house he had converted it from a tiny dull bungalow, painted inside and out the colour of elderly milk, into his own richly decorated lair. The kitchen where they sat was painted blue and the shelves were multicoloured. There were stencilled shapes and patterns painted around the shelves and the fridge was tomato red. A yellow phone mounted on the wall above the blue table sported sinisterly moving eyes and a nose, and a long sharp pair of horns. Like the rest of the house the kitchen was furnished with contraband and the old man hovered over the pots wielding a soup ladle which Leon had stolen from the kitchens of the Clayton Hotel.

The old man regarded Leon's telephone sculptures, the stolen hotel knick-knacks, the street signs, roadworks lights, the digital sign at the front door – now broadcasting the recurrent message FUCKOFFFUCKOFFFUCKOFF – the spray-painted bathroom, the multicoloured lavatory and all the other features of the house, with an air of disapproving and exasperated amusement. Leon's mother was an artist before she died, he told Maria. It was all her fault. He called his son the goon, and regarded him as insane, but turned up in the night to cook him soups and casseroles.

Once when Leon was arrested at Mount Maunganui after a New Year's Eve riot he was amazed to see his father appear in the public gallery at the court – the old man, in Hamilton on business, had heard about disturbances at the Mount in the night and had driven all the way to the courthouse where the revellers were appearing. 'I knew you would be here,' he said to Leon outside the court. 'You dumb goon.' He gave Leon a large amount of money for the court fine, then drove back to Hamilton again.

Vic Pavel came from Czechoslovakia after he was orphaned during the Second World War. He spoke four languages. There was a story that he had told Leon once: when he was a boy in Czechoslovakia during the war he had been taken to the back of some buildings and made to help bury the bodies of all the Jews who had lived in the village.

Vic lived by himself in a flat in Parnell. After his wife died he had never remarried. Now he was getting ready to go back home, clearing up the stove, storing some of his dishes in Leon's freezer. He searched around for his car keys in the cluttered kitchen, located them under a pig-shaped ashtray, then said good-bye and went off up the drive.

Leon said teasingly to Maria, 'You going to stay here?'

'Can I?' Maria was poker-faced, still gruffly ignoring him.

'Nothing could stop you.'

It was lucky he hadn't seen her on the way over, she thought. Fleeing across town in the cab, scarlet with disappointment and humiliation. She winced at the memory of Marcus's face, his look of disgust and rage when she'd stupidly woken him up. But the soup and the vodka were making her feel tough again now, she drifted and floated and decided that she didn't care, staring at the chains on the ceiling, her eyes following the patterns of telephone cord painted on the walls. Beside her Leon lounged and smoked and idly read a Telecom catalogue. He wore a T-shirt bearing the logo NZ POLICE.

Marcus was in pain, she thought. Pain makes you angry. Pain makes you irrationally mean. She shouldn't blame him for that. She felt sympathy for him all over again. But no! Forget about him! Let him stew, in his humourless prison, with his money and success. Here in the cheerful, gnomish, garlicky little house she was warmed and comforted. Here under the eyes of the telephone monsters, under the fronds of the stolen pot plants, corralled all round with stolen household goods, the newly minted lawyer curled up against the breaker of laws and drifted off to peaceful sleep, perfectly contented and blissfully secure, and slept without waking until the tui began to brow-beat the garden awake at dawn.

In the morning Maria took a cab across town and arrived at work in time to step into the lift with Ms Klara Leather. Exchanging morning greetings, Ms Leather's a frigid nod, Maria's a guilty one, Maria sighed with secret relief that she had declined Leon's offer of a morning shot of vodka.

She followed Ms Leather out of the lift on to the grey zone of the twentieth floor where the air-conditioning roared like a far-away sea and all other sounds were tiny and electronic, and the mutely separate world moved below.

A short talk from their gimlet-eyed tutor and then the recruits were to join their teams – the members of which, of course, they had met last night at drinks – and take their places in their own offices. Maria listened with dismay to the talk, which turned out to be about Quinn St John's sports teams, and winced to hear that Ms Leather had signed them all up for some sort of netball-fest in a week's time, on a Saturday, if you please, at 8:30 a.m.

Once again Maria felt called on to make an excuse. This was impossible. After all. *Netball*. You must be . . . Eyes sliding to the right, finger toying with the tip of her nose, Maria went to the front of the room, but faltered in the full glare of the Leathern dial, signalling as it was a reluctance to engage in anything but all-out war. Maria backed off with a fraudulent smile and followed the others out to the lifts.

Maria's team had sent a representative to collect her. He stepped forward and introduced himself as Somebody Peeks-Berlyn, a mournful young man who told her as they rode down in the lift that his name had used to be Berlyn until he married his girlfriend, whose surname was Peeks, and since he and Ms Peeks wondered why women changed their names when they got married, and since it didn't seem fair, they'd changed themselves to Mr and Mrs Peeks-Berlyn. He rubbed his hands together and beamed at the ingeniousness of this plan, while Maria considered the implications for subsequent Peeks-Berlyns, should the practice carry on down the family line. The lift pinged and they were there at the twelfth floor, occupied by Property Team B, under the leadership of the partner, Mr Giles Speer.

By now Maria had ascertained that Peeks-Berlyn's Christian name was not Flip or Flop or Flup, as she had first believed, but Phillip. Phillip showed her around the floor, and led her to her office, which was on the east side of the building, looking over an expanse of roofs and a green rooftop tennis court three floors below, on which four players were engaged in a strenuous game of doubles. She watched the slanting figures through the sepia light of the tinted windows, their mouths open with silent shouts as they swooped and dived and crashed across the Astroturf.

Her guide coughed behind her and she turned back to inspect the office. It was a small rectangular room, furnished with a pale stained-wood desk and matching cupboards and drawers, a tall metal filing cabinet, a slinky little phone, and drawers full of crisp paper and pristine stationery. The room smelt hotly of new plastic and electronic equipment. It smelt like a telephone. Maria sighed. So clean, so new. Everything in such straight lines. A shiny black diary on the desk, word-processing folders labelled with her name. Even a metal plaque slotted into a groove on the door, bearing her name, M. Wallis.

Maria beamed at Peeks-Berlyn and his baggy face suddenly hitched itself above the narrow bridge of his teeth to reveal grey gums under bulges of cheekbone and a dull light in the narrowed eyes, which facial rearrangement Maria optimistically interpreted as a smile.

When she was sitting at her desk a few minutes later she heard a scraping and thumping along the carpet and the partner Mr Giles Speer came skating along the hall, dragging his shoes. He stopped outside her door and she looked up to see him leaning in from the corridor and poking his head and one shoulder around her office door, as if his shoes had ceased to peel up off the floor when he walked and become glued to the carpet outside. After exchanging wary greetings with Maria he began reluctantly to drag the rest of his body into the office, inching around the door like a man clambering around the edge of a precipice. He held in his hand a number of sheets of paper. He slid uneasily into the chair opposite her, smiled, looked to the left and the right, dropped the papers on the floor, hurriedly retrieved them, and scratched the sunburnt tip of his nose. Then he crossed his legs one way and then the other, changed his mind and crossed them the other way, untangled his shoelace from the telephone cord and when he was finally comfortable spread the papers out on the desk and proceeded to assign Maria her first piece of real work.

Two miles away Marcus Klein was reviewing his options, while above him in a round mirror a concave brown face watched his every move. He tiptoed forward over the black and white tiles, running the finger of his good hand along the dusty shelves.

Two seconds ago, before he'd realised Mrs Tiwari was watching him in the mirror like an old brown hawk, he had considered borrowing a couple of her tins of food. Only borrowing, mind you. Just a tin of soup or baked beans and meatballs.

The thing was, he was off work, and the thing was, he was running out of money. The further problem was, if he didn't work he didn't get paid, not like these people who got sick leave, because for the past six months he had worked for cash under the table, and the question of sick leave naturally hadn't come up. His boss, Ron (that criminal), would laugh of course if such a fancy concept were even raised.

Marcus, having woken that morning not only in pain but ravenous, had just struggled through a difficult phone call with Ron, during which Ron had advised him to cut the crap and get in to work or fuck off for good. Marcus had thanked him politely and hung up, and had then spent a good ten minutes just staring hopelessly at the wall.

Mrs Tiwari hitched her cardigan up around her sari and came hurrying around the corner of the shelves. She stood in front of him with her hands on her hips, glaring at him. 'Can I help you?' she demanded. Marcus smelt a hot waft of vindaloo. His mouth watered. He stared at her raisiny neck and her plumply fragrant arms and imagined himself knocking her down, tearing a spicy limb from her body, sinking his teeth into the tender flesh.

He mooched past her with a certain wounded dignity. No use. It was no use. He wandered out on to the grey street and watched the useless rubbish blowing over and over past the shop, wheeling on down the street to nowhere. It would be days before he could go back to work. He spent a great deal of the time at Ron Audio Ltd carrying heavy speakers and amplifiers around, setting up sound systems for rock concerts and public meetings. But now he could hardly pick up a matchbox with his burnt hand, let alone a speaker.

Marcus stooped lower with a fresh wave of gloom when he realised that he might never work at Ron's again. Some fresh mule would take his place. He would have to go on the dole. Or back to Burger King.

The thing about Ron Reed was that he let Marcus use the office equipment after hours, and Marcus had spent three or four evenings a week with Ron's word-processor, working on his novel. *The Hard Men* had really started to take shape once he'd had a proper machine to work on. His old typewriter seized up all the time and he couldn't edit properly and Ron had laser printers and paper and everything.

Ron Reed's company made records that Marcus's mother (that acid drop) would scathingly call 'music', with her two tiny forefingers scratching the air into inverted commas. Marcus paused, remembering the lessons he'd endured as a musical child, plinking on the piano under heavy maternal surveillance on Monday afternoons in the school hall. He had played the piano (played it well, they said) until his first day of rebellion, when he'd given up co-operating for good, when he'd drowned out his mother's favourite classical singer (the sublime Fishydishcloth) with a cleansing blast of *Slut, Slut, Dirty Bitch*.

Now it was probably all over with Ron Reed. All that word-processing time, gone. He wandered on down the street gloomily smoking and looking at the ground. He could ask his parents for money. He could, but they wouldn't hand it over without a list of conditions. He would have to undergo rehab, deprogramming, he would have to apologise for the last five years of his life. Then they'd try to enrol him at university and if he refused they'd go into hysterics all over again. And so on.

He took a deep breath, and then leaned on a lamppost to recover from it. Now his lungs were going. *Jesus* he felt a wreck. He made it to a bus stop and sat down on the seat, and sat blankly for a while looking straight ahead. Gradually he realised he was looking at the window of a café where Chrissie used to work. There was the sign that had irritated him every time he had dropped her off: 'Coffee's, Tea's, Eat's'.

She used to wear a red skirt and a gauzy white shirt, her face would be damp with the heat from the kitchen and she had a particular way of flicking her delicate wrist when she wrote orders on her pad.

He would sit in there watching her trip around the room and to entertain himself he would grab her by the arm and read her order pad when she passed. 'Chip's × 2', it would say. Or '4 sousag'es 2 egg's'.

'What's wrong with that?' she'd protest, half angry, all that sexy pouting as she grabbed the pad back, brown legs, brown arms, the perfect little face. He would feel like dragging her into the Gents and fucking her to pieces on the floor. He thought of her as *sex*. When he tried to write about her she was *sex*. Everything about her. When he had first tried to write about her he was struck to discover that he sometimes had to sneak away and jerk off, and it was hard to write about her for this reason. It was exhausting. Her bosses were always trying to seduce her, all the Valerios and Antonios and Lucianos. He would pick her up in the car after work and she'd come running out of the kitchen all hot as if she'd only just escaped with her virtue intact. Bounce into the car and kiss him on the cheek, just like that, without thinking about it. She acted naturally, without thought. Without remorse.

Marcus set about emptying his pockets. He stopped after a while since there was nothing in them except the sad five dollars he held scrunched in his hot hand. He began to experience an unreality attack. He'd had a few of these moments lately, where he knew he was in a certain place, at a certain time, doing something, but reality suddenly faded away and he became detached from himself and seemed to be looking at whatever he was doing from a long way off. Waiting for it to pass, he watched himself sitting at a bus stop, clutching a five-dollar note in his hand. He watched himself watching the café across the street. Watched himself watching himself watching himself. Watchingselfwatchingselfwatchingself.

Marcus leaned suddenly over the pavement and vomited violently into the gutter. Unreality fled in a flash and he rediscovered himself, bent double and open-throated in the desultory street. Dead paper in the wind, spinning away, and an old lady walking-sticking towards the bus stop slowed and wobbled for a second, the papery old arm straining to hold the stick steady. She nodded tinily to herself and turned firmly back the other way, *not safe there*. Marcus gargling at the pavement, turning himself inside out, looked up as the bus slowed and then sped up and roared past him up the hill, *don't stop there*. Drivers glanced out car windows and wrinkled their noses in disgust, and accelerated away.

Shivering and retching, Marcus slumped down on the bench until the gaseous burps and violent hiccups had subsided. He sighed and rubbed his watery eyes and lay quietly until he began to feel light and empty, relieved that the storm had passed. I am not very well or happy, he thought sadly to himself. Another huge involuntary sigh rose in his chest. Watery sunlight broke through the cloud and he felt the sun shining on his shoulder. A woman dragged a child by the arm past the bus stop, glaring angrily at him as she steered around the vomit. The sun was stronger now, warming Marcus through, shining on his arm and side and right leg. He stared sadly across at the café sign with its misplaced apostrophes, thought of his mother with her sharp forefingers scratching the air, saw the ghost of Chrissie behind the glass of the café with her pen in her hand, mouthing at him, shaking her wrists.

He lay like that for half an hour, then got up and walked unsteadily home. Done the shopping he thought with faint hilarity, entering the dark hall at Connick Street. What's next?

The hard men were at work (they had found their niche in demolition) and the house was coldly silent. Feeling ludicrous and childish but determined, Marcus rummaged in his chest of drawers and took out a crumpled exercise book. He tore out a page, found a biro and began shakily to write a list:

1) Food
2) Apply for dole, emergency money (tell no one)
3) Ring Ron – lie, beg, whatever
4) Ring Maria
5) Find C.

He stared at the fifth entry for a while, then crossed it out. Then picked up the biro and wrote it in again. Then hurriedly scribbled it out, and so on.

Carrying his five dollars, his list and his jacket Marcus walked stiffly back up to the main road. He took tiny steps, shuffling along like an old man. He had decided not to take the car, he couldn't deal with the difficult steering with his arm the way it was. Now he waited at the bus stop where the warm sun was cooking his pale yellow vomit into an omelette on the pavement. Fraudulently he wrinkled his nose with the other travellers, stepping over it with expressions of disgust as he climbed on to the bus. He paid his fare and rode into the city, bouncing along on the back seat, his face pressed against the cold glass of the window. Strange taste in his mouth. Bright light in his eyes. At the terminal he changed buses and rode out through the green suburbs to Meadowbank. He got out on the long stretch of main road where hedges and white board fences and garages fronted neat houses and flat gardens. He shuffled along the empty street, the pale sun above playing a white glare on the weatherboards, spreading rings of light on a swimming pool behind a pine fence.

Marcus turned into his parents' drive and saw with relief that the parental cars weren't in the carport. They would be at work, the old man at the university, where he shed his mild and secretive domestic persona and became celebrity history professor D.K. Klein – Marcus's father hosted his own TV programme in which he explored New Zealand history, and even had, apparently (oh for Christ's sake, Marcus had harassedly exclaimed on hearing about it) a fan club – his mother at the gallery where she hung around making coffee and talking art and earning three dollars a year.

The key was in its usual hiding place and he let himself into the cool, stone-flagged hall. He de-activated the burglar alarm and looked around. Everything spotless, as usual, colourfully tasteful, everything expensive and decorative. Out in the green garden the spa pool gurgled and steamed, and red bougainvillea leaves floated on the surface of the swimming pool.

He entered the kitchen and stood under the hanging bronze pots, casting his weary eye over the heavy crockery, chunky breadboards, rows of steel utensils. Elaborate plumbing, complicated appliances, hanging herbs, glossy cookbooks. The clashing colours of the hanging tea towels, indicating cheerfulness, carelessness, *relaxed colour schemes for spring*.

Marcus took a kitchen chair and drew it up to the fridge. He opened the fridge door, settled into the chair and went to work on the parental concoctions within.

Half an hour later he sighed his way towards the shower. He selected a range of bath products and lathered as best he could with one arm stuck out of the shower door, flooding the bathroom floor in the process. Wrapped in a fluffy towel, sipping chardonnay and armed with a blowdrier, he scorched his hair in the tinted mirror. In the kitchen he attacked the fridge again, and drank the rest of the bottle of wine.

Out by the pool with a vol-au-vent in one hand and the phone in the other he stared into water, so bright in the sun that it hurt, and dialled seven digits. He listened to the phone ringing in the tiny house out west. Chrissie liked to lie on the couch with a cup of herbal tea and watch the soaps while she recovered from all the shifts of her night and her mother would sit at the kitchen table calling out clues for the crossword: 'Pigs, dear, five letters.'

'Swine, Mum.' Without taking her eyes off the set.

But there was no answer at the house in the west. He rang Maria. He was connected.

'Maria Wallis,' she answered, all brisk and corporate and slightly embarrassed. He sipped wine and listened with silent enjoyment while she described her new office and her new boss. Also described in overly strenuous detail a grey-faced colleague who had a stupid reason for his name. But she had to go, she said happily, she had to get on with what she was doing – reviewing planning objections to an Indian temple in Mount Albert, wasn't that funny?

'Oh ha ha,' Marcus said sourly. He frowned into the bougainvillea. Maria having to go?

'Bye,' he grunted, and quickly hung up on *her*.

A few minutes later he rang her back. He was connected.

No, Maria Wallis was in a meeting. In a meeting. *Bitch!* He lounged into the kitchen and went to work on the contents of a casserole dish that had caught his eye on the last foray.

Marcus stayed out by the pool for most of the day, going in every now and then to eat something more. Mostly he just lay in a chaise longue in the sun with his eyes closed, listening to the hum of the pool pump and the slop slop slop of the filter and the distant drone of cars on the main road. Six hours until they would come home, five, four, three. He dozed and lounged and soaked up sun and felt himself reviving, like a lizard slowly warming its cold blood on a rock. The sun crossed the sky, rearranging the shadows around the pool and reaching a pale intensity in the early afternoon, when Marcus woke to find the sleeve of his burnt arm unpleasantly hot, and giddily dragged his deckchair into the shade of the fence.

He slept again and woke to discover himself chilled in the shade and shadows creeping out from the ponga ferns and his own shadow slanting into the blue depths of the pool. He got off the chair and lay on the hot concrete at the edge, staring at the plastic-blue water, watching the dancing smoke rings of sunlight on the surface and the watery shafts of light below that were full of grains of dust or leaf or pool chemical, for ever floating down.

But he looked at his watch and realised it was late. He went round the house removing the evidence of his visit. They wouldn't miss anything. Couple of inches creamed off the top of the ratatouille, one of the wine bottles gone, half a salami where once there was a whole. He hoped that his mother (that sharp-nailed witch) wouldn't notice that most of a whole quiche had vanished into thin air. He hoped she'd just blame the old man, and the old man never confirmed or denied anything to her anyway, just patiently let her rave and scream and then changed the subject gently, or slipped out of the room before she'd noticed he had gone. She complained that the old man drove her mad with his secretive ways. That was what she loved about Marcus (she told him once) because he could be as vinegary as she was, and when he was a little boy he gave her as good as he got. But now that he was (her voice would rise to a shriek) throwing all his cleverness *to the winds* . . .

Marcus, who had entertained a brief feeling of fondness for his small and peppery parent, now pushed those feelings away and briskly completed his tidying. He felt restored, invigorated, why, he was even up to the next unpleasant task he had set himself. A painful mission, possibly even dangerous. A test of his ingenuity, daring, courage and skill. Shutting the door on the tidied house, gathering together the bundle of his jacket which was now loaded with tins of food (lucky the old virago was such a hoarder), blithely oblivious to the scrap of paper containing his five-point plan as it slipped from the pocket of his jacket to land, neatly scrolled, on the parental doorstep, Marcus took a deep breath and embarked on his next venture: to go round to Ron Audio Ltd and beg Ron Reed for money.

6.

In the mornings Maria roused herself, banged on Ernest's bedroom door as she passed it in the hall, showered, ate a virtuous bowl of cereal, donned her corporate clothes (long tube skirts, linen shirts, black shoes), took her briefcase, bought a newspaper on the way to the bus stop, and sat reading with lowered lids and pursed lips in the back seat as the bus roared and shuddered through the blindingly bright streets.

Climbing out at Customs Street she minced in her tube skirt through the city, and arrived, at high speed mince, in the marble foyer of Quinn St John at precisely 8:25 a.m. Rode up in the lift to the temperature-controlled tube of the twelfth floor, strolled along the corridor and entered her office, all spick and span in the tinted light with files and folders piled neatly across the desk, and usually a note from the partner, Mr Giles Speer, asking her to carry out a particular task, or to come into his office to discuss a file.

The Indian temple in Mount Albert had kept Maria busy for weeks with a record number of objections to the proposed construction, a sour whiff of racism hovering around most of the submissions. The public sentiment could be deciphered as follows: don't want some curry jamboree going on in neighbourhood, damned if going to put up with it, thank you very much. But the temple file was up to date and now Maria had conveyancing and commercial files arranged across the desk. Every morning she made a cup of coffee in the twelfth-floor kitchen, exchanged pleasantries with the deadly Peeks-Berlyn, then sat down at her desk and went with pleasure through the tasks of the day. She liked to write entries in her diary, she wrote and then stopped to admire neat and precise file notes, she liked handling the shiny stationery, she even liked the tiny plastic click of the phone as she put it down after completing a call.

Peeks-Berlyn was designated as her supervisor and was pompously leading her through the intricacies of commercial and non-commercial property, and other related mysteries: leases, tenants, landlords, mortgages, charges, caveats, and so on.

'How fascinating,' Leon sighed, rolling his eyes and stifling yawns when she told him about these things after work. It *was*, she insisted, it was just so satisfying. So orderly. So tidy and correct. And the money. No more sad student meals of soup or baked beans. Every night now she would buy something elaborate for her evening meal, or go to a restaurant with Ernest, or more usually drive to Leon's house with an expensive bottle of wine and eat with Leon and Old Vic, the old man seizing the wine off her at the door and threatening with much Czechoslovakian rolling of eyes to use it in his cooking as he ushered her into the steamy kitchen where his cauldron of vampire broth would be bubbling glutinously on the stove. That garlicky green soup. Elaborate casseroles. A stew, for example, cooked with chicken and olives, eaten in the kitchen under the antennae of the watching phones.

She would lean back and look contentedly around the strange room, inspect a new acquisition that Leon had brought home from somewhere, a new appliance perhaps or something he had made at work. He told her they were working on a television advertisement for air freshener, he had been constructing models of bits of garbage – a fish skeleton, a tin can, a toilet roll – which were going to come dancing animatedly out of a huge model trash can.

In his spare time he had transformed some old-fashioned dial phones into hundred-eyed insects, and he had painted colourful man-sized figures on hardboard, strange stiff people with the same sharp faces as his own. They stood in corners around the kitchen, slouching Leon-style, seeming to shift restlessly on their feet, all staring and grinning jaggedly, all waving with one large outstretched hand.

Maria ate her soup watching the figures watching her. Their eyes were painted with silvery paint, and appeared to glitter malevolently. Later, when she went to put the mustard away she saw that he had painted the same silver eye on the clear plastic shelves inside the fridge.

'Look at that,' Vic said, leaning over her shoulder. He turned to Leon. 'What's with the eye? You on a diet?' He laughed uneasily. 'You mad goon.'

After doing the dishes Vic wiped his hands, and stood looking around the room. He stretched and rubbed his arms restlessly and said to Leon, 'I need exercise, boy. Will you walk with me?'

Vic and Maria and Leon walked down on to Shore Road, around the edge of the cricket ground, past the dirty creek where drifts of oil lying on the water moved slowly downstream and the storm drain drip-dripped into the dead water, and a rat swam across the slow current and scuttled away into the grass. The night air carried the rich swamp tang of the mangroves and the mud. Vic Pavel, stumping along in his long frayed sandshoes, sniffing the damp air, holding forth: 'When Leon was a boy he gave art lessons. He advertised to the local kids. Made them pay for it. They loved it, they'd run home with their paintings. When Leon was a boy I taught him to cook. When he was a little boy Leon talked all the time. I used to have to say, slow down. Give a minute. Shut up.'

Leon kicked a stone sideways with his foot. Patiently. 'Yeah yeah, Father.'

'You know all this. You know . . .'

'Yeah, so you can shut up about it now.'

The old man walked faster, the old shoulders bent forward. He made a sudden agitated movement with his hands. 'You were a boy . . .' he said. He stopped walking, and grasped Leon's shoulder roughly. Leon paused, in his face a flicker of surprise, or pain.

Old Vic said angrily, 'But what are you now?'

Maria saw the rat again, darting through the shadows on the mud bank. Above them the white streetlight flickered and hummed. A damp gust of wind blew the trailing willow branches and a bank of cloud was gathering over the hill. Leon removed the old man's hand, stepped away and lit a cigarette. He threw the match into the creek, inhaled, exhaled, gave the old man a ghostly, wide-eyed, challenging stare. 'Older,' he said.

Vic sighed impatiently. He began to walk again. '*I'm* getting old,' he said, querulous suddenly. 'I don't want to be alone.'

'You're not alone.'

'Ah, don't listen to me. Sometimes I don't talk to anyone all day. I can't sleep at night.'

Leon went ahead, not looking. After they had walked in silence up the steep end of Portland Road and turned on to Remuera Road Old Vic stopped to get his breath back, bending over, resting his broad old hands on his knees. He coughed, looked up at Leon and asked in a humble voice, 'You think I'm losing the marbles?'

Leon flicked his cigarette away. 'Yeah, Father. All of them.'

'I fear it.' Vic sighed gloomily and reached out to put his arm round Leon's shoulders. 'Why you make me walk this far? I'm nearly dead.'

'Stay at my place if you want,' Leon said quietly, looking away.

'On that cranky sofa? Your paintings and their eyes, spying on me all night?'

Leon rolled his eyes skywards. 'I'll have the sofa and you can have the bed. OK?'

Vic Pavel winked at Maria. 'Is good bed,' he said, in a hollow voice, and was cheerful again.

Driving home along the back streets faintly drunk, parking under the pohutukawa tree, going up the path towards the welcoming light of her room, Maria reflected that life would be perfectly balanced in all respects if it were not for one thing. Perfectly balanced, she repeated to herself – fumbling for the key, dropping it, groping for it in the dark – between the cool dry order of her little office at Quinn St John and the pungent anarchy of Leon's house. Between the pristine condition of her room – surveying it now, straightening a picture, smoothing down the bed – and the rest of the shabby house. Between tonight and tomorrow, between the order of the day and the shenanigans of the night. All in order, apart from one thing: she couldn't live through a day without being seized by a shiver of loss, a tiny, desolate pause in her concentration, causing her to sigh at the long-suffering Peeks-Berlyn, it's nothing, no it's nothing. That Marcus . . . She would doodle his name on a page in her diary, tear it out and flick it into the bin.

He hadn't visited her for weeks. She knew because she was often at home in the late evening now, catching up on reading, getting an early night. Half listening for the sound of his big boots scraping on the verandah rail outside. She didn't go out so much now and Leon complained about it, the way she would only stay up all night in the weekends, the way she wouldn't come up to the Hyatt Hotel and check into a free room. Leon still used the skeleton key as often as he thought he could get away with it: recently he took young Carol from work and they spent an evening clearing the minibars and nearly getting caught, as usual. It was the nearly getting caught that bothered Maria now, and she couldn't understand why it hadn't bothered her before. Now that she was actually working in a law firm the idea of appearing in court on a criminal charge seemed distinctly disadvantageous.

Leon smiled dangerously and called her a *suit* but he invited her round every night and always wanted her to stay. Sometimes she stayed over and they would lie in his bed drinking vodka at 3 a.m. and Leon would turn on Talkback Radio to hear the sherry-befuddled old ladies who rang up in the dead of night and rambled querulously and refused to stay on the topic, and began each fuzzy new salvo with the declaration, 'Now, *I* don't drink . . .'

'I don't drink!' Leon and Maria would chorus with each new caller, their glasses raised.

One night, having got through a lot of vodka, Leon rang in and spoke as a whispery old Samoan, 'Ai ton't trink,' and talked for a long time about ruppish collection and the price of fitteo tapes while Maria listened to him on the radio, admiring his inventiveness and his ear for the Samoan accent, marvelling at the way the DJ never caught on, even when Leon brought the conversation to the brink of a satirical precipice and she was shaking with laughter and so was he.

'Goodbye, caller,' came the warm farewell.

'Good*pye*,' Leon whispered.

Callers in the night talked about the price of funerals, discussed undertakers – those who were caring and those who were pushy – debated cremation versus burial, and always came back to their fear of violent crime. The little old voices were irritable, argumentative, indignant, most of all they were afraid. Sitting at home alone over the sherry bottle, while out there in the shadows lurked rape and burglary and death.

Leon and Maria, horizontal with vodka, laughed at them and toasted them and took the piss out of fear. Leon suggested that he go out and roam the neighbourhood in his underpants carrying an axe – Maria rolling round the bed snorting with laughter and saying go on then – or that he should go out and set a phone booth on fire. He disappeared out of the room long enough for Maria to get up and peer with hilarious expectation through the curtain, but he stalked grandly back in having merely replenished the supply of vodka.

When they were lying companionably on the bed again Leon said, 'When I die I want to be buried in a neon tomb at an intersection, with flags and lasers and loud music and flashing lights.'

'Mmmph,' Maria said, hearing him but already going out and far away on a silvery shrug of vodka, a wave of liquid peace.

She woke early, and lay looking up at the bedroom ceiling where Leon's chains hung, strung with pictures and other decorations: studded belts, telephone cords, hotel signs. Outside in the hall the bathroom door bore a brass plaque: This building was opened by Her Majesty, Queen Elizabeth II. Maria got up and looked under the blind at the garden in the dark windy dawn, at the trees at the bottom of the garden tossing and blowing in the moving air, the clouds above them coal-black and streaked here and there with an inner glow of fiery red. The glow brightened, the clouds became livid, and from the tree branches above the window came the first single notes of the tui, extraordinarily clear, the bird tuning up for the first onslaught, the full pomp of the morning's performance. On the other side of the bed Leon stirred, groaned, then emerged suddenly from under the duvet, looked around, picked up a spanner and threw it at the wall above the window. 'Fucking bird!' he shouted.

There was a short affronted silence outside. Recovering, the bird emitted a couple of primly hesitant peeps. With a grunt of rage Leon picked up a large screwdriver and hurled it at the wall. There was a long silence from the garden. Then, as Leon plunged comfortably back down on to the pillow and closed his eyes, the bird let off one short gallant trill, before launching suddenly into its full repertoire, singing wildly up and down the scale, with all its squawks and peeps and toots jumbled and speeded up, while Leon, rearing up out of the duvet again, hurled boots and books and appliances and tools at the wall and the bird sang on, madly, defiantly oblivious.

They lay in bed.

'It's got balls, that bird.'

'Definitely.'

'Vodka?'

'I think not. On the whole.'

'Right.'

They ate breakfast in the garden, Leon in dark glasses, sipping his tea and scanning his diary, businesslike. The toaster and kettle sat in the empty birdbath, connected by extension cord through the kitchen window.

'Busy day?' Maria sat with her feet up on a deckchair, a plate of omelette in her lap.

'Average, really. Salt and pepper?'

'Thanks.'

'More tea?'

Work in the morning. Maria enjoyed the structure of work, she enjoyed having to turn up there after nights out with Leon, being forced to gather her thoughts and forget about irrelevant things. She liked the stunned cup of morning coffee in the office-brown light, watching the clouds move across the tinted sky, watching the mute tennis players below as they swooped and dashed and called.

She enjoyed listening out for the clomp and scrape of the partner's shoes as he skied along the hall, peered around her office door, hung ape-like off the door frame, smiled at the ceiling, and inched around the filing cabinet into her room. Always looking out from under his eyebrows, rumpling his hair, his shirt hanging out the back of his trousers. She liked him. Quinn St John, being a large and successful and glossy firm, was a place of bristling blow-waves and aggressive self-promotion, and Giles Speer, with his floppy hair and his ungovernable shoes, refreshingly broke the mould.

At eleven or so the team would stop for a morning break. They would gather in the secretarial bay, perching on desks and filing cabinets, and make joky and desultory conversation for a quarter of an hour before drifting back to work. Maria was earning bad marks, she knew, by reading the paper throughout this dull interlude. She knew because Peeks-Berlyn had gone red one morning afterwards and told her in a throttled voice that she wasn't showing herself to be a team player, just reading out there and not joining in. She looked cold and stand-offish, he said, leaning on a cabinet and flicking through the *Herald*.

Maria absorbed this news without surprise and continued to read the paper during the morning break. She wasn't a team player, if it meant you couldn't have a flick through the morning rag. She liked to read the paper. If Quinn St John disapproved, then let it disapprove. Let everything be in balance, she thought. Let them not have all of me.

But Peeks-Berlyn shrugged, and warningly shook his head. Remember Klara Leather. They wanted all of her. All of her or nothing.

Musing down on the tennis players, Maria imagined that Giles Speer wasn't interested in what people did at the morning break. He didn't seem disposed to comment or care, just skated off up the hall rubbing biscuit crumbs into his hair. She watched him go. She imagined he was freer than Peeks-Berlyn, more humorous, less conformist. She imagined all this. But she didn't know. She didn't know anything about him at all.

One Friday afternoon Maria was head-down at her desk, composing, with infinite care, a letter to the client: We enclose the . . . together with your . . . and a copy of . . .

Maria spoke quietly into her Dictaphone, not yet possessed of the courage to pace the room as the old hands did, barking gruffly into the machine, audible halfway up the hall.

'Paragraph,' Maria breathed. 'No . . . Just make that another sentence . . . Hang on . . .'

Then stop, rewind, fast-forward, sound of her apologetic laugh on tape, later to cause secretary in her headphones to pause and blow on her fingernails and sneer contemptuously down the hall.

Maria pressed on, diligently. Accelerating the Dictaphone down the dull home stretch of the afternoon, slamming on its brakes, u-turning, backtracking, driving the secretary (the efficient Clairene) mad.

Friday afternoon and the pile of work had shrunk to nothing, one last letter and home free. The sky was a hard metallic blue out there, it was a cold snap, down to twelve degrees or so, and the air inside was correspondingly hot, overheated air roaring through the great pipes of Quinn St John, turning the little office into a sauna.

Maria felt heat prickling on her thighs under her stockings, felt sweat break out on her nose. She pressed the stop button finally and sat languidly back, felt the itch in her thighs, sighed the sigh of Friday afternoon, felt energy gathering in the hot room behind the sealed glass, sun angling through the brown windows making the room hotter still.

Maria on fire under her nylon shirt, heard the scrape scrape of the partner in the hall, watched as he came into view, saw him glance amiably into her room, and delivered him the full louche stare of Friday afternoon heat. Hesitation, a wobble on the skis, a near crash into the glass wall of the word-processing bay before Giles Speer righted himself, accelerated, and shot off at an angle into his room. His door slammed.

Maria laughed into her own dilated pupils, reflected in the hot brown glass. Sorry about that, partner. It's just . . . Friday afternoon. It's just, that I must find him. I want to find Marcus.

And so Maria on the phone after work, couldn't find Marcus as usual, and felt the need of a Friday night drink. She dialled again and asked Leon the usual, Jwanna go out? I rang Marcus, she told Leon, but he's not around, I thought we could meet him too. Leon hesitated and she stared out of the window, surely he wasn't going to say no? Hello? she said. It's all right, he answered after a while, I'm just looking through my tapes.

They arranged to meet at a bar in High Street at nine, and at 8:59 she found him already there drinking vodka at a table outside.

'It's cold out here,' she said, and Leon smiled behind his sunglasses and told her, 'You need some wodka.'

They sat close together, sheltering against the wind and Leon carefully draped his jacket over her shoulders. 'I've ordered something disgusting,' he said, and soon the waiter brought it out, a large dish of glutinous nachos – the cheese and mince and tortilla chips all welded together into a rubbery microwaved mass, and they sat and drank and tugged elastic strings of the stuff out of the dish. Leon drank vodka, lime and soda, and Maria ordered vine-gary white wine by the glass and became tipsy and told Leon stories about the repressed Peeks-Berlyn and the nervous partner, Giles Speer.

But soon she was complaining that it was cold and that they should go somewhere else. She thought (with Marcus in mind), pretending to consider the options for a moment, that they should go to Quays. It was too early, Leon said immediately. It wouldn't be open.

They argued for a while, idly, but Maria began to feel impatient, to shift in her seat and frown. She could feel Leon's reluctance. His resistance. He knew she hoped to find Marcus and she knew that he wanted to stop her, that he wanted to keep her to himself.

But she wanted to see Marcus more than anything now, urgently; it was as if life depended on it, she thought, and she meant it literally – she felt, at this particular moment anyway, that Marcus *was* life. He represented life. For the first time she didn't want to roam home through the night with Leon, happily waiting for the mayhem to begin. She would look for Marcus, she wouldn't be put off, and finally Leon consented to move.

They walked towards Quays, Maria pulling and tugging him along the streets. She turned the corner on to Quay Street and found the door of the nightclub only just being opened by the door-man, Wiremu Ihaka, and a large queue already formed along the street outside.

Dragging Leon by the arm, keeping an eye out for Marcus, Maria approached the door. She moved experimentally into the doorman's field of vision. Wiremu Ihaka's massive frame was compressed into a black suit, he wore a white shirt and a black tie, and his head was freshly shaven.

Craning over the heads of the crowd at the door she smiled up at him winningly. His eye fell upon her and he assumed a grim and authoritarian expression. Maria fluttered her fingers in a tiny wave. He frowned darkly and looked away. Maria bounced impatiently up and down behind the tall man in front of her.

Wiremu Ihaka glared down at Leon and Maria. Then he began to shoulder his way briskly through the crowd, which parted fearfully as he came through. He reached them and stood over Maria with folded arms. She greeted him, holding Leon firmly by the elbow as he tried urgently to melt off into the crowd. 'Hello,' she said. 'How did you get on in court?'

Leon slumped despairingly beside her. Wiremu Ihaka loomed over them, curved Maori mouth parted and showing teeth, one pop eye closed in a squint, the other wide and glaring out of the great slab of his face. 'No problems,' he growled at Maria.

'Oh good.' She beamed at him. She wasn't scared of him, not in the least. You could always tell with men, after all, which ones were problematic and which were not. All around her men shrank in terror from the doorman's huge bulk, sensibly, since he would do *them* over if necessary, and enjoy doing it. But Maria smiled and felt quite at ease as he scowled and glared and loomed, and beside her Leon prepared quietly to be minced and eaten alive. She looked up into the gargoyle face and asked politely, 'May we come in?'

The doorman looked briefly away, and then looked back and laughed. 'Why, certainly,' he said, and with an air of courtly ceremony took them each by the arm, and led them past the riff-raff and through the door.

Maria stepped on to the crowded dance floor at ten past three a.m. with Leon at a nearby table, cheering her on. At three thirty she was grooving around with a long-haired stranger who had inveigled himself into her space, Maria executing dance moves to be recalled by her and cringed over in the morning. Leon laughed as Maria performed some sort of hula with the stranger, Maria laughing and pushing the stranger's groping hands away. The bass beat of the music shook the floor and throbbed in the throat, the red lights and laser beams swept the room, everywhere there was noise, vibration, overpowering heat. Now Maria appeared to be engaging in some sort of pushing and shoving on the dance floor. Leon stood up to see. Maria was appearing and disappearing behind the writhing bodies, moving in slow motion as if she were under the sea. The stranger's brown hair flew across Maria's face, then Maria's hands were across the stranger's face – was that a slap? Leon moved forward but the stranger came stumbling and weaving through the swaying crowd. He staggered off the dance floor as if emerging from the beach, shook his wet hair, and went panting off in search of the bar. Leon wiped sweat from his forehead, looked anxiously for Maria and saw that she was still dancing, in swinging slow motion, by herself.

Leon sank back down into his seat. All right then. No problem. From the door, Wiremu Ihaka glared darkly after the long-haired stranger. From behind the bar watched Marcus Klein. Around the room the strobe lights shone on the tortured faces, blind, sweating, upraised.

At four a.m. Maria came bouncing off the dance floor and threaded her way through the crowd to get a glass of water at the bar.

'You're not.' Maria reeled back in overexcited surprise.

'It pays well,' Marcus shouted over the music, giving her a wry look. More softened than his usual contemptuous snarl. She noticed that immediately and became animated.

'So you're working behind the bar.'

He ignored this statement of the obvious, so typical of Maria, and poured out a glass of water, smiling slyly. He was quite deft with the glasses now, despite the thick bandage on his wrist and arm. She was so pleased to see him. Practically leaping over the bar, rabbiting on, how funny that you're a barman, can I get free drinks now?

'Yeah, it's hilarious, and no you fucking can't.'

Look at her, beaming at him. Jesus. He felt almost embarrassed. But he was pleased to see her too. Marcus leaned over the bar and shouted into her ear, 'Did you miss me?' (as expected, she shouted coyly, '*No!*') and, 'Can I come to your house when I've finished?'

As expected, she replied . . .

Marcus polishing glasses, only a hundred to go. Only fifty, forty, only twenty-four . . .

Back at the table Leon held out a glass.

'I got you a drink. What happened on the dance floor? Did that long-haired guy give you . . .?'

But she shrugged and laughed and shook her head. 'Marcus gave me a free cocktail. He's working here behind the bar.' She slid into the seat and began applying make-up.

Leon put his arm over her shoulder and shouted over the music, 'Shall we walk home?'

'What?'

'Do you want to walk home?'

'No, you go.'

'What?'

'*You – go,*' she shouted with force in his ear.

His eyes flicked up. He sat still for a moment. Then he got up and turned away without saying any more, leaving his drink on the table. He made his way towards the door.

Maria watched him go, admiring him, with his striking dyed hair, the broad shoulders under the bright jacket, his characteristic swinging walk. How graceful he is, she thought. And how clumsy I am – how stolid and graceless and ordinary. He made her feel suburban and obvious, always yearning for things that, she knew, his whole being rejected and mocked. Things that he didn't want, and would never have. Ordinary things. He was so subtle and satirical, so quick to perceive the ridiculous that he made her feelings seem laughable and awkwardly expressed. But still, but even so. Inelegant as they were, her feelings were real. They were real . . .

She watched him feed money into the cigarette machine at the door, the advertising sign lighting the extraordinary face, colouring it red and gold. He was tall and handsome, neither masculine nor effeminate – he was something else again, something other. He was skinny and foreign, he was rich and strange, and his eyes, flicking up suddenly with their strange penetrating force – his eyes were electric.

Maria hesitated. She stood up to follow Leon out the door. But there was Marcus behind the bar. She turned away and sat down again. She sat for a while, thinking, then applied lipstick, and pushed her way back through the crowd to the bar.

An hour later as they came out of Quays together Marcus said to Maria, 'I've met that guy before.' She looked: ambulancemen were loading an unconscious man into an ambulance by the bin-bags outside the club, the figure wrapped in a red blanket, his face covered by an oxygen mask, his long brown hair straggling down the side of the stretcher. Nearby Wiremu Ihaka squeezed and flexed his great right fist, and looked coldly on.

'That's Dave,' Marcus said, putting his bandaged arm around Maria and pointing out an ambulance officer with a large moustache.

'Hi, Dave,' Maria said happily, and waved.

Leon, walking home along Quay Street, stopped and listened in the empty dawn. He heard birds singing in the ragged pohutukawas, the roaring of machines on the docks far away. The sky was turning faintly pink at the edges, colouring the white concrete walls, lightening the rusty red of the freight cars lined up in the railway yard. Leon walking in the grey street under the shell-pink sky, looking ahead towards Gladstone Road, the tennis court, the park, looking along the long dead stretch of Quay Street before it curved up the green hill to Parnell. Over his head the sky broke into silver streaks, dawn sun shooting across the city, hitting mirror buildings, lighting up the bridge, the low metallic light glancing off the windscreens of cars. Hands in his pockets, jacket draped over his shoulders, Leon made his silent way home through the sharp wind, turned into the gate of his house some time around six, took a deckchair and sat out alone in the still, green garden, listening.

7.

When Marcus woke one Saturday morning the bed was shaking, the cold wind was blowing the curtain across the room and he had no hangover. This was very rare, it had to be said. Stuck in Quays all night – his ears ringing from the musical hammering they'd received – and no hangover. And what was she doing, lying there beside him, shaking? She was laughing, of course. The madwoman.

He poked her roughly in the shoulder and she turned her face up out of the pillow all covered with straggling hair. Eyes squeezed shut, teeth clenched.

It was the dancing, she explained, subsiding into snorts. Remembering the funky moves on the dance floor last night. Blame the demon drink for that sideways bump and grind routine, with the night-fever arm thrusts. For that can-can. That whooping hula. For the sing-along head rolling and arm waving, the clapping and ass wiggling, the stompin' high kicking. She flopped down, tee-heeing into the sheets. Maria going on and on about it, overdoing the detail – once she starts laughing she can't stop. With her, mirth and agony are never far apart. What a riot she was in the hay, Marcus thought, practically having a breakdown at nine in the morning, over something like that.

'Granted, you were quite a sight.' He lit a cigarette politely. Maria's screams of hilarity were mercifully stifled by the pillow.

No hangover. He lay back, savouring the experience. He felt almost cheerful. He could lie there and sleep in, if the mad bitch would stop writhing around in the bed. Get her out of it and into the kitchen, that was the ticket. Get her rustling up something hot and rich, with bacon. But first. To calm her down. He effected a headlock and half nelson and pushed her face into the pillow. She fought free and wriggled around to face him, suddenly serious. 'You're here all the time,' she said. 'Why don't you move in?'

Rather than answer he kissed her, then wangled her out of her underwear and let her peel him out of his. No hangover! He felt like pushing her head under the covers and showing her what no hangover looked like. Cop a load of *that* rude health. He put his arms around her and kissed her again. I'm a gun, he thought with grateful simplicity, moving in underneath her and pulling her on top, I'm a missile, I'm a nuclear warhead, oh, what it is to be fucking with no hangover, and when he came at last – and she seemed to be squeaking and shuddering and moaning as well – he felt as if he was in command and in control, and that everything was going to be fine.

She lay beside him absolutely still. No more hysterics. With great satisfaction he pulled her up on to his shoulder. 'Let's go back to sleep,' he said calmly, 'and when we wake up I'll take you out to lunch.' The curtain blew over the bed, cold air chilled his shoulders and face and soothed his injured arm. The wind scraped dry pohutukawa leaves over the wooden deck outside. She breathed deeply beside him, the madwoman sleeping. The madwoman. He leaned over and kissed her cold cheek.

They ate lunch in a Turkish café on Mount Eden Road, Maria strangely calm and unhurried over her falafels, talking normally about everyday things. He could even look her in the eye without feeling as if he were being hungrily scrutinised, inch by inch.

He drew a desultory comparison between falafels and sheep dung and she merely smiled in tolerant assent. He made a politely deadly observation about her hair – the way she resembled a bag lady or Rasta – and she just remained relaxed and said 'yeah', or 'hmm', where she would usually have rushed in hysterics to a mirror.

She looked all right actually, under the mangled steelo pad of hair. She was good-looking. Smooth face, thinly plucked brows, the neurotically observant blue eyes. She was taller than Chrissie. Marcus had glanced quickly at each waitress in the café, by habit, searching for Chrissie. But he was happy, with his healthy appetite, his throbbing no-hangover. When Maria asked him to come back to her house to stay over again he wanted to. He wanted to.

And, he paid for lunch. Her falafels, his kebab. He had money at last. Although his final visit to Ron Audio Limited had not been a resounding success, what with Ron scoffing and snorting and indignantly booting him out the door, and although he had had a lean time of it, and had been forced to pay a humiliating visit to the offices of the Social Welfare – bowed in the cubicle under the scornful eye of the semi-literate clerk, replying in monosyllables to the stream of insulting interrogations – he had survived and paid the rent (emergency benefit), and managed not to tell anyone just how ill and poor and fucked up he'd been.

And now he was working behind the bar at Quays (his friend Branko being the cousin of the bar manager's wife), and he would work his way up from there. Save some money and look around for a proper job, with Ron Reed's rival perhaps, Shane Saloon, of Saloon Sound.

He had visited the out-patients' clinic at the hospital and they had given him a prescription for more suitable painkillers. 'How did the last pills make you feel? Nauseous?' the doctor asked him.

'Afraid.'

He was no longer in so much pain. When he rang the seven digits of Chrissie's little house out west he couldn't get through. 'The number you have dialled has changed,' the robot voice gently explained.

So he left it alone. He didn't look for Chrissie, except in cafés by force of habit – frisson as he glimpsed the agile, narrow-hipped waitress from behind, anticlimax as she turned, wrong-faced – he didn't look. He walked contentedly through the cold spring streets, arm in arm with Maria. Maria, whom his mother (that ball-breaker) would whole-heartedly approve of, and would want him to invite home.

So they were officially together. They got on well. He stayed with her on Friday nights, stayed all day Saturday, went to work on Saturday night. Usually he hung around all of Sunday. Mondays they separated, both bright eyed and bandy legged after a final rip-roaring session in the hay. She went to Quinn St John and he went home to work on his searing novel. *The Hard Men* was turning into something big, he could feel it. He was thinking of developing another character now, an ambitious career woman who spurned the company of ordinary folk. He was planning his next chapter, containing fraught and harrowing sex scenes, which he hoped Maria would never ever read.

One Monday morning Marcus lay in Maria's bed crimson-eyed, smoking, listening to the phone ringing in the hall. The answerphone clicked on, and a strange voice left a brief message. Marcus got up and headed for the shower. On the way he passed the answerphone and pressed the play button. An old Islander spoke into the tape. 'I don't drink,' the voice whispered.

Some old fruitcake. Coconut.

Shrugging coldly, Marcus erased the call.

Maria burst out of her office and dealt briskly with the admirable Clairene.

'Four tapes, two to be typed by four,' she instructed, dropping them crisply on to the desk. Clairene glared out of the riot of her cosmetics. She hated Maria, on principle. She hated all new recruits. Maria looked gently into the secretary's face. In her imagination she insulted Clairene. You really need to tone it down, don't you. You look quite a clown. But there's the acne problem, isn't there, all those bumps to cover up. Maria smiled over the secretarial bay.

'And I need a bank cheque for this, and a copy of this, and I need two copies of this transfer straight away.'

She was becoming more confident with the property transactions. She was learning every day. Things were going well at work and at home. She kept her office spick and span and her files in order and every day Giles Speer had something new for her to do. She was doing some interesting research for him – she had tried to tell Marcus about it last night but he had mockingly ignored her. He lay sprawled on her bed, smoking and preoccupied. He was always preoccupied – he explained that he was planning a new section of his novel. Maria tried idly to launch a conversation.

'Just between you and I,' she began, and he looked up and grinned slyly and corrected her, 'Between you and me.'

'Oh. Just between you and me. Just between . . . Between . . .'

'What?'

'I forget now. Look at your boots.'

They looked at the deteriorated wreckage laced to his feet. The woollen threads of his old rugby socks poked through the holes.

'I could buy you some new ones,' she said.

'Now you're a rich lawyer.'

'Yeah. Why not?'

'That would be very nice,' he said politely, and leaned his cold face against her cheek.

Now, in the secretarial bay Maria looked down and saw that Clairene was breathing with effort, her frowns growing ferocious. And when you've done that, Maria thought, cheerily gathering up her files, you can take this Dictaphone, Clairene, and shove it up your fat . . .

Singing under her breath, Maria skipped off down the padded hall, narrowly missing the ambling figure of Giles Speer who pulled up short, rumpled his hair in alarm, reached around the back of his pants to tuck in the flapping end of his shirt, and rolled himself quickly along the wall into his room.

One afternoon Maria left Quinn St John earlier than usual and hastened to a Chinese supermarket that Ernest had recommended to her as his favourite supplier.

She wandered along the stacked shelves. Seasoned claws, pickled tongues. Eye of newt, wing of bat. She had invited Marcus for a meal, and she wanted to cook him something unusual.

She emerged at the checkout some time later clutching a wire basket of questionable ingredients, smelling strongly of Marmite or blood. Bypassing with a shudder of horror a sign which offered rat foetus wine (New! Full-Bodied!) she had also bought crisp chardonnay and decent coffee. Down the street she bought herself costly new black stockings, with seams. How corny, she thought happily. Buying dinner, buying stockings. Rushing home from work with her briefcase and her ingredients – she felt like something out of a woman's magazine.

She waited for the bus, watching the light-show of late afternoon, the nearly black sky bulging from its buttons like a stuffed quilt, the sun weirdly angling in from a break in the clouds, turning the trees pond green in the sunlight, under the storm. The air was hot. Thunder, thought Maria, sniffing the air. *Lightning*.

At home she cleaned the kitchen for an hour. Then she worked on the rest of the house. She threw open all the windows, pausing to rest her elbows on the windowsill and look up into the straining sky. Pressure building up there, cloud upon cloud marching from the west, bank climbing upon bank, the whole of the air charged, darkened, thick with waiting.

Maria, stirring her concoction in the blackened kitchen, opened the window and let the blood-scented steam fly up into the sky. She put her head out the window and the sky glared back, pop-eyed. She found that she was sweating. The clouds peered darkly over the shoulder of Mount Eden, in the garden the wind had died and the trees were sombre, heavy-green, weighted with waiting.

Maria bustled around the bathroom, sat down on the lavatory and stared absently at the pinewood wall. She hummed and sighed in the woody silence. Above her she heard the noise of small concussions, as if someone was banging sticks together on the roof, thwack thwack, thwack thwack. She looked up and saw the first big drops hitting the dirty glass of the skylight, irregular at first and then more and more until the drops were hammering on the glass and on the iron roof and the iron sky behind the skylight was smearing and dissolving into dusty rivulets of tears.

She ran around the house banging the windows shut. A gust of wind blew a squall of rain on to the side of the house and rain roared on the corrugated iron. Purple lightning flashed, the hedge outside lashed and tore in the sudden flurries of wind. She wrestled with a window, then leaned on the glass and watched the underwater garden, plants swirling in the currents, fern fronds tossing and waving, Ernest battling his way up the path under the clothes-line, head down, hair slicked to his head, glasses fogged, blind, half drowned. She opened the door and he fell gasping weakly into the hall, 'Nearly made it . . . ran all the way from the bus.' Complaining weakly, he squelched off to his room.

Under the roaring rain Maria diligently sipped and stirred. The kitchen was hot with exotic scents and tangs. Rain streamed off a broken section of guttering outside.

The doorbell rang. Her scalp tingled. She dawdled to the door, flung it open while looking away down the hall as if she had just broken off a fascinating conversation, turned casually and said, 'Oh, it's you.'

He greeted her in his usual ironic, half-smiling silence. His hair was plastered to his head, eyes blinded by his wet fringe, his body weighted down by his sodden clothes. The rain danced on his shoulders and drummed impatient fingers on the top of his head.

Overexcited to see him, Maria pretended to slam the door in his face. His polite snarl deepened – oh ha ha – and he pushed his way into the hall. Maria talked, spouting jokes and platitudes as she helped him out of his soaked clothes. Eventually he stood, stocky and long-suffering, in his underpants and socks. She was amused at his predicament, he grimaced. She made jokes, he smiled balefully. She bustled about, she dropped things, she laughed at her own clumsiness. She coy, she jittery, she eager to please. And he a constant. He unchanged. He was fatally, musically tuned to detect *false notes*.

He was also charmingly comical – donning an absurd bathrobe, eating his meal with a furry towel wrapped round his head. Peering out from under his turban like a malevolent troll.

He was, Maria thought, terrifyingly honest. To talk to him was to tiptoe through a minefield – the constant pressure to rein in her blundering transgressions of style, her charisma errors. No one else was so noticing, so uncompromising. One mistake and he was reaching for the sick bag. With a fond sigh Maria presented him with her next creation, one of Ernest's actually, bamboo and fried chicken, in Grasshopper sauce. They talked and ate companiably.

Later the rain eased to a drizzle and they walked up the steaming street to the shops. They shared an umbrella and he draped his arm around her shoulders. At the dairy she bought some cigarettes. Marcus wandered outside on to the street to wait for her.

When she came out of the shop he was talking to a pale thin-legged person in tight black skirt and black stockings. Maria stared into the vampish face, sensing hostility and resistance behind the green-eyed stare. The woman extended a thinly wristed hand.

'Darlene,' she explained coldly. Maria shook her hand. She had heard of Darlene (Darlene the Greeter) but had never met her – she had always been at work when Maria visited Connick Street.

The Greeter turned back to Marcus. He was staring at the ground.

'Don't you believe me?' she asked.

'No,' he said. He sounded wounded, appalled.

'It's true. Three months.'

'Fuck off.' He drew his hand across his mouth.

'No,' said Darlene, looking back and forth from Marcus to Maria, her chilliness suddenly congealing into ice, 'fuck you.'

And then she was clicking away on her heels and Maria was staring after her, her fists involuntarily clenched with the memory of that voice. The phone voice, long ago. *No, fuck you.*

She looked up to exclaim to Marcus, but he was already yards up the street, hurrying away in the direction of the city. She ran after him and caught him by the shoulder, asking what was the matter, where was he going? He stopped and rubbed his hand over his face distractedly. He seemed to change his mind and turn to go back with her, then shrugged off her hand and stared off along the road.

'There's something I have to do.'

He farewelled her with an odd, formal stiffness. Turning away, refusing to say any more. He looked distressed.

But Maria couldn't leave it like that. He began to walk off and she kept up with him, asking him for an explanation, what was he doing, when would he return? He didn't answer, just walked and ignored her and walked faster until she began to despair and pluck at his sleeve, panting along the road past the dairy, the video shop, the used-car yard, past the kitchen emporium, House of Knives. There she suddenly saw red and shouted at him, 'You're so bloody contrary!'

She danced around him agitatedly by the window of the knife shop. Behind him on posters cool kitchen blondes wielded gleaming blades. Maria persisted, demanded, hot faced and furious. Where was he *going*? He detached himself roughly.

'Something's come up,' he muttered. He wouldn't look her in the eye. Maria exploded, all self-restraint flying away as she demanded, 'Are you coming back?' Her face was screwed up with indignation, her hands were planted on her hips. At that he stared back at her. In his eyes there was a hunted, angry look. They were both silent for a moment. He touched her arm and began to say something, and her expression lightened. She folded her arms and stood back, expecting him to be reasonable, to explain.

Seeing this, he said with a sudden surge of desperate rage, 'You're a *bootlicker*, Maria.'

Marcus rushed away. Maria stood frozen. She stood as still as stone. Marcus turned the corner and was gone, out of her sight.

There was nothing else to do. There was nothing to be done. She walked home in the gathering dark, through the empty streets. She cleared the remains of the Chinese feast away and threw herself on to her bed in a fever of tears. She loved him. She loved him. He was gone. She saw that he might never come back.

Marcus hurried away. He felt sick. He was resolved. He would go downtown, he would get on a bus. He would ride to Connick Street, he would jump-start the old car. He would take all the money he had earned and drive to the little house out west. He had money, he had no hangover. He was ready. *I will not cheat life. There will be no more cheating.*

But the phone rang unanswered at the house in the west. Where had they gone? He saw in his mind the house turned to post-holo-caust rubble, himself searching in the ruins for clues. Chrissie and her mother gone on a train, flown on a plane, gone up in smoke, no news, no news. Armed with a faded photo he searches railway sta-tions and bars. A woman in her fifties, her daughter, thin and lithe. They are this tall, have no money, read the future in the dregs of tea. They have dreams of Disneyland, they *see* it sometimes in the leaves.

And the daughter (thin and lithe), yes there is something else. She is in a certain condition, Monsieur – si Señor, it is true. The young woman he seeks (with terror, with love) the young woman is *with child*.

8.

Life, that bitch, and the hard course of her days! Marcus was gone. No one knew where he was, especially not his mother. The Meadowbank matron rang Maria searching for news of her son and together in rare camaraderie the rejected mother and the forsaken friend sadly cursed the love of their lives.

Maria was wounded. She was also angry. She gloomed through the days. You're a bootlicker, he'd said. A bootlicker. She was furious and hurt and yet, perversely, in one part of herself she admired his nastiness, because it was coldly accurate – he noticed, pulled her up, he let nothing past – and she couldn't control herself, she knew. She couldn't remain calm and in command. She couldn't take anything lightly either, because she felt everything so much. She wondered how he'd learned to be so consistently tough and detached.

What he had and what she lacked, she thought bitterly, was dignity. Her dealings with Marcus were a test that she failed every time – if she could only be wittier, colder, sharper, harder. Or, equally perhaps, more innocent, more heedlessly and unconsciously straightforward, like his beloved hard men, like Chrissie. He loved them because they lived strictly in reaction to life, without noticing or thinking or consciously acting, and so, in them, he found no false note. It was a strange fastidiousness he had. Strange puritanism. He couldn't take the sum of the behaviours that made up Maria Wallis, as intelligently self-conscious, shapeless and uncharismatic as they were.

Sitting on the bus on the way to work – and she looked forward to work, work cheered her – she decided that Marcus was naive, that his fastidiousness amounted to rigidity, even that his novel was going to be false if he could only deal with 'pure' notes. (*The Hard Men* was, after all, a risible title and she was never sure whether it was a joke with him or not.)

But even as she felt her way towards that idea – that he showed some failure of imagination or aesthetic sense – she understood that that argument, even if it was right, was no use to her. What it meant, after all, was that he didn't like her enough, and there was nothing she could do about that. He was extraordinarily loveable. She loved him. And no amount of arguing with him would make him love her in return.

Over the days Maria absorbed Marcus's absence. She bore it stoically, partly because she was preoccupied with Quinn St John, and partly because she occupied herself in brooding on the contradictions and difficulties Marcus represented. There were so many things that she wanted to say. She paced intently in the kitchen in the mornings, waiting for the kettle to boil or the toast to pop, emphasising points to herself. But Marcus wouldn't argue back, of course, if he ever came back. He was allergic to argument: any 'intellectualising', any hint of round-eyed sincerity aroused the savage in him immediately – he would silence her swiftly, or send her off into hysterics, with a venomous and deadly joke.

The effect of her meditations was to reinforce, naturally enough (after all, she found him so interesting), her secret, patient, stubborn hope that she would open the front door and find him on the doorstep, smiling his bad old smile, and larger than life.

It was the 2nd May 1987. Maria woke with a feeling of unease, as if something fundamental were about to change. Maria had always reacted badly to change – when she was a child, her mother had told her, change of any sort would make her angry and prone to tantrums – and she felt inexplicably disturbed and angry now.

She was waking, she discovered, to the sound of the ringing phone. She flew to pick it up, answered to hear Leon's cheerful greeting, and shouted at him angrily to leave her alone. She hung up on the hurt silence and threw the phone at the wall. Picked up the damaged appliance and threw it energetically across the room again. Quietly disarmed by Ernest ('just give me the phone, Maria') she stalked off to the shower. Readied herself, ate nothing, trudged furiously up the road to the bus.

Everything bothered her, everything grated on her nerves, and she was at a loss to explain why. The old women on the bus, why couldn't they keep quiet? Jabbering away about church, children, prices, pets. Look at the bloated dalek at the wheel. Maria glared at him in the mirror. Maria, secret fascist, rested her hot face on the glass and found herself willing the devastation of the entire bus. Let there be flames, let there be maiming, let there be screaming and wailing. Let street and city broil and dance and writhe, to the tune of the pain of Maria.

At 8:45 a.m. Maria went whirling and spinning into work. Soon Clairene lay mauled and bleeding in her wake. With his internal barometer plunging towards zero Giles Speer skied into his room and firmly secured the door. Peeks-Berlyn looked up from his happy perusal of a commercial lease to find Maria fondling a paper stabber and staring at him in a predatory manner. Thus alienating and unnerving her colleagues Maria toughed it out through the endless waste of the morning.

'It's nothing,' she snapped at the nervous Peeks-Berlyn, 'it's just nothing.'

Later Maria was sitting in her office, calmer now and wondering at the violence of her mood – she couldn't think why she'd woken in such a state, unless it was just that Marcus's absence had gone on too long – when she received another telephone call from Leon.

After the recent hours of anger and the lonely morning, she cradled the telephone receiver with a tender delight. She felt unfamiliar sensations – warmth, affection, pleasure!

'Oh, you. I've missed you. I'm sorry about everything. I've been mad. I went mad for a while. That Marcus. He . . .'

Ignoring her, Leon asked her the usual, carefully, 'Jwanna go out?'

'*Yes*,' she said with a feeling of relief and joy. 'Oh, yes.'

'Come over tonight,' he said briefly, and hung up.

Maria sat with the receiver under her chin, listening to the electronic pips. He was hurt, of course. But that wouldn't last. Everything would be the same. She hadn't realised how much she had been missing him, and she waited impatiently for the long afternoon to end.

At seven-thirty that evening Maria hurried with happy anticipation down the drive to Leon's front porch. He opened the door and ushered her in. She smelled a wave of vodka and cigarette fumes. He wore a red jacket, thin trousers, black leather boots. His eyes were bloodshot, there were dark purple shadows under them, his hair stood up in fine blond spikes.

She sat in the kitchen with a glass of wine and talked incoherently about Marcus. He was temperamental. Sensitive. A writer . . .

Leon smiled jaggedly. 'He give you VD?'

'No. Only lice. And fleas.' She sighed and smiled. She looked at Leon with love. He was clearly drunk. He swayed around the room, cigarette in the corner of his mouth, eyes narrowed against the smoke.

He manhandled his stereo, pulling tapes out roughly, shoving tapes in, playing fragments of songs and then switching them off. He was careless about his left hand; more than once she saw the tiny withered fingers and the abbreviated thumb. The painted hardboard figures watched as he sat fast-forwarding, stopping, rewinding, thumping the machine with his fist. Fucken thing, he said smiling at her. Fucken thing. He swigged his vodka, refilled the glass. Standing over her with his hand on her shoulder he poured her more wine.

Maria stared around at the strange, cluttered room. The smoke hung in a flat cloud, at head height. The colourful figures grinned and peered through the gloom.

Leon rummaged in a bag at his feet. 'I bought a new song for you,' he explained, and he played it to her.

'I like it.' She sipped and smiled.

'You have it.' He took the tape out of the machine, picked up her handbag and put the tape into it. Then he scooped up the vodka bottle and stuffed that into her handbag too. 'Be prepared,' he whispered.

They were going to a film down on the waterfront, a French romp called *Les Ripoux*.

They arrived at the cinema in a taxi just as the large crowd was threading its way in through the doors. They jumped the queue by habit – Leon and Maria never queued, saw a queue as a test of skill – and bought tickets.

They found their way to their seats in the middle of the row, with much bumping and groping and hissed apologies. The lights went out. Maria felt Leon reach for her handbag in the dark. She heard the scratch of the bottle top being unscrewed and smelled the raw tang of alcohol.

The first hectic trailer roared on to the screen in a blast of mayhem and flame. Over the sound of the gunshots and screams Maria heard Leon sigh and gurgle and swig.

Five trailers later, as they were unblocking their ears for the feature presentation, Leon leaned over with a breath of fire and announced in a stage whisper, 'Need the Gents.'

Maria snorted and smirked as Leon rose unsteadily and began to edge his way through the tangled mass of coats and knees, offering pungent and courtly apologies to the dismayed crowd around him. Maria listened with amusement to the whispers of protest around her, her attention thoroughly diverted from the comedy now playing on the screen.

Leon reached the end of the row to sighs of indignant relief, the whispered threats of violence subsided, and order was restored. The roguish French cops went on with their dirty business in the streets of Paris. Maria's eyes strayed back to the story and she settled down to watch.

But now odd noises began to float up from the foyer below. The crowd shifted uneasily and heads turned as sounds of a distant but violent altercation wafted up the stairs. Audible shouts, a crash as of something large falling over, and then a shaft of light as a tall figure threw open the auditorium door and leapt nimbly up the carpeted terraces.

Brightly spot-lit by the torch-wielding usher in pursuit, Leon began to wangle his way to his seat. The crowd groaned, there were shrieks as toes were trampled, pantyhose were torn. Realising he was in the wrong row, he vaulted over a couple of seats, booted and kicked his way across a couple more and slumped down, still spot-lit, in a dizzying fume-cloud of vodka.

'Shhh,' he whispered at Maria, finger to his lips. Then, fixing his eyes on the screen and sinking low in his seat, he felt around for a match and ignited a cigarette. At this fresh insult the crowd went wild. Fists belaboured Leon from behind, umbrellas and handbags were wielded, a middle-aged man stood up and shouted tearfully, 'It's just not on!'

In the midst of all the shouting and keening the house lights went up, security moved in, the crowd roared, and that was the end of the movie for Leon and Maria.

Now they strolled casually along an alley towards the main street. Their ejection from the cinema (out of the back entrance into a narrow street full of cats and bin-bags) had not been too violent. Leon had simply been plucked from his seat and frogmarched from the cinema to the cheers of the crowd while Maria sauntered along behind, whistling non-committally.

She looked Leon over fondly and plucked a piece of paper rubbish from his hair. The old chaotic Leon. Funnier than a film. She was just so pleased to see him. She caught a whiff of pizza from the Italian restaurants on the waterfront drive. She was hungry and led him, still swigging on his vodka bottle, to the nearest café, Tonino's, where they sat inside at a vinyl table and ordered a seafood pizza to share.

Leon was wild-eyed by now and slurring his words. Maria sat back and contemplated him. She could see that he was wrecked, as if he'd been drinking all day.

'Why are you getting so drunk?'

But she felt relaxed and warm. She watched him indulgently. 'You're a disgrace.'

'My legs will go,' he whispered.

'That's right, they will.'

He offered her the bottle and she took a drink. She wrinkled her nose and shook her head. She gave the bottle back.

He bared his teeth demoniacally at her, and went on sipping. The pizza came. He ate with his big right hand, stuffing olives and mussels into his mouth between swigs from the bottle. Maria took another sip of vodka, but she wasn't in the mood for drinking. She felt cheerful and lazy, released from the tension of the last days.

Leon finished eating and got up and wandered around the tables. By now they were the only people left in the café. He struck up a conversation with the Italians behind the counter. Like Maria they were indulgent, winking over at her, 'He pissed, eh? Take him home, sober him up.'

They patted him on the shoulder and joked with him, the striking lunatic with his blond hair, his luminously bloodshot eyes. He looked as if he was fleeing from something and laughing, eyes wild with adrenaline, intense with escape-hype. He lurched and swung around the tiny room, the nearly empty vodka bottle tucked into the crook of his arm.

At 1 a.m. the three Italians were closing up the shop. They stacked chairs, mopped the floor, talking comfortably all the time to Leon and Maria as if they were part of the establishment. Leon sat on the counter with a toothpick in his mouth. Maria lifted up her feet while the waiter, their new friend, genially mopped the floor underneath.

Finally the boss turned off the lights, and they all went to the door. Shouting goodnight, the Italians went off to their cars, and Leon and Maria forged out into the damp, black, salty night.

It was two o'clock in the morning. Leon slung his arm over Maria's shoulders. The tide was high, the sea was choppy and full and the wind blew spray off the sea. Maria looked without hope for a taxi, but it was late and there was no cab in sight. Leon began veering quickly along the road. She called out to him to wait as a car pulled up in the road behind them. The driver cranked the hand-brake abruptly and peered out of the window. It was the oldest of the Italians, the boss.

'You want a ride to town?' he called out wearily. 'You get in.'

Gratefully Maria bundled Leon ahead of her into the car and they drove slowly around the bays towards town. Leon put his head out the window and smoked. Maria closed her eyes and leaned on his shoulder. When they got to Quay Street the old Italian stopped the car. He turned his head with effort and smiled thinly.

'You get out here. Not smoke in my car. Anyway, I go to the bridge.'

Leon turned vaguely and blew a stream of smoke into the front of the car, into the old man's face. The Italian reached over the seat, opening Leon's door.

'Hey, you. Time to go.' Weighted with vodka, Leon smiled sweetly and didn't move.

'You get out,' the Italian said, suddenly exasperated, tired, urgent. He wrestled and fumbled with the door. 'Get out, you . . . faggot. You fucking *poof.*'

Leon flicked up his eyes. For a second he sat still and pale. Then they clambered out and the old man drove quickly off towards the harbour bridge.

Across the road the all-night BP coldly pulsed like a landed spaceship. Leon leaned heavily on Maria's shoulder. 'Let's go,' he said hoarsely, rubbing his hands over his face.

He stood back and swayed gracefully on the kerb, his face coloured orange by the streetlight. He frowned with concentration, lit a cigarette, threw away the match. He took Maria by the hand and she felt the hard, wrinkled skin of his deformed fingers.

'Hang on, have you got any money?' Maria said. She disengaged her hand and felt around in her handbag.

'None left,' he said with a sigh. He stepped off the kerb and walked on towards the gas station's glowing neon core.

Maria stood rummaging in her bag for her purse, humming to herself. In the background the sigh of the city and the wind blowing through the freight yards and the all-night birds singing in the neon sunshine in the trees near the BP.

She heard a car on the empty road, driving at speed. The whine of its engine, urgent as a drill. She looked up and saw Leon on the centre line, standing quite still. The car coming like a rocket, and Leon on the empty road.

She waited for him to move. She waited until she heard the shuddering impact, the explosion of glass as the missile connected. Leon upright and still, then flung in an instant into wild motion, Leon's limbs flying up, flying apart, his head whipped back, the scream of high speed sound as the car wobbled in its tearing trajectory, as it swerved, and carried on. Maria watched as Leon was borne past her on the spangled litter of the bonnet, lying in a lolling web of blood and limbs and glass, flying past her along the road until the car swerved violently into the kerb, skidded and nearly rolled, and his body was flung off and landed face down in the gutter.

Over the sound of screams she heard the panicking gear change, the shrieking accelerator, watched as the car juddered and jumped forward, gathered its speed and tore away like a screaming black bomb along the flat stretch of Quay Street.

Maria screaming alone in the broken glass, ran this way and that in her panic, now towards Leon, now towards the lighted BP. Fighting to breathe, she realised she was screaming; with a terrible effort, she stopped. Heaving, gasping, she heard the tearing sobs of her breath. The street was flat, black, silent, the trees were sick and sullen under the orange lights. Maria heard screams again, and couldn't draw breath.

Then she was in the BP, running between the shelves. The petrol station attendant already reaching for the panic button as she tried to vault over the counter, tearing at his clothes and face. 'Come come come,' she gasped and screamed, 'come come come . . .'

She dragged him out into the street. She pulled him along the road to where Leon lay.

They lifted him up, so that they could see his face. Most of his cheek was ripped away. Dull red of flesh, yellow white of bone. The strange limpness and heaviness of his shoulders, limbs falling curiously awry. The remains of Leon's face priestly, pursed-lipped, the poor skull, small under its slicked-down mat of bright red hair, broken up in places with crockery-like shards of protruding bone. The withered hand, palm up, loosely curled.

The petrol attendant laid Leon quickly back down on his face. 'No no,' he muttered, wiping and wiping his hands on his jeans. 'Ah no.'

Maria crouching in the road laid her hand on the shoulder of her friend. Head down, hand on his shoulder, she talked to him. She stayed with him, she waited with him, she wouldn't leave him alone. Around her while she waited, while she watched the still face, calls travelled through the reverberating air, messages flew, sirens screamed, engines roared in the echoing streets. In ten minutes the street was a teeming ant-heap of life. Cordoned, surrounded, spot-lit, Maria crouched with Leon in the road.

A hand touched her shoulder, Maria looked up. The street had gone, in its place a red and blue disco filled with uniforms, plastic tape, plastic cones, a hundred blue and white vehicles, carelessly parked.

A man with a large moustache put his fingers to Leon's neck, shook his head, peeled off his crimsoned, gloves. Maria shifted on the asphalt, her knees were soaked with blood. Large hands covered

Leon's body with a plastic sheet, impatiently she tore the cover away. Hands reached down and stood her up.

'He's dead,' they told her, as if she didn't know.

They took her to a room in the top of the Central Police Station, a mean grey boxy office with a view of the city. She watched two neon arrows on the skyline flashing alternately, like lightning bolts. They brought her cups of tea that were so full of sugar she spooned them up with a plastic spoon. They asked her if she wanted anyone to come down. She said no. Then they left her alone. She sat and watched the arrows, crunching the sweet crystals of the tea. She thought dazedly, now look what he's done. How's he going to get out of this? She looked out along the empty corridor. They would bring him out soon, black of fingertip, wild of hair. Grinning. She would find a taxi, ferry him home, they would lounge and laugh and watch morning TV . . .

She heard voices. The door opened and a slight, grey-haired man marched into the room and slapped a file down on the desk.

'John Hughson,' he said. He glared at her as if she would question his right to the name. 'I'm in charge here. Right?'

Maria looked at him without interest. Two other men had entered the room. He introduced them, pointing them out with a biro, Detective Teddy Nu'U, Detective Teina Light. He picked up another file and slammed it down on the desk. Maria flinched and sighed.

'Siddown,' he said.

She was unaware she had stood up. She sat. Detective Hughson cleared his throat, scratched his head with the biro and glared over the desk. The tone of his voice was angry and nasal, with a soupçon of injury, as if she was keeping him up late.

'You said the car was . . .?'

'A Ford. I think. Black. Like an Escort, or Cortina. Four door.'

'Your friend was . . .? Where?'

'In the middle of the road. He was . . .'

'You were?'

'On the side of the road. Nearest the railway yards. I . . .'

'Which direction it drive off in?'

'Towards Gladstone Road.'

'Up Gladstone Road?'

'I think so. I don't know.'

'He was pissed?'

'Yes.'

'You're drunk too.'

'No.'

'Take drugs?'

'Who?'

'You . . . Or him.'

'No. Never.'

'You sure?'

'Yes.'

'But now you're pissed.'

'No.'

'I wasn't born yesterday.'

'So?'

'So are you . . .?'

'*I am not fucking drunk.*'

Maria, surging with confused rage, jumped up out of her chair. But the large hands of Detective Nu'U forced her gently down into her seat.

Hughson twirled his biro violently between his fingers. He waited for her to sit down, pointed the pen at her and said, with a triumphal roll of his shoulders, 'Don't you swear at *me*.'

She stared at his face. A thin line of saliva shone on his lower lip. He was thin, athletic and deeply tanned, with an arid grey chiselled face and hot hard little black eyes.

'Why not?' she said. She stared at the ceiling.

'Say again, your friend use drugs?' Biro turning and turning in the knotty hand.

'No, and why are you asking me that fucking irrelevant question, *fuck* . . .' Maria spat out the words, choking, threshing in her seat, while behind her Detective Nu'U shifted on his feet, cracked his knuckles, cleared his throat.

'Try again. You drunk?'

Maria stood up, and the little grey man rose out of his seat and barked, '*Sit down!*'

She remained standing. With terrible effort, with her last piece of strength she said, 'I am not drunk. The car was a black Ford. It drove off along Quay Street. Do what you're supposed to do, find that car, and leave me fucking alone.' She sat down. 'You fucking cunt,' she added bleakly, with her last breath.

She saw Detective Teina Light look away from the window briefly and smile. Detective Nu'U went out of the room for a moment and Detective Hughson threw himself about behind the desk for a while, taking notes, shouting for minions, issuing instructions, and eventually commanding Maria to draw a series of diagrams of the street.

She drew in the figures, got it wrong, drew them again. There were old tram-lines on the road, she couldn't remember where they were. She couldn't remember where the gas station was. She forgot where she was, looked out the window and saw the lightning bolts on the horizon and the dark city spreading away to the Waitakere Range.

She glanced at the clock on the wall, it was 4:45 a.m. She stood up and paced around the room, talking vaguely to Detectives Light and Nu'U. She remembered things, tried to get them right. At one point she exclaimed, 'Of course,' and laughed out loud as she remembered something, then looked into their faces as they paused with their pens raised and stared curiously at her.

She felt something descend on her then, some inkling of gravity, of weight. Dread weakened her legs, forced her down into a chair. Her head felt as heavy as lead. She felt again that it was hard to breathe. She fell silent and sat until 5:30, when Detective Hughson re-entered the room and announced jauntily into the silence, 'School fees for JPs!'

She rubbed her face, uncomprehending, as the grey maniac slammed another file on the desk, grinned at his silent brown cohorts and sang out again with an air of sprightly malice, 'School fees for JPs!'

He glanced over at Maria, scratching his nose with his pen. 'Know what I do when I get home?'

Maria conveyed heavily sour uninterest.

He gestured at the other two detectives. 'Those guys sleep all day, lie round in front of the box. Not me. I run. I run around the bays every day. Not an ounce of fat on me. See?' He thumped his chest.

Maria looked at the wall. He left the room, rolling his shoulders. Detective Nu'U looked faintly embarrassed.

'We need to take you somewhere now, just over to Ponsonby in the car.'

'Why?'

'You seen him dead, you see. You can sign the form.'

They waited in the office for Detective Light to get a car. Maria stood at the window and watched the arrow lights on the horizon flicking on and off. The odd disjointed thought surfaced, where *was* Leon? If she could see him, if she could tell him what was going on . . .

Maria gasped suddenly and rocked on her heels. Detective Nu'U looked up from his notes.

'What?'

'Nothing.' She stared at the arrows, off/on off/on. The horizon was beginning to get light. She became aware of a bad smell in the room. Had the detective *farted*? Had *she*? The smell gathered intensity, the detective shifted in his seat. Maria felt that she was losing herself, flying away, flying apart. Where was Leon? What was she doing here? The arrows were fading as the sky became delicate pink. She saw black cloud on the skyline, moving from the west, bruising the pale red skin of the dawn.

Detective Light came back and the three of them rode down in the battered steel lift to the car. Maria walked in a dream, blank faced, utterly silent. The policemen were quiet too, occasionally speaking in low monosyllables in the front of the car.

She rode along through the damp cardboard suburbs, looking out at the tangled trees in the Ponsonby park, the crooked trunks leaning in frozen agony, hairy clusters of tree fibre hanging like women's long hair.

'Two-four,' the car radio announced. 'A four-five on a nine-eight, probably a six-ten . . .' The big car sighed over the slicked black roads.

In Grey Lynn they turned into a small residential street. They parked, got out and the detectives went up on to the porch of a wooden house and knocked on the door.

A hunched bald man in a tartan dressing-gown emerged, rubbing his eyes. Detective Nu'U turned to Maria.

'This is Mr Grogan, JP . . . Justice of the Peace,' he added.

The little man beckoned them into the narrow, stuffy hall. Detective Nu'U produced a form, put it down on a telephone table and invited Maria to sign.

'Dessertificate,' he explained. He handed her a pen. She signed. Leaning down the JP signed on the line beneath.

'School fees,' she murmured stupidly. The JP glanced up irritably.

'I'm sorry?' he asked.

'Forget it.'

They led her back to the car.

'Now where?'

'Home.'

They drove in silence to Ashton Road. The detectives spoke listlessly, in low voices. She opened the car door. Detective Nu'U leaned his head out the window and winked, 'Be in touch.'

'Goodbye,' she whispered without moving her lips, and watched as they U-turned and drove quickly away.

She went in and knocked on Ernest's bedroom door. She shook him awake and told him. She sounded like a robot. He groped for his glasses, open-mouthed, appalled. After thinking for a moment he got out of bed and said he would make tea.

'Of course,' she said, 'it's what you do when people die.' She laughed harshly. Her voice sounded alien to her, metallic like the voice on the car radio.

'It's a ten-four on the four-five,' she said. She laughed again. He stared, her throat constricted. She followed him mechanically into the kitchen. He fumbled anxiously around in the debris and she disappeared out on to the back lawn and began to pace up and down. When he came out she was agitated, pacing along the length of the hedge.

'I'll tell you something.' She grabbed his arm, tea spilled on to the grass and scalded his hand.

'What what?' Flapping his hand, deeply upset.

'I can't feel it.'

'Feel what?'

'Grief.'

He put the cups carefully down on the grass. 'Well, the shock . . . you will . . .'

'But I can't feel it, I can't see it, I can't understand . . .' She looked distractedly at him, rubbing her hands through her hair.

'You need to get some sleep . . .'

'No, you don't understand . . .'

He stepped back. She looked insane. She advanced on him, tripping over the cups.

'Maria, for Christ's sake . . .'

'I can't feel it. Can't feel what it means . . .' Her eyes were red and screwed up, spit flew out of the corner of her mouth. A kind of snarl or growl came out of her. Her hands, when she put them to her mouth, were like claws.

Ernest went into his room and came out with something in his hand. He held it out. She looked at it uncomprehendingly.

'Take it.' He pushed it into her hand.

'What is it?' She slurred the words. He noticed red-brown stains on her neck and shirt and arms.

'It's a Valium.'

She said she didn't want it. Then she grabbed it from him and swallowed it. She lay down on her bed. Sleeping heavily, she dreamed. She was flying away, high over a red desert. She saw cold bronze light above a red horizon, dry stones, red dust, red rock. Shadows over dead dunes, arid rock, wild light.

Every person and every thing she had ever known left behind her for ever.

9.

Maria slept for four hours and woke to the sound of the birds fighting in the trees and the moans of the iron clothes-line turning slowly in the yard. She crept from her room to find that Ernest had tidied the house and gone to work. She looked out at the garden, at the dry bare pohutukawa twigs sticking up among the glossy green leaves like old fingers caressing new notes, at the looming hedge, the sullenly damp and tangled sponge of the lawn. All the same. All unaltered. Maria frowning at the garden with her elbows on the sill, thought wonderingly, why has it not changed colour, gone black. Why has it not withered and died? Should the world not register the unalterable change?

But what change? The dull garden remained defiantly green, the sky the usual fluid battleground, of retention and release.

She went quickly to the bathroom, peeled off her clothes and stuffed them into a plastic sack. Full of DNA, she thought, staring with sick fascination at the bag. She thrust it quickly into the rubbish bin out the back.

Before she did anything else she rang Giles Speer and explained, surreally, why she wasn't at work. She tittered and stumbled her way through the humiliating call, struggling with the feeling that everything she said was grotesquely inappropriate.

'It's a "bereavement",' she said conversationally, as if scratching the air with raised index fingers. 'Yes. Actually. Last night. Ha ha.'

Twisting the phone cord in her fingers, tapping her foot on the floor.

His voice hoarse with horror and embarrassment, Giles Speer

said carefully, 'You must take some time off. Of course, as many days . . . as . . .'

'It takes?' Maria couldn't shake her tone of jaunty shame.

'Yes. Ha ha . . . I mean . . .' She could hear his seat creaking as he fidgeted and writhed.

'Thank you very much,' she said politely, dropping the phone back on to its cradle as if the receiver were poisonously alive.

Back in her room Maria lay down and entered a curious state of suspended animation. Now she felt that any movement, any loud noise would jolt her into territory that was unimaginably dangerous. If she stumbled, if she moved clumsily, if she coughed or sneezed, the glass silence would break and information would come, knowledge so overwhelming she would be swept into its madness and lost. She lay carefully with the pillow over her head, so still that she might have been dead. Hours passed, and she thought about nothing. At times she surfaced, became aware that she was thinking about nothing, considered this briefly, then drifted again. She floated, limp and heavy as a drowned corpse, carried on the current of the stunned afternoon.

The phone rang and answerphone messages buzzed inaudibly. Several times someone knocked on the door. A man called her name, waited for a while, looked through the letterbox and then went away.

She lay there until a sideways glance at the shadows on the wall told her it was late afternoon. Then the yellow afternoon light on the walls, the dark shadows slanting across the floor seemed to signify something hidden, to carry a terrifying weight. Night was coming. Night, and its black comedy, its terrible *shenanigans*.

Maria came alive and flew around the room, locking the outside door, securing the windows. Swiftly she rang the Central Police Station and asked to be connected to Detective Teddy Nu'U. He answered.

'I want to see him.' She enunciated clearly, carefully. She had made a decision.

'What?'

'I want to see him. Where is he?'

'He's in the morgue. You can't . . . You're not supposed . . .' She heard the detective chew, finish a mouthful, moistly swallow.

'Not supposed to what?'

'Well, he's being . . .'
'What?'
'He's being cut up.'

She drove. While the sky darkened and the lights came on. With speed and accuracy through flickering shopping centre, shop verandah, dark car yard. Randomly at first, with no destination in mind. But after an hour she found herself speeding on an empty road near Piha, the odd pale streetlight shining on the dripping skeletons of the ferns and hedgehogs scuttling ahead on the road, flashlit and doomed. The terrible, tangled bush with its headachey tang of tea leaf and damp crowding and pressing at the edges of the road.

She stopped the car. Sat on the cold vinyl wanting silence, moon, understanding, grief. She listened. Darkness but not silence, in the stalled black night the bush breathed and moved, the bush was alive with dripping and rustling, with secretive whispers and sighs. Down the bank a possum made its unearthly staccato threats, ak ak ah, such a harmless little animal, such a sinister sound. There were no stars, no moon, only a faint lightening of the smothering black blanket of cloud over the city lights behind the hills.

Then she saw something move at the edge of the headlights, and fearfully locked the doors, and revved the car into life. She turned it around and drove back to the city, increasingly afraid that the car would break down, that she would be stranded in the suffocating blackness of the bush.

The petrol gauge was low, she accelerated and sped. She leaned over the wheel, whispering to herself, she knew now what she had. The infection. The disease lying low in her, waiting to take over, the thing that would eat her alive – it was fear. From all sides the bush pressed and crowded, rustled and moved on the high banks. She hurtled through the ghost tunnel of the bush road, small animals veered and leapt, froze and stared and died under the wheels, dead ferns dangled and whipped the car, twisted branches loomed low over the narrow road. She drove, aimless, unhinged, undone, terrified, she didn't know what to do. She didn't know what to do. Back there (the chew, the moist swallow, the faint burp of farewell) back there they were making phone calls, eating hamburgers, cutting him up. They were cutting him up.

She ran out of petrol at the top of Leon's street. The car coughed wearily and died. She coasted to the kerb, parked and hurried on down the road.

The lights were on in the tiny house. Full of terror she knocked on the door, feeling as if she were knocking on a coffin or shaking the shoulder of a corpse, would the door spring open, would the pale zombie rear jerkily into life . . .

The door opened and she looked into the yellow-lit face of the dead. The burning eyes with their strange defiant power, the savage-comic mouth, the patrician forehead.

'Oh, Maria,' he croaked, stretching out his arms, 'I've waited all day for you to come,' and she lurched forward and clung to him and they held one another fiercely, with relief, with bitter desolation and terror, with a kind of ragged grief at last.

On the morning of the funeral Maria lay numbly in Leon's bed and listened to Vic Pavel making final arrangements over the phone. She had been with the old man for two days now, eating his casseroles, sitting in the kitchen late at night watched by the secretive hardboard figures, as she looked through Leon's things. Stopping to sigh and look away, creased-faced, the dumb tragedy of items left behind, hairs in his comb, his unwashed socks on the floor, half-used cans of hairspray, half-smoked packs of cigarettes.

The old man looked through Leon's childhood photos, at the bright keen little boy in his spotless shirt, full of bravery and smiles, not yet knowing what he is, what tricks and jokes life has in store. Then the later photos – through schoolyard taunts and jeers he has learned about his deformed hand, that it must be hidden at all times. The stance lopsided now, the hand no longer seen, the eyes already sly, savage, ironic, the eyes old before their time. His father and mother were both foreigners, speaking at home and in the street like a pair of magpies, those harsh foreign sounds, and the house always full of strange paintings and cooking smells. The mother an artist, loud, brightly made-up, warmly eccentric, but soon to wither away from cancer in the bedroom upstairs. One day during a dispute a neighbourhood boy rounded on Leon unexpectedly, with childish venom: 'What's that smell round your place? Smells like your mum, didn't they bury her yet? She died of embarrassment, looking at *you*.'

Foreigner, faggot, cack-handed, wrong-handed. The eyes with their powerful knowledge, ghost of the smiling boy gone wild. Leon crazed with rebellion, eyes burning out of the faded snapshot, laughing with his teeth – he had courage. The eyes, the whole face, blazing with it. Courage and flair and colour, and then – gone. Lost, on Quay Street. *Quay Street* . . .

On a speechless humid afternoon Maria drove with the old man to some anonymous suburb – flat streets, sagging houses, black-birds on the power lines making sheet music in the white sky – and looked at what they had left of Leon. Poor leftovers, after the meal they made. Her mind stuck on the same horror, Maria swallowed and sighed.

The coffin was mounted on a trolley with criss-cross metal legs, allowing it to be cranked up and down, to cater, as the pallid attendant explained, to the comfort of tall and short mourner alike. The coffin lay in a small square strip-lit room, under a vase of synthetic flowers, on a carpet of sickly beige.

Maria and Vic entered with fear. Leon, in full make-up, bore the same look of priestly forbearance and surprise that he had worn on the night he died. His face was grossly misshapen, the forehead bulging and the jaw askew, and on his cheeks a red paste covered the places where they had pieced together his face. The old man inhaled sharply and bent forward.

'Oh, you don't look too bad,' he whispered. 'You look OK. Oh, don't worry, boy.' He leaned over, whispering into the box.

When it was her turn she brushed the cold forehead with her lips. He was just a shell, she knew. The things they did. Took everything out, packed the body with cotton wool. There was something under his eyelids, she bent closer to look. Freckles there on his nose, under the ghastly powder. And a white plastic covering, like half a Ping-Pong ball over each eyeball, under the lid. He smelled of chemicals. Look what they've done to you. The look of a body so terrifyingly final. Death, the fearfully abstract concept, suddenly concrete. He was vanished, no trace. Looking at Leon she believed in it now. She believed in the absoluteness of death.

Maria and Vic walked back to the car through the desultory streets. Now the old man was crushed and bent, all his self-control was gone. Maria silently helped him into the car. What to say to the old man, breathing raggedly now into his handkerchief in the passenger seat? That Leon was with the angels? She didn't believe it for a minute. She never had believed in any of that stuff.

They sat in the car. 'He's in heaven now,' she murmured experimentally, glancing sideways. (Even though he wouldn't qualify. Even though he wouldn't want to turn up in heaven now, looking the way he did.) Old Vic looked up, blew his nose. 'Ah, come off it,' he said, blinking and sighing. He smiled bleakly at her and squeezed her arm. 'You don't want to believe any of *that* crap.'

Now she lay on Leon's bed, listening to the old man talk on the phone. He spoke in a foreign language: Czech, she supposed. Earlier she had rung her mother to tell her what had happened and listened to Celine struggling with the invasion from the outside world. Celine had managed to make the right noises eventually, horror, sympathy, all that. Then she had said, with desperation at the edge of her voice, 'Now Maria, we must keep calm. At a time like this . . . We mustn't fall apart . . .' Maria could sense Celine urgently casting her eye around the concrete flat for the nearest book. A shock like this, what would it take? *Poor Fellow My Country* perhaps, or *War and Peace*, again . . .

Vic came into the room, looking pale and intense, papery old skin bulging around the strained blue eyes.

'All set?' He smiled bleakly down at Maria.

They drove east to the cemetery and parked on the hill where the land rolled down to the railway lines and the graves stretched away in all directions in long rows, culs-de-sac, subdivisions, the orderly suburbs of the dead. Far away a gardener drove a lawnmower through rows of winged angels and speckled plaques, down there the lawn was a rich and cosmetic green, sinisterly well-nourished. It was a hard, bright, autumn day, cold wind blowing up the hill, the autumn sun on its low trajectory sending long shadow statues sprawling among the graves. The wind turned the water in the estuary to silver, the seagulls screamed and turned in the hard light.

Maria followed the old man away from the hillside of graves and down the chiselled drive to a white building which was in all respects like a church, except for the blackened vents in the spire and the discreet curl of smoke winding up from the vents and over the roof of the building.

Maria sniffed sharply. Immediately she regretted this detail, the cremation choice. The old man's choice, of course. But why couldn't Leon have a place in a quiet avenue, in a row in the city of the dead? She hurried after him over the gravel. This oven thing, the miserable urn afterwards, nowhere to put it and no grave to visit. The dead sitting around in the house, mixed up with the crockery and sporting trophies in a glass-fronted cabinet, or on a windowsill on a ludicrous stand, gathering dust. The loved one reduced to a chattel, an uncharismatic piece of ugly bric-a-brac – isn't it time we threw Mum/Dad/Rover away?

Bury me on a green hill, she thought, let the wind blow over my grave. A faint memory rose – had Leon said something, once, about where he wanted to be buried? But she couldn't remember. She couldn't recall. She walked on under the cold shade of the dark cypress trees, forcing herself forward against the urge to run the other way, down the hillside into the sun, by the racing water, by the silver tracks.

The old man had vanished into a crowd of people gathered at the front of the church. She heard different languages. It was quite a big crowd; the old man seemed to have numerous friends. She even saw Leon's old enemies the Camcooks from next door; perhaps, Maria speculated, merely satisfying themselves that Leon was really dead, that this wasn't some trick cooked up by him before a final pillaging of their house. Maria imagined Mrs Camcook with a crowbar, eagerly levering up the coffin lid.

A furtively whispering functionary in black and white plucked Maria's sleeve and handed her the order of ceremony. It looked like a menu. And the specials are. The chargrilled, the seared. But this is disgusting, she thought with misery. She went inside. The coffin lay on a trolley at the front under a spray of quivering flowers. Maria looked around. The interior was churchy, with a disguising overlay of fake wood panelling and plastic stained glass. She sat down in a pew, sure that she could feel the heat from the furnaces beneath the floor. It was a logical progression, she thought with a hysterical smirk. They had *cut him up* and now he would be *cooked*. She eyed the metal pipes running up the walls. Look closely, the place was a kitchen. Something caught in her throat and she began to cough, an old woman looked round and frowned. Maria stared back, the old woman looked away.

The service began, the vicar opening with the surprise observation that Leon had been a practising Christian. In fact, one could actually say he had been *devout*. So rare, he continued, narrowing his eyes, so heartening in one so young. Looking sideways, Maria saw a bitter smile cross Mrs Camcook's face. She wondered whether the vicar had got his lists confused, but saw the old man's head unconcernedly bowed and concluded the distortions must be for the benefit of the old relatives and friends, who were nodding and smiling in fuddled satisfaction. It went on, surreally. Leon's tireless work for charity, his community spirit. His work among the elderly. Maria thoughts were becoming incoherent. She stopped listening. She stood and sat and kneeled and stood, no longer caring what was going on. Community spirit. The *community*. But the community hated him . . .

They sang, the old voices quavering pitifully in the metallic acoustics. This place is awful, she thought. But what did it matter? You couldn't make it better. You could never make death better. But I killed him, she thought suddenly. *I* killed him. The appalled, stinging tears swelling painfully behind her eyes.

The congregation began to shuffle slowly towards the front of the church, beckoned forward by the vicar. She heard a faint squeaking. With a rhythmic creak the coffin was sliding backwards, jerking slightly on its rails. Abruptly it braked, then there was a whirring noise as it began to descend slowly into a square hole in the floor. The vicar poker-faced at his pulpit, smoothly operating the controls. Maria wanted it to stop. It was all too quick. *Wait*, she whispered, clenching her fists. *I wasn't listening*. The coffin reached the bottom with a tiny bump, and as the trapdoors began to close it was trundling away into a horizontal tunnel. The trapdoors closed, the crowd relaxed and murmured and stepped back. Nodding, hands on shoulders, turning away, the hard job done.

But Maria was already walking out of there. Elbowing her way past the old foreign ladies in their crocheted black ponchos, before the trapdoors closed. Pushing urgently against the heavy wooden doors and out into the cold light, clicking up the drive on her heels,

turning abruptly right and down the hillside, to stumble wildly
down through the broken concrete graves, past the drunken angels –
up close they sported beards of moss, missing noses, missing
wings – over the sagging stones with their faint writing and long-ago
dates, through the long spindly shadows criss-crossing the green
slope.

Above on the hill, blinking out with the crowd into the light, the
old man looked down and saw Maria fleeing like a goat among the
concrete crags, down through the jumble of white rock and shining
marble, the ice floe of graves, slow-moving glacier of the dead (inching further every year) down the sunlit valley to the dark mud
mouth of the sea.

Maria smoked a cigarette down by the mudflats, by the railway line.
Bright light, photographic clarity. Gravel on the embankment sliding drily underfoot, blinding light arcing off the curving tracks. The
turning tide sluiced water through the channel, the water flowed
towards the estuary mouth. Sticks turned and turned on the surface,
milky bubbles in the moving current rose up through the salt and
floated swiftly away. By the railway line she smoked and watched,
while the deep green water ran down to the sea. Seeing the sticks
turn and turn, watching cars through the sunstrike creeping slowly
up the saddle of the hill. Cars moving, water moving, wind over the
water and nothing changed. Smoking and watching she saw it bitterly, that everything was beautiful, and nothing had changed.

By the railway station a car slowed and she heard yobbish hoots
and lewd wolf-whistles, she glared at them smearily, how *could* they?
As she walked back up to the cemetery gates a jogger swerved past
and clipped her shoulder, she stared after him in dismay, how *could*
he? Practically pushed her into the hedge, and the sharp sticks
scratching her face. She swore at him weakly. *Fucking* joggers. He
passed on with a swish of air and a waft of sweat and didn't look
back. Great overdeveloped hams, tautly shuddering buttocks, legs
pistoning away up the street. How could he? But why should he not?
Why not?

She hurried on through the bland garden suburb, the indifferent
streets. She caught the old man as he was driving his car through the
cemetery gates.

'Sorry,' she said, getting in.

'It's OK.' He patted her knee. Then he squeezed her knee, relaxed his hand, squeezed it again. At the touch of his hand the hairs rose on the back of Maria's head. Her nose tickled. She raised her handkerchief to her face and looked at him – it was Leon's profile, the same features but thicker, heavier, more masculine. Leon grown heavy and male. The big fingers continued to flex on the scratchy nylon of her stocking and Maria suddenly entertained a vision of herself sprawled up against one of the broken graves, her pantyhose around her knees, the old man with the son's eyes fucking her to pieces on the surreal grass while the grey angels watched through mossy eyes and startled blackbirds rose over ruined bouquets and empty jars and blackened slabs.

But he turned his head and his eyes were weak and watery and not intent but hopeless, and the flexing of his hand was an involuntary wringing and nervous stroking, weak fluttering of an old man who was lost for words, who came to himself with a shake of his head and took his hand away and fumbled with the keys, accelerating the car forward with many muttered apologies and distracted sighs.

Shielding his eyes against the light, he turned out into the impossible blinder of the afternoon sun. Driving straight on into the west, the sun sunk low and burning, burning.

Golden light in the cemetery, yellow light on suburban rows. Weatherboards, neat hedges, rainbow sprinklers over the glowing grass. Maria rode with one hand on the dashboard, flinching when they stopped abruptly at red lights. Those Jews. In your village that time. Did you bury many? Were there many? Did you see? *I was a little boy. But the men worked hard all day*. Were there many? How could you bear it? How could life go on? *I was a little boy. There were twenty of them. Or thirty. Life went on. How could it not? How not . . .?*

They arrived at a brick house in Orakei. Leon's cousins greeted them at the door. Don, a builder. Vaclav, a dentist. Aleta, plump mother of five wiry boys. All tall and amiable, long-nosed and blond. The old people gathered on the bright lawn, carefully enjoying the late afternoon sun, eating lemon cake, drinking coffee. Maria walked about the garden and the terrace, sat on a chaise longue on a concrete verandah and listened to the ugly-beautiful sounds of foreign languages: Czech, Polish, Yugoslav. She nodded and smiled, murmuring. Yes, I was the girlfriend. I'm the girlfriend. I was. Yes, I adored him. Yes.

An old lady on crutches tottered over and lowered herself down. She looked a hundred years old, dressed like a fortune-teller in heavy eyeliner, bright lipstick, a black scarf over her head tied tightly under her chin.

'I am aunty,' she whispered harshly, rolling her eyes to heaven and fastening claw-like hands on to Maria's arm. 'When he was this baby, I rock him on my knee . . .' She drew in a sharp, rattling breath and peered beadily sideways at Maria. 'You are the girl-friend?'

'Yes.'

The old lady nodded and sighed, closed her eyes, pressed her claws to her lacy breast. 'My dear, already you must have cried a thousand tears!'

'Oh yes, a thousand. *More*!' Desperate spray of cake crumbs, flapping of the unfurled hanky. In the reflection of the glass French door Maria glimpsed her own wooden and humiliated smile.

Nodding and blinking and sniffing exhilaratedly, as if a funeral were a stiff walk in the alps or a cold swim in the sea the old lady wiped tears from her own milky eyes, rose and crutch-walked efficiently away. Maria smoothed her hair automatically, silently consumed more lemon pie.

But I haven't cried, Maria thought. Not like that. It won't come. And I don't know how to. Maybe it's just – and forgive me if this sounds strange – maybe it's just because I'm so *afraid*.

10.

Marcus rehearsed it in his mind. He pictured himself, reasonable and forceful and calm. First (after the knock at the door, Chrissie's footsteps in the hall, his cool silence, her gasp of surprise), he would arrest her panicky flight. She would be hysterical, defensive, the lithe brown arms flailing, pushing his manly hands away. Gently he would pin her to the wall. She would shrink from the anticipated blow. And he would be forgiving. Strong. Showing her – see how the arm is healed. They made it better, the clever doctors. Just a scar (to make me more of a man). And I understand now, I *understand*. It's all going to be all right. We'll be all right. All *three* of us . . .

He heaved the last crate on to his shoulder. An empty bottle rolled and spun under his feet, he pitched forward in the dark, nearly losing the heavy load. Fuck. He paused to balance the crate again, and winced as the weight tugged the tender skin on his injured arm. Swearing and fumbling in the hot gloom under the weak lights he set the box down and flopped on to the bottom step to rest. Automatically he began to re-screen the Chrissie scene again, this time with less satisfaction. But Wiremu Ihaka stood at the top of the stairs, his massive bulk blocking out the light.

'Hurry up, mate. M'dying for a smoke.'

'Hang on. Jesus. Why don't you give us a hand?'

'Come *on*, mate.'

Fucking big bastard up there, muscles like balloons. Not lifting a finger to help. Laughing at him, flicking his cigarette lighter near Marcus's hair.

'Ow. Fuck off. *Cunt*.'

The big man gave his teasing Maori laugh. 'Y'sound like a girl. Girl.'

'Total *arsehole*.' Marcus struggled to the top of the stairs. He straightened up with dignity and spat out a cobweb and a string of expletives.

There was a big party tonight. The club would be full of the usual crowd, ecstatically dancing and weeping and throwing up into one another's mouths. Arrests, the odd drug death, one hoped (it enhanced the reputation of the club). He'd had to bring practically the whole cellar up and stack it behind the bar. Groping around down there with the spiders while Lord Huge Arse there shouted instructions from the stairs. Marcus lit a cigarette and wondered for the hundredth time when he would get away from this never-ending round of manual labour.

'Why don't you give me a hand?'

'I'm Security, mate. You're the bumboy.'

Marcus flexed his arm. It *was* better, almost completely healed. Although permanently scarred. Every night in bed after writing the latest instalment of *The Hard Men* he ran his fingers musingly over the rough skin. When he walked he felt the scar tissue tinily scraping in his armpit, like sandpaper. His underarm hair was loathe to return. Follicular death. Meltdown. He seemed to have a permanent rash under there too, as if he'd shaved it with a carrot peeler.

But he had survived what he considered to be a very bad time, a black time, and things were not as bad as they had been. He had the job at Quays, and the pay was reasonably good, given that you had to stay up all night and go deaf and dumb with shouting, and cancerous and mad with all the smoke and free drink and drugs.

Even better, the tenants of Connick Street had been granted a month-long rent holiday when something had gone pungently wrong with the drains under the house. After a long period the hard men had tired of going around the house holding their noses and saying jokily to one another '*Pooh*', and '*Phwoar*', and had summoned up enough initiative to ring the landlord. Then the whole Health Department turned up. In force. Then it turned out they were lucky not to have cholera and typhoid. The water supply running through the equivalent of a dead horse. Or forty possums. The council workers were down there in the gully for days, in gas masks and protective suits.

A further miracle had occurred when Ron Reed had rung up and begged Marcus to come back to work. It had been a struggle but Marcus had been entirely restrained, resisting the urge to jeer and crow, and merely accepting the terms with a sob of tearful relief.

So he had two jobs, and the use of Ron's word-processor again – and *The Hard Men* would be a number one hit, he was sure – and the only thing he didn't have was Chrissie. He longed for Chrissie now, with a tug of pain and anxiety and nostalgic love. And fear. And . . . what else? Something else. Was it the lingering desire to beat her up? After all, he had suffered so. Days and weeks of pain. Or was it a niggling dissatisfaction with the scene he enacted in his head, day after day? – She weeps with contrition, *I was desperate, I was mad*, he folds her in his manly arms. Tenderly he places a hand on her rounded belly, together, in wonder, they look down . . . This wasn't the sort of thing he would ever put in his *book*. What was this feeling that came over him, of being ensnared in cotton wool, in candy floss? Involuntarily, treacherously, his lip would curl. Little Chrissie's Disney dreams . . .

But he still had no memory of what had happened that night, when he had gone on fire, when she had disappeared out of Connick Street for good. Somewhere in his thoughts he came back to the fact that he didn't know what had happened, and knowing that he didn't know made him afraid. Then he would replay their reunion in his head, automatically, and it would comfort him at night. And then there was the other thing, the *other thing*, inside her. The other thing. When he thought of that he felt sick and weak and he longed for her in the night when he lay alone in bed at Connick Street with the workmen's orange lights flashing outside and the rain roaring on the roof, and he thought of it, carried around, tiny, defenceless, blind, *out there*. Then there was no room for doubt or detachment or any other ignoble thought, there was only urgent longing for action, for contact – send out the rescue party, dial one-one-one – and still there was no trace of her, just no trace.

'She fucking dead, man,' Branko said one morning, unexpectedly, as they ate their cornflakes in the Formica breakfast shanty at the back of the house. Marcus stared across the table while Mike and

Mike went into a moistly warm flurry of headshaking and denials, 'Na-ah, nah mate, no way,' and Marcus said coldly, 'Don't be such a fool.' He'd sounded exactly like his mother. He'd nearly added, 'You *moron*. You *yob*.'

Also unhelpfully, Branko had ditched the chilly Darlene, or she had ditched him. She too had disappeared and left no forwarding address. There was a new greeter at Darlene's work, Marcus had gone and checked. The new greeter had told him with elaborate froideur that Darlene had been 'let go'. She hinted at some crime, embezzlement perhaps. Asked to elaborate, she had haughtily sniffed, 'I'm afraid I'm unable to divulge.'

Sighing, Marcus shouldered his load again and elbowed past Wiremu Ihaka who was leaning on the security door and fatly smoking.

'There'll be a big crowd tonight.' Gently Wiremu inspected his immense fists, balling and flexing, testing the flesh. Marcus paused. There were white scars on the great fingers, white notches. The blue–black swallow tattoo was ugly on flesh that would have been brown if it weren't pale with endless nightlife. All over Wiremu was the colour of milky coffee gone cold.

'Should be fun. For a big bad fucker like you. Few scalps.'

Wiremu smiled mildly. He gave a light laugh and smoothed beads of sweat from his shaven head. He narrowed his huge eyes. 'Take them as they come, bro. Take them as they come.'

Marcus trudged up the corridor after him. Wiremu with his TV-speak. *Bonanza*, *The Virginian*, *Star Trek*. Every evening, when Marcus sourly ascended the stairs and bashed on the heavy door, Wiremu opened it with a cowboy wink and two pistol-shaped fingers. When you were that big you could carry on like that without everybody laughing, or beating you up. Nobody had ever even tried to rough Wiremu up, they wouldn't know where to start. He was simply too enormous. And when he was angry, or feigning anger, he was effective all right. He was terrifying. His Maori mouth, the curving upper lip designed for maximum bearing of teeth, the great muscular jowls, hysterically rolling eyeballs, the brutally shaven head. Every night he loomed in the doorway glaring at the maelstrom of the dance floor, while the revellers tiptoed nervously around his bulk.

But Marcus spent long nights behind the bar watching Wiremu. He'd made a study of him. And Wiremu Ihaka was always the hero in TV. Bailing up the baddies and running them out of town. *Any trouble and you're history, pal. This man bothering you, ladies?*

Wiremu loved to wade lifeguard-style on to the surging dance floor and carry out the fainting girls, the small white faces lolling over his great arm, the long hair wet and streaming in the underwater light. Tenderly he fanned them back to life in the back office and packed them off home in a taxi, with much shaking of head and harsh words for their errant mums.

Then he would go growling back to his pop-eyed vigil and wreathe himself in cigarette smoke, until he looked as if he had emerged with a puff and a flash from one of the many old bottles lying at his feet.

Chrissie knew Wiremu, Marcus remembered suddenly. She had talked about him. Didn't he let her in free a couple of times? Let her sit in the DJ box, all that juvenile stuff. The 'Security' at Quays – she used to call him *Wi*. She would go to Quays with her girl-friends, not with Marcus because he wouldn't dance. (Girls danced, fags danced, all sorts of people got out there and waggled themselves about, but not Marcus: he didn't want to be seen looking like that.)

But now his thoughts were interrupted by the unwelcome arrival of the bar manager, Klint Steel. Klint barged his way into the bar area as usual, jingling his keys and threatening beatings and sackings, and Marcus began disgustedly to arrange the shipload of alcohol he had brought up from below, pausing now and then to lift his head up and peer over the bar at the doorman who stood in a fierce huddle with the management, planning strategies for keeping mayhem and death at a minimum for the night.

Three hours later Marcus, bathed in sweat and gasping for air, rested his pulsating temple against the cold wall of the back office. His first break and he was already deaf and dumb and nearly blind. He drew deeply on his active cigarette, his first after six thousand passives since eleven o'clock. He sipped on his beer. Braced himself. Twenty minutes and then back out there. Only he didn't feel up to it tonight and it seemed he would have to get drunk. He downed the beer and poured himself a staff whisky. Stiff. He leaned back and closed his eyes. Few whiskies. Take the edge off the nerves. He ran a hand over his weary brow. Stiff one. Calm down. But an instant later there was a shocking smash outside and the door handle was wrenched practically out of its socket.

As Marcus winced and feebly brushed spilt whisky from his shirt Klint Steel thrust his boiling face around the door. Klint wore a headset with antennae, and a tiny curving stalk of a microphone quivering about his mouth – a recent acquisition with no practical function whatsoever. Klint simply *wore* the headset, which didn't work, at all times, to impress girls perhaps. Marcus smirked. Looking like an ant or wasp under his waving feelers Klint peered through the gloom. With a triumphant hiss he clocked Marcus in the corner chair. Then, with much denouncing and screaming, and deaf to all reasonable protests, he kicked and cuffed Marcus along the corridor and back to work.

Marcus stood at the edge of the bar. Now the crowd out there in the hot dark was undulating like a many-armed sea creature, buffeted by waves of sound and heat, blinded by flickering strobe and laser lightning, shuddering with the deep vibrations from the floor. On the other side, in the pale light, Wiremu Ihaka shaded his eyes and stared fiercely into the storm.

Marcus watched as the great creature swayed in the current and dashed itself against the tables, the formation bulged and surged and broke and spent dancers, washed out, were sent scrambling towards the welcoming light of the bar. Marcus stood back as a bedraggled figure sleepwalked past him. Thin arms, wild hair. He saw the outline of her profile, the sharp ridges of her shoulder blades in thin tight cloth. He hesitated, stepped forward. Then he reached out and caught the end of her sleeve before she was sucked into the current swirling round the bar. Effortfully, hand over hand, Marcus reeled Maria in.

She sat on a wooden crate in the stockroom. Silently Marcus handed her a glass of water. She stared up at him out of huge eyes. 'Thanks,' she whispered. Then she laughed. Then sipped. Smoothed her wild hair.

'Did you come here by yourself?'

'I drove here. Straight from Tauranga. Speeding all the way. My mother . . .'

'What?'

'She makes me mad.'

'What did she do?'

'Nothing. We fight. Cat and dog.'

'So they don't know who, um, ran him over? Who was driving the car?'

'They have no leads. No clues. They probably don't even care.'

'They have to investigate.'

Maria looked around the dingy stockroom. She lit a cigarette and said flatly, 'So you didn't know about it?'

'No.' Suddenly Marcus could hear Klint shouting in the corridor outside. He started to edge towards the door. Maria looked emptily up at him through the curtains of her hair.

'Stay here,' he said, opening the door a crack and peering uneasily out. 'I'll get you a drink. What do you want?'

'I don't know.' She tossed her head and looked at the ceiling. 'Just a bottle of something, I suppose.'

Back at the bar Marcus managed to fill a jug with vodka. He found a bottle of tonic and took it back to the stockroom. She accepted it wordlessly and he wondered suddenly, what are we doing? What was she doing? He didn't want to go home with her, did he? Actually he did. Yes, he really did. But the way she looked . . . Just as sexy, but pale and defiant and strange. Definitely madder than usual. This Leon person, this fag she used to hang about with. She used to talk about him all the time. Always telling him anecdotes about what she got up to with him and ruining the story because she was laughing so much – half the time he could hardly understand what she was saying. Obviously she was shaken up (and by all accounts they'd had to scoop him off the road into a wheelie bin). And she'd been right there. Jesus. Right mess. And her so mad anyway, so *highly strung*. He wondered whether he should have locked her into the stockroom. He didn't want her roaming around out the back there and running into Klint. Delirium.

He served a few more drinks, shouting the prices out into the wall of noise. It was 4:30 a.m. Closing time. Some shithead wanting a cocktail. Fuck off, he thought. Think I've got time for all that poncing and shaking. He glared and screamed and gesticulated and ignored his way through another half an hour, then sneaked off to check what was happening out the back.

There were voices in the stockroom. His skin crawled. Not Klint surely, trying his feelers on her. Not fucking Buzzy Bee . . .

He opened the door a crack and peeked in. He saw Wiremu Ihaka down on one knee, his great head cocked sideways. Maria leaning back in her chair with her feet up, twirling her glass in her hand. Wiremu kneeling, listening. With his great paw he was stroking Maria's hand.

With a harsh cough Marcus flung the door open and strode into the room. Maria looked at him with faint amusement. At least, her mouth was amused. But her eyes were mad. Wiremu looked up at Marcus and said, warningly, 'We're in the middle of something here.'

Then he looked piously back at Maria. She opened her mouth, looking between the two of them. Marcus poured himself a vodka. He said politely to Maria, 'I'm still working, but I've nearly finished. I'll try to get back as soon as I can.'

He struggled to control his voice. He could hear the discomfort and anger in it. He wanted to get her out of the stockroom. This was all wrong, the sordid room and her strange expression, as if she'd lost all sense of where she was. *Who* she was. After all. Couldn't she see how basic this place was, how incredibly dirty, how the people were criminals and low-lifes – white and brown? He (Marcus) belonged here (didn't he?) because of irony, because of his *work*. Most of all because he had decided to be here, for a purpose. His calling. But she . . .

He couldn't stand that stroking of her hand (the TV pose), it made his skin crawl. Maria, who missed nothing, who got all his jokes. Clever, quick Maria. She was just sitting there with her dead white face, letting the doorman touch her. And what would he do next, down on one knee like that, wrench her knees apart? Burst into song? But look at her . . . she didn't look altogether well. She was opening and closing her eyes and staring from one to the other . . .

Maria put her hand over her mouth. She gave an ugly laugh. She drew her knees together tight. Then she laughed again, sneezed three times, burst into tears and threw up, all in the time it took

Wiremu Ihaka to pick her up and propel her firmly out of the door and into the corridor that led to the back exit.

The doorman held Maria from behind, supporting her under her arms. Marcus bounded after him and elbowed his way around them in the corridor. Maria's thin white arms dangled disgracefully. Her head lolled on the doorman's chest. Marcus planted himself in front of Wiremu Ihaka and held up his hand like a crossing guard. 'What do you think you're doing?' he demanded in his coldest, poshest voice.

Wiremu stared down at him. He said dismissively, 'Take her home. Give her a seeing-to.' He heaved her higher on his chest.

'Now hang *on*.'

Unstoppably Wiremu moved forward – it would be like trying to stop a bus. 'Stop. You great *moron*. You *yob*.' Ridiculously Marcus pounded on the great shoulder.

'Maria, for Christ's sake.' He tugged on the skinny arm.

She opened her eyes and turned her head on the immense pillow of the doorman's chest. She looked at him with cold blue eyes. Then she pulled her arm away. 'Fuck off Marcus,' she said. She wriggled free and stood unsteadily on her feet. Marcus tugged her arm again.

'Let's go, Maria, we'll get a cab.'

She turned to him with her intent eyes. 'Go to *hell*,' she said and carefully put her arm on Wiremu Ihaka's shoulder.

Out in the back alley the night was warm and black. The sky was packed down close like a shroud over the dead city. No dawn, under the thick sky. Soon the air would be full of rain. He stood helplessly at the top of the stairs and watched the two shadows, Maria and Wiremu, move through the alley towards the lines of cars until the smaller shadow, stumbling and wavering in the dark, leaned into the larger, and was engulfed.

Whistling under his breath Wiremu Ihaka installed Maria in the recovery position on the back seat of his majestic black sedan. Then he started the engine, leaned out to brush a mound of advertising pamphlets from the windscreen, and cruised grandly out into the humid night.

What should he do? Call the police? But she'd told him to go away. He did nothing, he watched them go. He watched her go. I you he she it. Amo amas amat. He was filled with confusion, indecision, shame. The incoherent thoughts ran round and round in his head. I learned *Latin* at school, remember that? I learned to read music, all those years ago. Walking to school in the mornings, past the rickety wooden houses, by the waving toitois and the shining flax. I thought nothing would ever change. Maria and *Chrissie*. She got all my jokes, but *she* understood none of them, *she* loved star charts and sitcoms, took dull things seriously, things that made my lip curl. She was thin and nervous, *she* was calmly heedless (and insatiable in the sack!).

'He's fighting the class war,' his mother told her friends, pointing a mocking finger at his filthy boots. Only there isn't one. Not really. There's no class system here. All the accents are the same. There are only the details, and the sprawling streets, and the endless sky, what you make of it, what you don't. And freedom, and multichoice, infinite agony of choice. We're all the same. *No one will know you if you fall*.

And here came Klint. Busy Nazi Klint. Coming to bully Marcus in his nine- or ten-word range. I'm coming to the end of all this, Marcus thought. Things are going to change. *All this is coming to an end*.

He pushed past Klint and returned to the bar. He finished his duties and signed off. He walked down the steps and out into the close black dawn. He made his way slowly through the dark, along Quay Street.

11.

The flat was above a takeaway bar at the end of Karangahape Road. Maria fumbled up the steep stairs behind him in the grainy dark. When he got to the top Wiremu Ihaka unhooked a bunch of keys from his studded belt, picked a key and unlocked the top lock, picked a key and unlocked the next lock. And so on. Four deadlocks. The door was dented and dirty, bruised and scratched, as if city marauders came calling on busy nights with battering rams and baseball bats. What had he appeared in court for? That time, when she had met him, on her *tour*. Perverting . . .

The heavy door swung open into a hallway. He stepped inside and switched on a light. He took her by the arm and pulled her quickly inside. He locked the locks again. In the white glare of the swinging lightbulb he scowled heavily down into her face. The skin of his inside arms was furrowed, tiny silvery rivers running in the muddy brown. Stretch marks. The course, she thought. Perverting the course.

He led her along the smelly hallway and into a kitchen with neon strip lighting, vinyl floors, a Formica table. The bare white walls were battered and peeling. On the table were a loaf of bread and a jar of peanut butter, and a packet of sweating butter. She sat at the table and he stood glowering intently into the kitchen cupboard. There were sheets of newspaper lying on the floor. The greasy smells from the takeaway below rose on blasts of hot air through the light-well. The old pipes whistled and sighed. High above the kitchen cupboards a tiny window let in the cold dawn light. Early morning rain, the blind and tattered city, smeared with tears.

He leaned against the sink. He hooked his fingers into the top of his fat man's suit trousers and glared at her with pop-eyed concentration. He lit a cigarette. 'No food, eh. Only that.' He pointed at the bread. He laughed lightly, showing his teeth, passed his hand over his bristly head. He looked around the kitchen again, rummaged under the sink.

She saw the blue swallow tattooed on the great hand. The massively strong biceps, bulging over the sleeves of the cheap white short-sleeved shirt. The thin black bouncer's tie, the studded belt, the basher's boots. Dull silver skull earring in his big left earlobe, the brutal square force of his shaven head. The eyes that could protrude and roll with such maniacal basher's hysteria – 'Calling me a cunt? You calling me a cunt?' She had seen him last night squaring and looming over a customer too drunk to contemplate the danger he was in, shouting about legal rights and how dare you while wiser patrons winced and averted their eyes. Wiremu Ihaka had let him off lightly, with a broken leg, or something. A dislocated shoulder. Justice. The course of. The necessary perversions.

'Tea?' he offered, glaring down. 'Milk and sugar?' Then he fixed his great hands around the neck of the jug and wrenched the lid from its body. Gouged the last chunks of sugar out of the cracked and fragile bowl. Forced the tea bag under the water until it let out a tiny despairing bubble, and dyed the water brown. In the hard tired light the butter sweated and sank, and went to the pack. All over the silent city the raindrops fell, blew crazily around the tiny window.

'Let me do that,' she sighed. 'You're making a mess. Your big hands . . .'

He climbed out the window of his bedroom on to the verandah roof that sheltered the street below. He gave her a hand to clamber out. They sat on the ledge and looked over the drenched and empty street, washed in the grey light of the wet morning. She began to cry even harder, peering up at him, her face as wet and desolate as the dawn. She had been crying like this for an hour and a half. Such tears. Such floods. Ever since he'd picked her up. Ever since they had got into his car.

He had gone down on one knee and stared into her eyes, he had squeezed and stroked her hand. *All it took* . . .

Sitting in the grimy stockroom she had told him about driving from Tauranga, driving madly away – she had argued with her mother, of course, nothing would stop them arguing, not even death. She had roared out of the driveway shouting, 'You're mad, you're *mad*!' – and floored it down the open highway, looking out for cops. All along the road under the leaden sky, vigilantly, she looked out for cops. And none came. None came.

'You're lonely and scared,' Wiremu Ihaka had said as he stroked and fondled her hand. 'You're *hurting*.' And his voice had gone deep, and his accent changed, reminding her of someone, was it an actor on TV? What would she say now in TV-land? '*Help me. Hold me. I'm falling apart . . .*'

Now on the verandah roof with the fine rain whirling around he said, frowningly, 'Your man have any enemies? Anyone wanted to rub him out?' He gave her the pop-eyed glare.

But the fresh air had cleared her head. She blew her nose and said impatiently, 'No, of course not. I suppose it was a drunk driver . . . And *he* was drunk too. Blind . . .'

But warningly he held up his hand. 'Anyone he'd ripped off? Anyone ripped him off? Any problems with the *ladies*?'

Maria laughed. 'I doubt it.'

Wiremu scowled out over the slicked and washed street. 'You stay here. There's the bed in there. I'll stay out here for a while and keep watch.'

'Keep *watch*?'

He laughed and relaxed his face. He took her hand again, tenderly. 'Yeah baby, I'll watch over you.'

So she climbed into the pungent bed and stretched her feet down into the tangle of cheap and scratchy sheets. Yellow striped shadows of car lights prowled on the dingy walls, the room was as bleak and cold as an ashtray, and around the room ashtrays were precariously balanced on sills, lopsided and spilling on the ash-grey carpet, up-ended into piles on the cushions of ash-grey chairs. She sniffed sharply. Some dreadful additional odour . . . perhaps an old lung somewhere, ripped out professionally by Wiremu and boyishly dis-carded under a pile of clothes? She sniggered miserably. What was she doing here? What was it doing to her? Fear. She knew she was here because of fear. Because there wasn't anyone else and there was nowhere else to go. Out there on the roof Wiremu puffed on his cigarette and growled secretively at the dawn. What had he said to her, before tucking her in? Whispering. The great hands smoothing the crackling sheets. I'll take care of you, Maria. I'll protect you. *You're a bird with a broken wing.*

She slept and slept, hour after hour, as if she would never surface again. She woke with a clear head in the late afternoon and cast an appalled glance around the room. Wiremu Ihaka lay massively asleep on a sofa a few feet away. She heard the cars on the road outside and saw the heavy sky through the tattered shreds of the old gauze curtain hanging over the greasy window. Jesus. She thought of her work colleagues, Giles Speer, Klara Leather, Peeks-Berlyn. Trying not to make any noise she began to look around for her things, but he stirred, snored, lifted his huge arm over his face and woke up.

He turned with effort and raised himself on his arm. His big face was so creased and round that he resembled a plump red cabbage. He stared at her with fiery eyes.

'I need to get home,' Maria said hurriedly, trying to force on her shoes. He sat up.

'Why?' he said.

She paused, shoe in hand. 'I've got to get back, get ready to go back to work. I've been off for a week.'

She stood up. He didn't move. He put his arm back over his face, muttering, 'There's a movie, a woman in a movie you remind me of.'

'Oh, really. Well, thank you for the bed. By the way, what's that awful smell?'

Slowly he lifted his arm away from his face and stared at her again with his terrible crimson eyes. 'What smell?'

'Well, sort of like decaying meat.' She hesitated. 'Can I get out that front door?'

There was a short silence. Then he stood up. He narrowed his eyes, bared his teeth, and gave a convulsive roll of his huge shoulders. 'You think I *smell*?'

'Not you, your room.' She began to move towards the door. He stood in front of it.

'Are you all right now?' he asked coldly, one arm across the door.

'Fine thanks. I'm quite normal now, no more weeping and wailing.'

He looked down at his hands. 'I want you to stay.'

'Yes? Well, no thanks. Too noisome. Oh, come on. Hurry up and open the door.'

'Please stay. I'll do something about the noise.'

'No.'

He stared strangely at her for a moment. She stared back. Then he sighed and scratched his head, put his hands on his hips and looked frowningly around the room. He said, 'It's probably an old burger.'

'What?'

'The smell. Probably stuffed down somewhere, you know. I've probably just forgotten to eat it.'

'Great. Let me out of here. Now.'

Sighing heavily, he fetched his bunch of keys. Out on the street he asked again, 'Are you sure you're all right?'

'I'm fine.' Maria was hurriedly scanning the street, imagining she could see Giles Speer on every corner. Or Klara Leather making notes on her clipboard – *now what have we here? This huge criminal is a close friend of yours?*

She had to get home, have a shower, she had to get away from this disorder and chaos. Suddenly she thought with pleasure of her orderly room, the shelves full of novels and textbooks, the immaculate bedding, the tasteful furniture and pictures on the walls. Order. Purpose. Life must not lose its balance. Life must go on.

'Thanks, Wiremu,' she said with patronising firmness and strode off along the street. But at the next intersection he hurried up behind her. 'Listen,' he said, 'there are keys to my flat in the alleyway behind the takeaways. Under the DB crate. Four keys. You can have them. You might need them. I want you to come back.'

He looked down at her, wrinkling his great forehead.

'If you want to,' he added humbly.

'Thanks,' she said dismissively and walked away towards Grafton Bridge. Deliberately not looking back: if she had she would have seen him standing alone on the busy pavement, shading his red eyes with his hand and staring after her with fierce, intent concentration.

Evening shadows around the pohutukawas. Ashton Road, her dark street, shaded even in summer, even at noon. The landlord was a tree freak who never trimmed the trees (he liked to hug them and listen to them talk): the branches hung low over the house and dry leaves blew on the wooden verandah boards like dry fingernails, scraping.

She unlocked the front door and the house smelt unused, as if it had been empty for some days. She found a note from Ernest in the unusually tidy kitchen. 'How are things OK. Gone on journo course, Taupo. Lots of . . .' He hadn't finished the note. Perhaps the taxi had turned up early.

Deprived of the need to tidy the kitchen she entered the bathroom. It too was very clean. Ernest had outdone himself. She peered one-eyed into the lavatory. Extraordinary. Quite clear. No need to tidy a thing . . .

Maria lay on her bed in the silence and carefully consumed pasta and tomato.

The lightbulb had blown in one of her lamps and the room was dim. The shadows were black in the corners of the room. Outside on the white painted wall the shadow of the tree branch made the shape of a moving claw. She heard small animals scuttling in the dry-stone wall outside and crickets relentlessly sawing. She had tried watching television but the choice was unbearable, blaring game shows, some wearisome Australian surfing soap. Before retiring to her room she had gone round the house locking all the windows and doors.

She dragged out her old portable stereo and looked for her tapes, and remembered the one that Leon had given her. She found it in her handbag and put it into the machine. It was an old New Order song, melancholy and obscure. She wasn't a New Order fan, and she'd never heard the song before he had played it to her the evening before he died. 'Every Little Counts' was the title. She played it while pacing around the room. Then played it again, and again. She played it until she thought she would never stop hearing it in her head.

Later she heard a car stop outside on the road. The engine idled and the car door opened. She waited for the engine to turn off but the door slammed again and the car suddenly accelerated away. She opened the curtains. The street was empty. She turned on the outside light and went down the steps towards the street. The wind had blown the leaves into piles at the side of the path. The crickets sang and rustled in the hedge. Sticking awkwardly out of the letterbox was a large bunch of flowers wrapped in cellophane. She wrenched it out. Slowly she turned the damp bundle over and over, shook the bunch, more urgently looked in the letterbox and over the pavement. But there was no card. No message, nothing.

Shivering she raced back inside and slammed the door shut. No card, no card. What kind of a person leaves no card? What kind of a . . .

She lay angrily and fearfully awake, eyes wide open, listening, while all around the small house the leaves scraped and the mice ran in the rock walls and the grass sighed in the blustery air.

She forced herself to think of Quinn St John. Peeks-Berlyn. Mr Giles Speer. The wonderful Clairene. The satisfying sharpness of legal files. Her files . . . But when she tried she couldn't remember what any of them were about. It was time to get back to work. She imagined she was sitting in her orderly little office at Quinn St John, hearing the muted click of the keyboards, feeling sunlight through the hot brown glass warming her back as she bent over the crisp documents spread across the desk. Listening for the scraping shoes of Giles Speer . . .

She felt a hot rush of tears. Desolation. Self-pity. Life had become alien, terrifying, everything was ruined and black. And she was lonely. She realised it with a feeling close to panic. She feared loneliness, she could sense its terrible destructive force. She didn't know whether she could survive it. Loneliness was near and whispering: *I am here. I am with you. And all I ever do is get worse.*

Tomorrow is Sunday, then back to work. She repeated it for comfort, and wasn't comforted. She thought she would never sleep, but finally, around four o'clock, she went into an uneasy doze. Sleeping more deeply she dreamed that Leon was living in a woven hut above a great plain in China. The hut was decorated with kites and banners and coloured flags. Below the window a vast crowd, millions and millions of people all carrying bright silk flags, moved in a slow procession across the land. She sat with Leon at the window and watched the bright moving mass stretching away under the sky. Leon wore a red and green and yellow silk shirt. He turned to her and smiled, but there were three brisk thumps on the door, and he vanished. She jumped awake and looked at her watch. It was just after eleven o'clock.

Creeping to the door Maria felt about as crushed, as fragile as it was possible to feel. Aching, reduced, defenceless. She felt as if she would shatter into pieces. She opened the door a crack. On the doorstep Detective Hughson jogged on the spot, rolled his sinewy neck, cracked his knuckles and glared at her out of the tiny black slits in his face. Maria sighed.

'Rise and shine, Ms Wallis.' The old tyrant grinned through the crack, licking his wet lips. She opened the door wider and he came prancing in on his gaudy trainers, his large silent brown cohorts following behind him.

'Nice place you've got here.' Maria closed her eyes. The guy was like a terrible cartoon. Look at him, his trained eyes raking the room. Flexing all his muscles at once. What a nightmare. And he had nothing to say, as far as she could tell. Except that there were still no leads, no clues.

Maria leaned against the wall and folded her arms. You could do that, mow someone down, fling them practically into your back seat and out again, drive off with your windscreen smashed all over the road, and get away with it. How could it be? What about detective work, what about forensics?

Sighing, Detective Hughson asked to use the bathroom.

'It's not that simple, Maria,' Detective Light told her in a deep voice.

'Not as simple as you,' she muttered angrily.

'*Pardon?*'

'Nothing.'

She stared out of the window at the sunny suburban street. Someone was out there, someone who had scraped the evidence out of his car. You out there, she thought, who killed a man on Quay Street. What did the morning hold for you? (Bland face of the sky that morning.) What was it like for you? Morning of criminal blundering, hellish chores of the aftermath, the messy business of crime. Morning of washing and scraping, disposal and disguise. Was there self-pity, disbelief – fear in the stalled hours? The long wait for the knock on the door? Or were you tidy, efficient, coldly resolved? Do you know who I am, who saw and didn't see you? If I chose to walk out along Quay Street today, would you see me, and know who I am?

The detectives were watching her. In a rush she told them about the flowers.

They looked at them enquiringly.

'Nice gesture,' offered fat Detective Nu'U.

'But there was no card. No note. Don't you see? Someone who didn't want me to know who they were . . .'

'Discreet.' Nu'U looked plumply approving.

'No, no. Don't you see. *Guilty*.'

They cast silent glances at one another, shifted about on their seats.

'*Here*,' she shouted. She took the bedraggled bunch off the table and threw it into Detective Light's lap. He sat looking at it with distaste. Then Detective Hughson came back in, daintily wiping his hands with a tissue. His eye fell on the flowers.

'What's this? A gift?' He let out a dry tee-hee.

'Hardly.' Maria scowled at him. She opened her mouth and closed it again. Angrily she looked away.

Jogging on the spot the sprightly Hughson signalled to Light, who handed him a manila folder. Holding up his hand, Hughson jogged and read from the file.

'Well, let's see. Leon Pavel. He was blind drunk. Completely. Very high reading. Wouldn't have felt a thing. He an alcoholic?'

Maria looked at her hands. 'Probably.'

Detective Nu'U made short notes in a notebook.

'You know he had criminal convictions. Light-fingered. Theft. Drunk and disorderly. Other things. You're a law clerk. Funny sort of friend for you to have?' Hughson jigged and exhaled, waving and flapping the file.

She thought of the old man. The tiny, fantastic house with its colour and paintings and phone sculptures. The radiant little boy in the photos, with his shining smile.

Hughson stopped jogging and threw the file back to Light. He looked brightly at Maria. 'He really was completely antisocial, wasn't he? In *every* way.'

There was a silence. Hughson looked Maria up and down, insinuatingly, seemed about to say something more, then decided against it. He smiled and shook his head lightly. He picked up the file again and weighed it in his hand.

'You know something?' he said, nodding deliberately. 'In my experience, people like this . . .' – he nodded again, at the file – 'it all catches up with them in the end.'

At the door Detective Light handed her the flowers. He wiped his hands on his trousers.

'Be in touch.'

'Yeah, let me know.' She looked after them in silent despair. Detective Hughson stopped and came back up the path. He leaned on the door jamb, rolled his neck, fixed her with an indulgent look and opened his mouth to speak.

'But you know something else . . .' he managed to say, before Maria in a sudden rush of fury got hold of the door, stepped back, and slammed it resoundingly in his face.

When they were gone she rushed around the house, found her purse, slammed the door again and set off up the road. She walked fast into the racing wind. It was a sharp blustery day and the moving clouds darkened and lightened the sky. She needed cigarettes. Some supplies. Some things to eat. Hole up with a few luxuries. Then tomorrow, work. Don't think about how long it takes to get across the terrifying gulf of night from one day to the next.

She bought cigarettes and smoked one leaning on the wall by the bus stop, sheltering from the wind. She remembered how he used to give her half a packet of smokes before striding off down the road home. How he would put his arm around her and laugh at her, and the sharp humour in his wild eyes, and the crumpled shape of him face down on the road, his broken hand palm up and exposed. She shivered and threw the cigarette away, staring up at the dark slopes of Mount Eden. These thoughts must be pushed away to the back of her mind. She must maintain order and balance. She thought of her mother, Celine, hiding in her books as if some things in life were too damaging to be borne. In her mind's eye again she saw the small ruined three-fingered hand. *People like this, it all catches up with them in the end.*

She remembered how they used to laugh at the talkback radio, at the little old ladies and their night fears. All those hilarious nights a long time ago, before life reared up like a snake and showed her what fear was, and all the terrible little tricks it could play . . .

Oh, but *stop* this. She felt angry, desperate suddenly. She rushed home, flung open the door, marched into the pinewood silence, and dumped her purchases on the kitchen bench. Mental discipline. A good dinner, some wine, a nice book. Then in the morning a tasty pile of complicated leases, some difficult agreements for sale and purchase and a stack of directors' resolutions, say, to see her through the rest of the day . . . But how *fascinating*, he used to say, rolling his eyes, when she described the contents of her property files. She saw the elegant shape of his wrists, as he dismissed her, laughing at her, benignly. Always benign. Always there in the night, the one who never gave in or held back or had to get some sleep, or stopped laughing, or flagged, or let her down: the unshockable Leon, he had all Maria's energy and anarchy, her desire to break into life and shake it up and test it to see what it could do. The one who would be there when all other friends had gone. Her last friend.

For a second, somewhere inside her she felt the prickling threat of tears. Proper, understanding tears. Grief. Not the drunken, bewildered, non-specific tears of last night. But grief was a long way away, locked inside, at the other end of the arid red plain in her mind.

She turned on the answerphone. There was a message from Celine Wallis, tremblingly apologetic, asking her to call. Maria felt a twinge of guilt. She was always beating her mother up, not literally, but every time she opened her mouth. Or burst into Celine's flat, disturbing the atmosphere, giving off charged and angry and restless vibrations. Celine was so fragile, she could be bruised by the whirling molecules in the air. Celine would close up like a flower at the change in atmospheric pressure, and Maria would resent the retreat and begin to give off hints of thunder, intimations of lightning. Consequently Celine was rarely at the door to wave her off when Maria swept swearing from the small flat and roared with car engine screaming out of the drive.

She fast-forwarded but there were no more messages. No one more. Now she stood, hesitating, in the quiet, sunlit hall. Through the frosted glass of the front door she saw the bushes blowing in the wind. Tiny dust motes drifted down through the bright air. The wooden walls shifted with a faint crack and twigs scraped on the iron roof.

The sun went behind a cloud and the yellow light in the hall dimmed, and Maria felt her eyes adjusting to the sudden change in the light. Her bedroom door stood open, cold air blowing through the window and rustling the papers on her desk. The answering machine clicked loudly beside her and she jumped at the noise. The sun brightened the hall again and there was a cold sunlit fur over the carpet and walls, dust and hairs and bright air woven into glowing webs and balls, and the top of the telephone book was decorated with a sparkling layer of dust. It was no good. No good fighting it. She had to get out again.

She gathered up a few things, locked up, went out to her car, got in and drove through the bright and dark Sunday streets in the direction of the central city.

Maria parked, non-committally, in the Domain. She walked along the Domain Drive. She reached the duck-pond where brightly clad children trailed by parental paparazzi hurled lolly papers at the agitated ducks, and little family groups sat on the grass with their picnics anchored down against the bullying wind, and overhead the racing sky burst out in warm sunshine and frowned into sudden chilling shade.

She walked on, to the drab stretch of shops on Karangahape Road and spent a long time in the afternoon surf of a crowded McDonald's, drinking bitter coffee and reading the paper in the hard pale neon light.

She sat sternly and waited for the urge to return home but it didn't come, and as the afternoon turned late and evening came near she picked herself up again and went out into the street shrugging and sighing hard, as if finally admitting defeat. Behind the takeaway bar she found the stale and cluttered alleyway, and under the beer crate she found the keys, all four of them, in a bunch.

She groped her way up to the top of the stairs. After much struggling and blundering she undid the reluctant deadlock at the top of the door, then the second, then sat abruptly down on the step and reconsidered for a moment. This was madness. What was she doing? This criminal. This criminal *squalor*. She should just go home. Put the kettle on. Read a good book.

But loneliness pushed her on, and something else, an inexplicable urge, like the desire she always felt as a child to touch the hot element on the stove when Celine warned her, *it'll hurt*, she selected the third key and inserted it in the third lock, and the fourth and pushed the heavy door until it opened.

She put her head around the door and listened. She heard faint thumpings and scrapings. She entered the hallway and stopped abruptly as a groan issued out of the bedroom at the end of the hall, and a dull thump, and a high-pitched yelp, and a sharp smash. Then chilling, despairing exhalations, as of extreme suffering and pain.

Maria froze. Oh torture. Oh murder. She put her hands over her mouth, and dropped the keys. And as she bent to retrieve them her handbag became entangled in the door and as she pulled and tugged in her eagerness to escape the strap of the handbag broke and its contents spilled out on the floor.

She threw herself down on her knees frantically scrabbling in the dark for the scattered items, but oh, forget it, she thought, let's just get out of here, and she straightened up to find the great heaving chest of Wiremu McDonalds Ihaka inches from her face. He held his fist upright, and blood trickled down the great fingers, gathering in the hairs of the massive brown wrist, and fringing the shirt sleeve with a brightly obscene red dye.

With a jerk of fright Maria stepped backwards. Items of make-up that had spilled out of her handbag crunched on the carpet under her feet. He was muttering and growling, not looking at her but inspecting his gory wrist. She fumbled behind her back and tried to open the door but he looked up and reached quickly for the door handle. 'Where are you going?' he said.

'Just out,' she sang, struggling with the door.

'You've just got here.' He narrowed his red-streaked eyes.

Tugging on the door with both hands now she pleaded, terrified, 'Let me out!'

'No,' he said, looking down at her intently, holding the door with his great red hand, 'I want you to come in *here*.' And he took her by the upper arm and pulled her towards the bedroom.

'I've made a mistake, let me go, please,' she begged, struggling to free herself, her feet dragging along the carpet. Ignoring her, he pinned her with his huge shoulder against the wall. Slowly he opened the bedroom door.

'Close your eyes,' he said.

12.

Wiremu Ihaka covered Maria's eyes with his hand and propelled her through the bedroom door. Struggling to breathe behind the hot fleshy palm she stumbled a few steps into the centre of the room.

He stopped pushing, released his grip on her arm and took his hand away from her face. She fought him off and jumped away from him, breathing hard, waiting, fists raised, heart racing. The room was quiet.

'*There*,' he said triumphantly.

She rubbed her eyes. Her vision cleared. She looked quickly around the bedroom, struggling to understand what she was seeing.

The grimy chairs, old boxes, old couches and dead ashtrays had been cleared away. The floor had been vacuumed and shampooed, the windowsills dusted, the torn curtain replaced with a new dark blue blind. The window, previously so dirt encrusted that very little light had penetrated, had been cleaned and polished so thoroughly that the window looked glassless, and the bed had been made up with fresh clean sheets and a new floral quilt. Maria looked around in amazement.

'Well?' He put his hands together and looked out at her from under his eyebrows.

'It's . . . much improved,' she managed to say. She spread out her hands. He laughed.

'I thought . . .' Maria rubbed her quivering hand over her face.

'What?'

'Nothing.'

'I worked on it for hours. Since you said it stank in here. I worried about it. Then I got keen, went out and got cleaning stuff, got some

new things from along K. Road. I found a big mirror, see, on top of
the wardrobe, but the fugn thing fell on me and broke just now
when I was getting it down. It was really heavy, eh, cut my hand.
And I got these pot plants, and this nice poster, and a little bedside
table . . .' He bustled around the room, showing her.

'It's amazing. I can't believe it's the same room.'

He looked at her sideways, putting his hands together again. 'So
do you like it?'

'It's very . . . nice . . .' She hesitated, then went on, 'Really, it's
incredible . . . I mean, the room was so *disgusting* . . .' She looked
quickly to see if he was offended.

He lowered his eyes modestly. 'I did it for you.'

'For *me?*'

'I wanted you to like it. Because I wanted you to come back.'

'Thanks.' Not looking at him she scuffed the clean carpet with
her foot, politely fingered the new pot plants, admired the shelves on
which his CD collection and his books (*Jaws I* and *II*) were newly
displayed. He saw her looking at the books. He sidled over to stand
beside her, looked down at his fingernails and said casually, 'I've got
a cousin who's read those. Both of them.'

'Oh?'

'Cover to cover.'

'Well. How about that.'

'Yeah.' He nodded vigorously.

'Well . . . I'd better go.'

'But you've only just come.'

'I have to go to work in the morning.' She was backing towards
the door.

Looking deeply disappointed he said softly, 'I suppose you'd
rather be alone.'

Out in the hall she picked the contents of her handbag up off the
floor. She handed him the keys and he led the way down the gloomy
stairwell. She stepped out into the cold air and turned to face him.
Now it was evening and the street was empty and desolate, the shop
signs blew creaking in the wind and rain clouds were gathering over
the Domain.

All over the suburbs lights would be shining in the wooden
houses and the wind would draw curtains of rain across the empty

streets. She would walk under the dark trees into the dark wet heart of the Domain. She would unlock the car door, hearing the melancholy wind in the trees, she would drive home, glancing behind her at the back seat full of sliding shadows, the empty seat crossed by the sliding shadows. She would sleep alone, hearing scuttling in the stone wall outside that was sheltered by the eaves and always dry, hear the sifting of ashes and shifting of dust, the earth disturbed by the busy mice, dry paws on dry earth, dry as the plain in her mind – the red desert once crossed uncrossable, arid as bones.

She looked up at Wiremu Ihaka and her face creased childishly as if she tasted something sour.

'I'm going to go mad,' she whispered. 'I don't think I can go home.'

Together they walked back up the stairs. They stepped into the hallway. Jingling the heavy bunch of keys Wiremu Ihaka locked the great, battered door behind them.

Over the dirty shoulders of the city the shawl of clouds packed down close. The city was waiting for rain. The evening wind tore down over silent gardens and shadowy streets and rattled the milk bottles on the walls but towards midnight the wind died away. Then the air was still and charged and still the rain didn't come.

Terrible night. It was humid, breathless, without air. Marcus frowned sternly over his typewriter. *It was midnight*, he wrote. *Mike fumbled for the blackened spoon. By the light of the single greasy light-bulb he could see her eyeballs moistly shining She lay inert, her young face yellow and wasted. Mike touched her shoulder gently and whispered her name. Kristyl . . .? But there was no reply.*

Marcus read what he had written. He made a few brisk changes, then lay down in his rumpled bed. He tossed and turned, restless and dissatisfied. After a few minutes he got up again and went back to his typewriter and read what he had written. He felt a wave of frustration, irritation, impatience. He threw away the last page and took out a fresh piece of paper. He thought for a minute, his hands hovering over the keys.

'*Smoke?*' he typed.

Three hours later Marcus fell exhausted on to his bed. Sitting over his typewriter he had listened to the wind howl and he had listened to it die. Outside his window the orange lights flashed on and off, counting the seconds away. He lifted the blind and saw the dense black lid of the sky over the still garden, and time flicking past in orange beats, counting down, as if something were going to happen, beyond the sky breaking up and falling on to the house. Time flickered past while the earth held itself still. Over the western ranges the storm clouds would be gathering. Time beat a dull rhythm in his head.

Marcus dreamed that a bundle was brought to him and put in his lap. He could see that it was the shape of a baby. He opened the bundle, peeling away the layers of cloth. His fingers touched something cold and strange, and he saw that the bundle contained a tiny human carcass, that his fingers were touching a cage of bones, half cooked, half picked clean. He jumped back in horror, the bundle fell to the floor and he woke up. He sat up sweating and sick, got up and dizzily crossed the room. He turned on the light. It was 4 a.m. There was still no rain. He left the light on and slept again.

The telephone woke him. Now there was grey morning light behind the blind and the cars were roaring up on the main road. He rolled over and waited for the ringing to stop but it was late and the house was empty and the shrill ring persisted until he rolled out of bed and went into the hall. He picked up the receiver, resisting the impulse to throw it against the wall.

'Yeah,' he croaked, feeling his dry mouth peel apart. He heard crackling and interference, then a distant female voice.

'Marcus?' it said. He straightened up. There was a silence on the other end, then he could hear the tiny electronic voice again, far away. He shook the phone.

'I can't hear,' he shouted. 'Is that you? Chris . . .'

'It's me . . .' The tiny voice tailed away under a barrage of static.

'Hey! Hey!' Marcus shouted into the receiver, pacing along the hall. He banged the phone against the wall.

Then a voice said clearly, 'Hang on. Is that better? Can you hear now?'

He stopped pacing. He slumped down in a chair, biting his nails and staring at the wall.

'I can hear you,' he said. He paused, then asked, 'Everything all right?'

'Yes, fine,' Maria said brightly. Then she said, 'Actually, no. Things are very strange, and bad. Can I meet you somewhere?'

He looked at the brown pattern on the wallpaper, ugly brown flowers. Sepia, the colour of pain. The flower patterns hung in vertical sprays, making the wall look as if it were melting and dissolving downwards. Through the glass panel in the front door he could see that the world had filled with blinding rain.

'Are you still there?'

'Yes.'

'Can I meet you? Are you doing anything?'

'Yes . . . No.'

'Is that yes or no?'

'I'm going to be . . .' He looked along the long dark hall. 'I'm going to be moving house.'

'Why?'

'Things are going to change.'

Maria was crying into the phone. He sat and listened. I can't seem to get. Things are all. Everything has gone out of. Marcus leaned forward in his chair, frowning at the floor.

He tried not to. But he had to ask. 'Did you stay with him?'

'Wiremu? Yes.'

'Did you *fuck* him?'

'Mind your own business. No. Of course not. Can I meet you. Please?'

'You didn't fuck him?' He was unaccountably relieved.

'What do you care? *No.*' She quietened down suddenly.

'Why are you moving?' she asked. 'Are you going away?'

'I'm not sure. I'll have to ring you back. I could meet you this afternoon.'

She was crying again. He decided to meet her later at the wharf. But she was rambling. Going on again about chaos and squalor, something about *doors too*, or was it *jaws*. Wiremu's *jaws*?

The rain drummed on Marcus's roof. She was repeating something. He looked quickly around for a cigarette.

'*What?*' he said.

Maria whispered, 'When she rang out of the blue, it reminded me of you.'

Marcus stood up and walked along the hall. 'You spoke to her.'

'Not really. She said who she was and asked for Wiremu. She called him Wi.'

Marcus's mouth was dry. He asked tightly, 'Where was she ringing from?'

'I don't know. Who cares? *Disneyland* probably.' Maria tittered mirthlessly. He heard her blow her nose.

'But Wiremu would know where she is?'

'Why do you want to know? I thought you . . .'

'Chrissie's . . . got something of mine. Something I gave her.'

'You want it back? A ring, I suppose? No, that's not really your style . . . That would be very Disney.'

He could feel her struggling to keep control. Maria at her rawest, her most unsmooth. Why did she want to meet him now, when it was Monday morning and she must be at work?

'Where are you?'

'I'm in my office but I can't do anything. I can't concentrate . . .' She was off again, sniffling into the phone.

'Jesus. You'd better pull yourself together. They'll think you're mad . . .'

'I *am* mad.'

'I have to go and do something. I'll ring you this afternoon.'

'Wait . . .'

'Bye,' he said and hung up on her. He winced. It felt like punching her in the face.

But he couldn't do anything until the evening. He spent the day clearing out his room. Most of the stuff he just threw away. He lined the black plastic rubbish bags along the hallway, marvelling at how little he owned of any value and how much junk he had secreted in his room during his two years at Connick Street. He enjoyed throwing it all away.

The rain stopped and the sun came out. The garden steamed wetly. He worked fast, carrying the black bags out into the street and lining them up on the grass verge. He got hot with his exertions and rolled up his sleeves. He whistled while he worked. Even the vague throbbing in his arm was somehow pleasurable, it buzzed hotly and made him feel the weight of everything. This was a new beginning. Things were going to change.

In the late afternoon, when the room was a bare stripped cell and he had stopped for a cup of coffee and a deserved cigarette, he turned his mind for the first time to the question of what it was that was going to change. Where was he going? What was he going to do?

It was obvious, he decided, lounging on the bed in a shaft of afternoon sunlight. He was getting out of the whole thing. Not only out of the slovenly bedroom and the unsavoury house, but out of the sprawling box-land of a city as well. The endless suburbs under the endless skies. He was leaving the country. His parents might give him some money. They would welcome the idea of a new start. And he was going to take Chrissie with him, take *them*: it was what he had to do.

He lit another cigarette and blew smoke upwards into the whirling motes of bright dust. The whirlwind of reunion. Chrissie's little face, bright with happy tears. Dangling the airline tickets in front of her nose. *No, I'm not joking. Yes, it's really true. London. London . . .*

Abruptly the phone in the hall rang one ring then clicked off. He winced again. The bright scene vanished from his mind.

At 10 p.m. Marcus climbed the steps on Quay Street and bashed as usual on the metal door. He waited. He could smell the harbour salt in the sharp wind. Across the road at the wharves the heavy water slopped and shifted around the moving piles. Over the dark rusty hulls of the container ships the white upper decks were stacked like Lego blocks. He watched a ferry move across the dark water, plunging into the buffeting wind. Wiremu Ihaka opened the door and silently let him in. At the end of the long corridor Marcus saw Klint Steel, his keys jingling on his belt, headphone aerial waving, jigging about with his usual air of strenuously suppressed violence.

'Theresa's been fired again.' Wiremu Ihaka stared down at Marcus, looking amused. 'You'll be next.'

Marcus manoeuvred himself around in the narrow corridor. 'Listen, I need to talk to you.'

The big man lowered his eyes, glanced briefly at the quivering figure of Klint Steel and said, 'Not a good time.' He turned away.

'Fuck it. Come on.' Marcus pulled the sleeve of Wiremu's suit. Wiremu looked coldly down at the offending white hand.

'Oh, come *on*. Don't be so bloody . . . theatrical all the time. *Shit* . . .' Marcus tripped over a stack of beer crates.

Wiremu held up two fingers. 'Two minutes.'

'Jesus. Pompous bastard.'

They went into the small back storeroom. 'Shoot,' Wiremu said deeply. He squinted down.

'Jesus. Look, apparently you know where someone is.'

This sounded ridiculous. Wiremu looked piously non-committal.

'The thing is . . . I've been trying to find a friend. Chrissie. Chrissie da Silva.' He swallowed. Even her name was embarrassing somehow, said out loud like that. And look at the teasy bastard, weighing up whether to tell him, enjoying his discomfort.

Wiremu said softly, 'Christal. Does she *want* you to find her?' Gently he inspected his gigantic fists, spread out his hands and began to clean underneath his nails.

Marcus took a deep breath, half closed his eyes and said with epic self-restraint, 'Of course she does, you big dumb shit.'

There was a charged silence in the stockroom. Marcus looked up and saw with a start of alarm that Wiremu was staring at him with astonishing coldness. The ugly tattoo stood out starkly on the huge hand as Wiremu carefully wiped his beaded forehead and straightened himself up, the way he always did before he broke someone's nose and threw him into the street.

Marcus stepped back. Wiremu's violin-shaped mouth was stretched above his upper gums and his eyes bulged threateningly. Silently he rolled his great head on his muscular neck.

In consternation Marcus stepped back another step. Shit. After all. Wiremu had always been okay. Ridiculously good-natured. Marcus had never really been one of those on the outside, in the queue on Quay Street, reeling in terror before the sickening plunge into the bin-bags, the shocking connection with the concrete pavement. He had never taken Wiremu seriously: Wiremu was a cartoon. Wiremu was the sort of monster feared by people who lived in Wiremu's world, on Wiremu's terms. Melodramatically they would whisper, 'That *dude* at Quays, that *big fulla*, he'll kill you, eh. He's killed before . . .' They said things like that because people did kill you, where they came from. South Auckland. The hard life. Ten of you living in the Skyline Garage. Or the car. Marcus prepared himself to explain exactly what it was that he wanted. Just a telephone number, actually. As it were. Even better, an address . . .

And Wiremu said, almost in a whisper, '*What* did you say?'

'Say? I . . . Nothing . . .' Marcus began to explain about Chrissie again.

'You call me a cunt?'

'A . . .? . . . No.'

'*You calling me a cunt?*'

Marcus fell silent. He looked enquiringly into Wiremu's face and trembled at what he saw. He felt like a child suddenly, helpless before parental rage, innocent of all charges, condemned, waiting. The big man was going to beat his head in. Just like that. The great weight of the balled fists. There was nothing he could do. Closing his eyes he thought, unexpectedly, of Maria.

But it was Klint Steel who rescued him, Klint of all people, who broke the terrible silence just before the violence was about to erupt by kicking the door open with his steel-capped boot, bursting in shaking all over under his aerial, and announcing in a series of barks and snarls that in view of continued unreliability Marcus Klein was fired.

'You can work this shift,' Klint sneered. 'Then fuck off out of it. Comprendy?' The aerial waggled. Jingling and quivering he swept from the room.

Wiremu relaxed. He opened his fists. He smiled mirthlessly and waved his great hand. 'Way it goes, bro.'

'Oh, great.' Marcus leaned his head defeatedly against the wall. He was crushed. 'Now what?'

Wiremu was rummaging around in the drawers of a desk in the corner of the stockroom. He pulled out a bit of paper and a pen and wrote something down. He looked expressionlessly at Marcus and handed him the paper.

'What's this?'

'What you wanted. Her address.'

'But . . . you . . .'

'Second thoughts, bro. Be a good idea if you call around.'

It was a Parnell address. Marcus put it in his pocket. He felt hot all over, then cold. He rubbed his hands over his face, reached into his pocket and crumpled the piece of paper into a ball. Wiremu Ihaka watched him, a sly look on his massive face.

All through the agonising shift, as he toiled at the smoke-bank of the bar, as he shouted out into the wall of sound, as the music vibrated painfully in his tender head, Marcus could feel Wiremu Ihaka watching him. Through the smoke and the lights and the flickering darkness, across the churning tide of the dance floor Wiremu was watching like a great brown goblin, ogre-ish, tigerish, glaringly pop-eyed, and laughing occasionally to himself as if at some private, hilarious joke.

When the shift finished Marcus got out fast, stepping over the unconscious figure of Theresa, who had drunk herself into a coma after a marathon screaming session with Klint, during which she had been heard to denounce and pour scorn on him, to the secret delight of the remaining bar slaves.

Marcus ran down the rubbish-strewn back alley and out into the sharp grey dawn. He got into a taxi and rode home through the empty streets. He unlocked the door and went into his room, stopping in surprise at the sight of it, all stripped and bare, the floor striped by the shadows, all his things in cardboard boxes, packed away. He got into bed and lay there anxiously, willing the slow hours past.

At seven o'clock he was out in the back kitchen choking down a cigarette and listening to the birds fighting in the trees in the back gully. He heard a thump and a groan as Mike turned over in bed, then a sleepy command from the domineering Brendelia. Followed by Mike's valiantly good-natured, 'Fuck off there, babe.' A pause, rearrangements, then the usual crescendo of rhythmic shrieks from the bed springs. Marcus smiled tensely to himself. Domestic bliss. Getting it at home. The kitchen wall trembled. Marcus watched a piece of wallpaper slowly detaching itself from the wall and the crumbs spreading in the vibrations on the Formica table. He chewed his toast with effort: the bread was a week old, veined with furry mould, most of which he had scraped off into the bin. He shivered as a needle of wind blew through the uninsulated walls.

At what point, he thought, does it all become one? At what point does one become part of it all? He had set out to get away from the big house in Meadowbank, his child self in the horn-rimmed specs leaning against his mother in the photo, claustrophobic niceness, middle-class life; everything that stopped you being a man. He wanted to write about life, he had gone down into life and got dirty with it, took drugs, spoke in monosyllables, thought nothing, talked about nothing, believed nothing. He'd been stoned for a long time, beating his brain up with it, barely recovering his senses after a big session before getting into it again. Smoking, inhaling, snorting, popping. Only in these last months (after going on fire) had he started to think again.

He thought about Maria disappearing down the alley into the black mass of the doorman's shadow. He sighed and pushed the breadcrumbs into a pile on the table. *Life*. Get down and dirty with it. Flirt with it, slum with it. Don't take it seriously. Then, it'll hurt you. It'll bite back. Then there'll be nothing there to catch you when you fall.

Under his sleeve his scarred arm itched and burned. His head was so clear that everything seemed to hurt and jar. The early morning light through the window stabbed him in the eye. He winced. Clarity. Pain. The yellow light bored through his fluttering eyelid, into his brain. Clarity.

Chrissie hadn't burnt his arm. Chrissie wouldn't hurt a fly.

If not her, then who? Marcus shivered as if he would never get warm again. He closed his eyes and thought of Wiremu Ihaka. Face of the laughing gargoyle, lit up with storm light, criss-crossed by the hysterical strobes.

It was ten o'clock in the morning. There was a weird light. After the bright morning light had hit him in the eye he looked out the window and found to his surprise that the air was full of fog. Columns of mist moved through the lower air, the gully trees shone with drops of water and banners of mist hung over the tops of the houses. As the mist moved and parted, beams of sunlight shot down through the clouds and illuminated the spiralling vapour. It was hot, hard to breathe. Full of water, the air writhed, and the city was like a tropical aquarium, a habitat, full of green leaf, water, droplets, shifts in the steaming tank of the sky. Over towards the east great shafts of light angled down through a dazzling gap in the clouds, the puckered sky-hole up there too bright to look at, less like God's eye than God's arsehole blasting its bright searchlight right across the wooden box-land of the west. The city seemed to gasp and stagger under the collapsed tent of the air.

Marcus swerved cautiously down the narrow street in the old veering rattling car, wiping his forehead with the palm of his hand. He was sweating. Hot mist hung over the cars parked along the steep road. The fog blew lightly in all directions, spinning down the street, curling around the hanging plants on the wooden verandahs. Mist and sunshine, and rainshine, and steam on the hot asphalt, the light rain swirling and drifting and flying upwards.

The shuddering car stopped with a bump next to a rushing gutter, filled with racing leaves.

Blind fog. Blind mist. He peered out through the jewelled glass. Chrissie's fence. Chrissie's house. Why had he loved her? It was because of her eyes. Round, steady, soft brown eyes. They were at the heart of his sexual obsession. They were the thing that made him love her the most. Chrissie's *eyes*, he loved them because of this: he could drag her into the sack, he could love her and adore her (and she could love him), and he could stare deep into those round brown eyes and know that she didn't really *see* him, not properly. Not clearly. No hard light in them, no cold daylight, to make him turn away. She would walk in her shorts into the dark room where the hard men played poker under the swaying bulb and kiss him goodnight and flounce off to bed. She would lie on the bed and watch him undress, she would wind her thin brown legs around him, she would look into his face, and all the while she would never really see him, and he could be free. He could take her in his arms without a trace of irony, he could whisper in her ear . . . he could fuck her to bits, in private, and he could love her without fear.

He loved her now, stepping over the rushing gurgling gutter, wiping the sweat from his brow. *With* fear. Actually. He had wanted her for so long, so urgently.

He thought of Maria. The disquieting quality in Maria's eyes sometimes when she smiled. The eyes not changing expression, but boring steadily into him, observing him, knowing him, making him feel as if he were walking naked under a thousand-watt lightbulb, and his mind choking with the necessary defences: irony, small talk, quips, jokes. It was easier when Maria was drunk. When she was rolling pissed. When she was *blind*.

Clutching his small piece of paper Marcus paced up and down by the white picket fence of number 34.

He took a deep breath. He exhaled water and air. He went through the gate. He climbed the steps on to a large white painted verandah. There was an iron seat, pot plants, a wooden door with stained glass and a shining brass doorknocker.

He lifted the knocker up and dropped it twice, noticed ash on his sleeve and brushed it off, noticed mud on his jeans, scraped at it with his fingernails, heard footsteps in the hall. At once his stomach seemed to writhe and contract. He felt the burnt arm itch and twinge. The fog crowded on to the verandah, stopping his breath, the hot clammy air bringing sweat out on his forehead.

He stepped away. He heard brisk footsteps stop at the door. *She would open the door, she would see him there* . . . The handle rattled, and Chrissie opened the door, and looked out at him.

Her pale face with parted lips and pearly teeth, the brown eyes wide, neutral, bright. She saw. And said, in a hard, clear little voice, 'Leaving so soon?'

Chrissie with her open, arresting little face, with her arms folded, stopped him in his panicky flight as he backed away down the stairs. He hesitated at the bottom of the steps and she came slowly out on to the verandah to look down at him, at his ashy shirt, his dead white face, the dry vermicelli that was his hair, the defeated sag and droop of his jeans.

She was still small but not so thin, and her hair had grown into soft brown spikes and she wore some sort of tight chocolate brown suit, with a jacket and trousers. She was looking down at him rigidly, with her arms folded tight against her chest.

Slowly he came back up the stairs. He tried to speak.

'What do you want?' Chrissie said finally.

He was thinking out what to say.

'I haven't got much time.' She was alert and straight-backed and the fog clung to the waving spikes of her hair.

He looked up and grinned faintly at her. 'You've always got time.'

'Not now,' she said.

He looked down again, at the curve of her legs in the tight pants. She wore long black leather boots. He took a deep breath, gave a weak grin and said, 'I've just popped over to rape you.'

It was the wrong thing to say. He put his foot in the door as she tried to slam it. 'I'm sorry. It was the wrong thing to say. Don't shut the door. I'm . . . I'm going away . . .'

He found he was fighting back tears. 'You can't shut the door. There are things . . . I've got to ask you . . .'

'What things?' she said, coldly uninterested, through the crack in the door.

'Please open the door.'

'Fuck off.'

'Please.'

'Get lost.'

He leaned against the edge of the door. He closed his eyes and said with difficulty, 'I was told you were . . .' He paused.

After a moment she said through the door, 'I was what?'

'You were, you know . . . With . . . In . . . Up the . . .'

She threw the door open again, blazing. 'Told I was what? What? Told I was *pregnant*?'

He ducked away, out of reach of her furious fists.

'Yes.'

'Who told you? *Who*?' she demanded, violence in her eyes.

He held up his hands. Come on. Steady on now. 'Does it matter?' he said.

'Yes, it matters,' she spat at him.

'Well, Darlene. Darlene the greeter.' He gave another weak smile.

Chrissie assumed a pose eloquent with stunned disgust. Silent disbelief. Her lip curled practically up into her nostrils. Marcus struggled with a surge of irritation at this. For Christ's sake. What did it matter who told him, the thing was to . . . deal with . . . the practical considerations. She would come with him to London . . . He opened his mouth.

In a voice of ice, Chrissie said, '*I* told you.'

Marcus closed his mouth. He went absolutely still. Behind him a car droned busily past.

'You told me . . .' he repeated stupidly.

'*I* told you.' Now her voice was candy sweet with hatred and venom, honeyed rage. She said, 'You don't remember, darling. Do you?'

Tears in his eyes again. Confusion. Horror tears. Tears of horror. 'I told you the night before I left, when you came home.'

Chrissie leaned against the door. She smiled strangely. He looked into the animal hatred in her eyes. She spoke conversationally, with theatrical detachment, dropping the appalling words into the cringing air.

'I thought you'd be happy. *I* was happy. I lay awake, waiting for you. Excited and pleased. When you got home you were in a funny state. Remember, darling?'

'No.'

She stared at him for a moment, then continued. 'Well, you were just dying for a fuck. I said no. We argued a bit about that.' Chrissie laughed sweetly and held up her index finger. 'You tried to take a pee against the chest of drawers. Remember that, Marcus?'

'No,' he whispered.

'When you were calm again (after I'd persuaded you to use the toilet, and you had thrown up in there too, quite tidily), I decided to leave. But you wanted me to stay. You became weepy and affectionate. We had *sex*.' She spat out the word. 'Remember how we used to fuck all the time? That was all we did together, really, wasn't it? *Fuck* all the time?'

There was a terrible silence. He struggled to find words, any words.

Chrissie said, 'After that I said – and here's the funny part – I wished we could get married, or live together properly at least. And then I told you I was pregnant.'

'No,' Marcus said. 'Jesus . . .'

'You paced up and down at the end of the bed. You were stoned, you were ghastly, your eyes were mad.'

Chrissie took a deep breath. She went on, with elaborate candour. Her face cracked into a bizarre smile. Nothing in her eyes now but flat hatred. Worse than indifference: dead love. Love killed.

Marcus wiped and wiped his mouth with his hand. She looked carefully at him.

'Does this bother you? There's not much more to tell. You lit a pipe, one of those "bongs" you have so many of. You put something into it and lit it. Then you put something on a piece of tin foil and you were trying to light that with a lighter. You got frustrated, the flame wouldn't work. I could smell lighter fluid. You leaned back or passed out and suddenly your sleeve caught fire, and then the blanket and the quilt. You went up, *whoomph*.' She made a little jump at him, miming *flames* with her hands. He jerked his head backwards.

Chrissie nodded, smiling her terrible little smile.

'You got up with your eyes closed, still out of it, writhing with the flames. Tiny bubbles were coming out of your mouth. You woke up properly and screamed. Your shirt was melting into your arm, I could see. The smell was horrible. You were flailing your arms about. I grabbed the watering can and tipped it over you, and smothered the rest with the blankets. You got up, you stood up on the bed. Your arm, your clothes were smoking. You were writhing, jerking, your face was insane. I can still see the way you looked at me. Your whole face was twitching and you were grinding your teeth and your *voice*, it came out of you like a robot's voice, or a strangled old woman, without you even moving your mouth. You came for me, I thought you were going to attack me. I was terrified, I tried to call for Mike or Mike but no one was home, or everyone was too stoned to hear. You grabbed my chin and neck and held me, you stared at me and you were laughing and shivering and spitting, spit ran down your chin . . .'

Chrissie broke off. A spasm passed over her face. Her face creased with weird triumph, her round brown eyes shining with revulsion, misery, pain.

Marcus stepped forward, hopelessly. 'I'm sorry. I'm . . .'

She pushed him away. 'Your voice was like a woman's voice. You were clenching your teeth. You put your face right up against mine and you said, "Do you think I'd marry a *moron* like you? Disney-brain . . ." Then you laughed. You cackled, like a witch . . . As if it was the funniest thing you'd ever heard.'

Chrissie drew in her breath, in a tiny scream, her face grotesque with smiling grief. The loved face, with its salt water eyes, and her small shoulders shaking, the air like tears caught in her spiky hair. Marcus stood like a statue. Face of horror. Face of stone.

'Then you said to me, I want you to get rid of it. And I screamed at you no, and you shouted into my face, barking at me. You shouted "Never. Never. *Never*." '

Marcus swayed and put out his hand as if to fall on her, as if he would fall to his knees. She stood her ground and looked him straight in the eye.

'There's nothing left to say. I got rid of it. I didn't want it either. After that.'

The loved face, the longed-for face. The round brown eyes opaque with hate. All around them the weather whirled and wept and blurred as the sky drifted down and Marcus's vision bulged and distorted and swam until the green grass by the path was like a river of jewels. He wanted to take hold of her and cling to her and howl like a dog, but she fought off his pleading hands and wrenched herself away.

A voice called from the back of the house.

'Christal?'

There were footsteps in the hall. Marcus looked up and saw a tall man in suit trousers and a tie and a waistcoat, a square head with a brown quiff, a tanned, angular face and large teeth. Small grey eyes, like wet marbles. Slip-on shoes, with tassled fringes.

'Baby?' said the man deeply, eyeing Marcus with suspicion and putting his long arm around Chrissie's waist. She curled herself into his side, like a cat. Like a Burmese, with her soft chocolate brown spikes of hair.

'Hon?' Chrissie glanced up into the man's face. 'This is Marcus.'

Marcus rubbed his smarting eyes. Jesus . . . 'Hi *hon*,' he said.

Chrissie said, 'Marcus, meet Bryce.'

The man offered a large tanned hand. 'Bryce Ballseck? How you doing? You're good? Christal and myself are actually just off.'

Numb and silent, Marcus looked them both up and down.

Bryce folded his arms, looked down at Chrissie and said richly, 'In point of fact, Martin, in a couple of hours I'll be escorting my wonderful lady to Fiji.'

'Oh, really? So what are you going to do with *her*?' Marcus couldn't help it, he just couldn't, coming forward snarling and pointing his quivering finger right into her face and Chrissie was shouting something at him, grabbing his finger and pushing it away and the face of the tall impostor turned red as he swelled in the doorway and ordered him off the property, who did he think he was, and get your finger out of it and no way can you talk to my lady like that.

He couldn't help it, he couldn't let it end like that, he couldn't help fighting and swearing and kicking as the tall man manhandled him with astonishing strength down the steps and pushed him with brute force backwards along the path, until Marcus managed to graze him with a punch on the side of the jaw and the man hauled off and hit Marcus so hard that his neck cracked back and one of his shoes flew off and he staggered backwards through the gate and landed on his side on the footpath.

'You shit.' The man breathed heavily, rolling his shoulders with muscular contempt. 'You piece of *shit*.' He paced around on the pavement, nodding vigorously, inhaling, exhaling, uttering small explosive grunts as if an invisible audience in the hedge were being whipped into a frenzy of applause. 'Try it with me. *No way* . . .'

He walked off, then turned and came back down the path. He circled Marcus. 'You haven't even got a *job*, have you?' He picked up Marcus's battered old shoe, inspected it with sorrowful contempt and threw it hard into Marcus's face.

'A girl like that . . . A *lady* . . .' Bryce Ballseck shook his head wonderingly. 'Was always going *nowhere* with a loser like you.'

Lugubriously delivering a final kick to Marcus's slumped body he went shouldering away up the path to where she was waiting with clasped hands on the verandah steps. They embraced and hurried inside the little house, slamming the door shut.

Marcus got up slowly and hobbled away, down the steaming river of the suburban street. Lurching, reeling with sick rage, grief, hatred, shame. Clarity. Pain. Remembering what he had nearly remembered in the morning: the night he *went on fire*. He saw himself writhing in the ruined bedroom, his face contorted with terror and rage, his face turned to dog-snarl and foam and fangs, and the agony and drowning intoxication and the raw ego unleashed and raving, fighting for its life. Lash out at her. Fight her off. Break out, she's stifling me, she's dragging me down. And the smooth oval of her appalled face, the blind and black of her eyes, all pupil and tears, and her hands on the sides of her cheeks, her mouth set in a blameless frightened O. You came looking for me, she'd shouted. I didn't even want you at first. You came looking for *me*.

He had gone out into life, he had found life. He had made a life. And then the half-starved scarecrow of his own nature had reared up and killed it. Tore it down. *I went looking for life. Now look at the blood on my hands.*

Out on the road he sped away, through the drifting banners of the sky. Every atom in his body throbbing with grief and pain, and every inch of him tinglingly alive.

Marcus Klein drove like a demon out of Newton. He reached Connick Street and entered his empty room. He sat down at his typewriter and began to type at feverish speed, his pale eyes coldly blue, and burning.

13.

Maria pushes in the tape and presses play. New Order. 'Every Little Counts'. The song is like a lot of songs, banal on the page, less ordinary when heard, rendered extraordinary (or meaningful or nostalgic) by context. Place in time. What were you doing when. Where were you when. Does this song remind you of the time?

> *Every second counts when I am with you*
> *I think you are a pig, you should be in a zoo,*
> *I guess I should have known I'd end up on my own,*
> *Every second counts . . .*

How long ago did he die?
    Say, three months. Twelve weeks. (What *is* the date today?)
    How did he die?
    Instantly.
    Who killed him?
    Who knows?
    Did he kill himself?
    Good question.
    Was it your fault?
    The file is closed. Gather the evidence for yourself.
    Lying on Wiremu Ihaka's sofa she listens. On the TV on the dresser a science fiction video plays out in scenes so banal, so ugly that she almost retches, but she doesn't take her eyes off the screen.
    The song in the background:

> *Every second counts when I am with you,*
> *Even though you're stupid I still follow you.*

But on the video a being has laid eggs in the bodies of the crew, and when the eggs hatch a long, slimy, wriggling worm eats its way out of their foreheads. The enslaved spacecrew gather in the control room, each with a wet, one-eyed tentacle waving out of his head. When threatened, when shot at with lasers, the worms retreat inside the host brain with a moistly sucking plop. The captain is holed up in the storeroom – he is the only one left. His second-in-command has just been dismembered, his body parts sucked dry. Wetly, noisily whispering, the tentacle people are closing in.

Every second counts when I am with you. Every second. Maria doesn't block her ears, or turn away, but stares.

And Wiremu Ihaka glances up genially, taps the TV remote against his forehead and says, 'Wait. Just wait. The best bit's coming next.'

Wherever she goes in the city now, sooner or later she will hurry back to K. Road. He will open the metal door and usher her up the stairs – Wiremu Ihaka, obese-fisted monster, he's kinder, more devoted, than anyone she's ever known. Everything is falling apart now, everything is falling away. The threads that tied her to the world are cut, lost in an instant, on Quay Street. She lies on the sofa in the grey light, her face fixed on the video screen. She doesn't move, or speak, she hasn't the energy to look away. The doorman moves carefully around the room, humming, dusting, arranging his things. He frowns thoughtfully down at her out of his brutal face. She has never felt so loved, or so ashamed.

In the busy mornings on Karangahape Rd, wintry yellow sunlight streaming on to the grimy shopfronts, and the pedestrians marching briskly and the bright light glancing off the passing cars, a furtive figure can be seen opening the battered door and sidling and blinking out into the light. Well-dressed if somewhat dusty, tidy but haggard-faced, glancing nervously this way and that, now up the road, now down, now checking the time on her watch, Maria walks away from the metal door and sets off into the bright crisp air, looking back once with a scornful toss of her head, as if she is leaving something inferior and low, and heading towards something better and more worthwhile. From the window above the takeaway bar the great crumpled brown face frowns sternly down, with an expression that is gentle and tolerant, and distinctly proprietorial.

Maria comes late to work every day now. Today she arrives an hour and a half late to find Giles Speer, Phillip Peeks-Berlyn and Clairene eating crackers and drinking morning coffee in the secretarial bay. Fish-eyed with late nights, speechless with secret shame, she hurries past to the kitchen, makes herself a cup of coffee and carries it back to the group, only to find that she can hold the cup but can't bring it to her lips without a violent trembling of her hand, a quivering so extreme that the coffee threatens to spill all over her sleeve and on to the floor and she has to sit holding the cup with both hands and not drinking while the conversation flows and eddies and dies around her and the three pick up their cups silently and go back into their rooms, glancing at one another behind her back, with raised eyebrows and looks both significant and severe.

In her office she feels the hot air pressing in close, hot sunlight on her back through the brown glass, her throat harsh and furry with tar, her mouth dry, her head fuzzy and confused. She wants to lie back in her chair or lie down on the floor, or even better to sweep the statutes and textbooks and folders off the broad shelf along the window and lie there in the hot brown light watching the tennis players below, the muted game on the windy court, on the vibrant green, in the cold hot light.

Colours seem intense. She muses over colours, sunlight and sunshade, sky tone, cloud shade, shadows moving on the walls, deep shadows in the gorges and canyons of the streets, cloud shadows on the red cliff walls of the National Building and the watery plains of the Downtown roof. She wishes she was out in the hot light on the edge of the red brick precipice, leaning into the tearing updraught – in here the canned air is so stifling and close – or down on the court where the toy players lunge and dash and the white shirts flap and fill with wind. Aerials sway and tarpaulins billow and tiny figures on a flimsy platform lower themselves down a mirrored wall, cleaning the glass as they go down. She watches time pass, watches the cleaners descend the face of the reflected city. The timesheet on her desk is empty, files are unopened, calls are unreturned. Twice she lets the phone ring unanswered, until the call diverts to Clairene and is dealt with somewhere else, by Giles Speer perhaps, who sits frowning in his large office and debating what to do, and reflecting resignedly that very few staff go insane, and it's probably natural that one would lose the odd person to madness or ill health, but perhaps she could have had a spell in a health farm, or therapy group, before it was too late? But he is busy, and loathe to exit his room, and soon he is thinking of other things, and wondering with pleasure which of the firm teams he can poach a new recruit from when Maria is gone, perhaps that jolly, competent girl in banking and finance, or that serious young fatty they've been working to death in tax. That file he was going to give to Maria, he can't let her have it now. Let Peeks-Berlyn cast his eye over it instead. There's not much time left for Maria Wallis. Decisions have been made. She doesn't know it yet. She hasn't been informed.

Yet in the evening, when she meets Ernest at the doorway of the house in Ashton Road and sees the look on his face the thought occurs to her, not for the first time, there's not much time left. Things won't go on like this for long. Time passes and it all falls away.

Ernest is dragging her into the house and forcing her into a conference in the kitchen. Maria, do you live here or not? Are you still paying half the bills? I've got the power bill here, look, what are you going to do? Maria, if you're not staying here, why don't you move out? And where (if you don't mind my asking) have you been all this time?

I can't tell you, she says. I've been around.

Are you working?

Of course. I'm in every day.

Have you gone round the bend? (The sight of you. Jesus.)

Yes. Yes, I have.

She eats some dinner in the kitchen, gets up, stuffs some clothes in a bag. Already she can hear the fingernail ends of the leaves scraping on the iron roof, see the shadows moving over the bedroom walls, hear the mice scuttling in the dry-stone wall. The dark cars sliding by, unidentified, on the slicked wet road.

She sees that ants have made a trail through her room, forming a two-lane highway up the table leg and over the dusty piles of books. She hasn't read a book in weeks. She watches videos, and drinks too much in the evenings to read. She picks up a tattered hardback and slams it down on the marching column. Unperturbed, fellow ants march on over the flattened dead. Watching them, Maria begins to fancy that her neck is elongating, that her head is stretching further and further away from the ants, that she is looking down now from somewhere near the ceiling while her feet remain planted firmly on the floor. She can't stay here. There is no gravity here. There is too much to fear. Dust drifts across the floor, and in an old coffee cup by the bed the dregs have formed into thick milky clumps. There are muddy footprints on the wooden floor. One corner of a poster hangs loose and blows listlessly in the draught. The room is irredeemable, wrecked, lost. It smells of damp and mice.

She is sneaking out the door when Ernest catches her again. Exasperated. This can't go on. It can't. Decidedly no. His is the name on the lease, remember. The word eviction on the tip of his tongue.

To lie down, lie back, and let it all slide away: it doesn't take long. A moment to let go, then the gentle slide, down and down. Nothing to catch you and life falling with you, crumbling away. Lie down in the hot office light and wait for the juggernaut of Quinn St John to roll forward, and move on.

Ernest shouts something inaudible from the path. She gets into her car without answering and drives back to Karangahape Rd. In her head, the voice:

How long ago did he die?

Thirteen weeks. Twelve.

Are you filled with grief?

I dreamed I crossed a red desert and left everything behind. I have never cried.

Do you miss him?

I miss him. I loved him. I'm dying of loneliness.

You're young and healthy. Life goes on.

I have a sickness, a cancer, living in my head. It's malignant, and growing, I feel it pulsating, I feel its pressure behind my eyes. I look in the mirror and see it looking back, it controls me now. It controls me. Its name is *fear*.

Wiremu took a brownish saucepan from the shadowy depths of the kitchen cupboard. 'First assemble your ingredients.' He banged the pot down on the bench.

'I don't believe this.' Maria cast a scandalised eye over the pile of goods on the table. Corned beef. Eggs. Tomato sauce. Sausages. Tinned spaghetti. Baked beans.

'You're not going to put all of it in there.'

Wiremu smiled. 'Mais oui.'

'Mais oui. This is absolutely fucking disgusting.'

'Go downstairs and buy yourself a sea dog then. That's more disgusting.'

'I will. It isn't.'

He began to break eggs into the pot. Counting them, up to ten.

'You're not going to beat them or anything?'

He ignored her, businesslike. 'Pass the sauce.' She passed. He squirted. 'Feeling peckish?'

'Fuck, no. I feel sick. Your mother's recipe, is it? How much does she weigh?'

'My aunt's. Twenty-nine stone. Mum died of a heart attack when she was sixteen, I told you before. Give me the corned beef. No, the corned beef. And the coconut milk. And that packet of sausages. This used to go a long way at home, y'know.'

'I bet.'

'Last time I was there at the marae, up north, the court made me go, you know, instead of doing PD?'

'Yeah.'

'It was choice, all the kaumatua, telling us the old stories, showing us the old ways.'

'Sort of food gathering and that, was it?'

Wiremu frowned and stirred. 'Actually, it's all horticulture now. Marijuana. It's big business. The elders driving round in new four-wheel drives, buying new appliances. Aunty Mei lost control of her Road Warrior last month, drove it into a tree.'

'Injured?'

'Nearly dead, mate. Intensive. Give me the soy. They're all unemployed up there. The cousins have big dope plantations in the bush. You don't want to fly over in a helicopter, the cuzzies'll get up in the trees and shoot at you. Think you're cops. They ring the plants with booby traps. Razor blades on wires. Gin traps. It's Vietnam, mate.'

'Are you putting this brown stuff in?'

'Yeah.'

'Oh, right. And this?'

'That's soap.'

'Oh.'

Wiremu tilted the saucepan. The mixture moved with a glutinous, effortful plop. He squinted over at her. 'Why don't you move
in here?'

'I can't.'

'Why not? You're here all the time. Why pay rent at the other
place?'

Maria sniffed and sighed. 'I'm too sickened by your cooking.'

'I won't cook then. You're my best friend. I want you here all the
time. Why don't you stay with me?' He hitched his thumbs into his
studded belt and leaned back on the bench. He ran his hand over the
blue five o'clock shadow on his head.

Maria sat looking at him thoughtfully. He shaved his head every
evening with an electric razor, humming and singing in the sham-
bolic bathroom by the light of a small gridded window that looked
into the light well. He showered in the cubicle made of packing cases
and a plastic sheet, the bottom of the shower groaning and creaking
alarmingly under his feet as if it would give way any minute and
send him crashing hugely and nakedly into the takeaway bar below.

After his shower he would prowl along the corridor, one bath
sheet barely encircling his massive waist and another wrapped in a
turban around his bald head. Deftly he would lean into the kitchen
and light a cigarette, then stroll to his room with the fag hanging off
his lower lip, his huge eye squinting against the smoke. Inhaling
deeply, smoke shooting from his nostrils and curling around his
head, he would unhook the crackling black super-sized bouncersuit
from the back of the door, pull on the shiny trousers, and button a
fresh white shirt right up to his neck. Then the thin black bouncer-
tie and the menacing bouncerboots, and the viciously studded
bouncerbelt – you whipped it off and wound it round your knuckles, the better to maim and crush and pulp – and he would be ready
in time to flick on a soothing CD and down a quick cup of tea before
work, or run the Hoover over the floor and whip around the room
with the duster, before taking a cup of tea to Maria out on the verandah roof where she sat silently and watched the street below.

*

She came to his flat regularly. She arrived every afternoon after she had finished work, furtively looking behind her as she came in the metal door, as if she thought she was being watched or pursued.

In the evenings before he had to go to work at Quays they watched videos and drank wine and ate takeaways and he made her laugh by parodying himself and his own brutal hugeness (it always got a laugh) by wearing a frilly shower cap or bringing her tea on a tray or curtsying in his bath towel when he came in from the shower.

Every evening at six he watched out for her, and if she was late he would go out into the street to look for her, shading his eyes against the dying sun, full of anxiety until he could see her hurrying up Queen Street against the wind. Then he would go into a lunatic frenzy of waving and hallooing, playing the part of a hugely and dangerously overexcited simpleton or fruitcake – *Honey*! he would scream, *You're home*! – and every time he could see her waver between hilarity and horrified embarrassment as the crowds parted around him and people crossed the street hurriedly to get away.

She would cross the street too and then he would pursue her and catch her arm, and pretend he was dragging her into the alley, and all around people would point and talk and gesticulate and twice Wiremu and Maria had only just made it round the corner and through the metal door when sirens had begun to wail in the distance.

He knew what he looked like. People went pale if he sat next to them on the bus. People went pale when he got *on* the bus. It made him free, in a sense, because he never had anything to fear. Most people were terrified of him whether they needed to be or not, and made every effort to stay out of his way, and this gave him licence but it made him marked, and his dealings with the world were unsatisfyingly predictable. He never had to wonder how people were going to react. Often he was lonely.

But Maria had never been afraid of him – she knew instinctively that he would never do her any harm. He felt that this made them close, that she had known his secret self straightaway. He knew she liked the fact that he never needed to be afraid. He liked – he loved – the fact that she had never feared *him*. Maria had a problem with fear, he could tell. She had it generally, non-specifically. And now she needed him, the ferocious mass of muscle and aggression, covering her back, guarding her door, and he was flattered, he wanted to protect her, he wanted to keep her near. He had loved her as soon as he'd met her.

He knew that she had two reactions to him, that one side of her nature was entertained by his outrageous and antisocial appearance and the other was bothered and oppressed by it. That was why he teased her by appearing at the top of Queen Street and shouting like a maniac. Telling the world he knew her. Her face would be twisted with amusement and shame. He understood, without thinking too much about it, that they'd become friends so easily because every-thing seemed to be going wrong for her – she'd told him she was going mad. The thought had occurred to him recently, as he stood glaring coldly at the queue outside Quays, that she might eventually recover some lost part of herself, and that when she did, she might not want to know him any more. This was something he *did* fear, and he pushed the thought away. Increasingly, as she spent more and more time at his flat, he worried that he might lose her. He realised that losing her was something he wouldn't be able to bear.

Yesterday evening she pointed and said, 'Look at the sky out west there. All those extraordinary swirls of colour.'

'Almost like a beautiful painting,' he said briskly. 'Can you do these?'

She buttoned the stiff cuffs over the bouncerwrists then looked away over at the west again.

'I can see there's a lot going on in your head,' he offered. She glanced at him, infinite calculations going on in her eyes.

Once she was storming around agitatedly and he'd taken her chin between his forefinger and thumb and said, the way they do on TV, gently, commandingly, before delivery of the wise advice or home truth, 'Look at me. *Look* at me.' Then watched the sudden rearrangement of forces in her eyes, minute changes of light and shadow turning the expression in an instant from neutral to remorseless, from open inquiry to savage derision and scorn.

She pulled the cuffs down over his wrists and did up a button on his pocket. 'Have a nice time at work,' she said.

'Will you be all right?'

'I'll be fine. I'll pop down and get an onion sea dog. Maybe a magazine.'

Wiremu looked her over and rubbed his head anxiously. She looked at him with dead eyes sometimes. Eyes without expression.

'There's a party tonight. Why don't you come down?'

'No. I have to go to work in the morning. You have a lovely time.' She patted the tattoo on his hand. Then she smiled at him and said, 'Ever heard of eggshell skulls?'

'No.'

'Well. Be careful. Don't hit too hard.'

He leaned over and rested his great sweating face against her shoulder.

'Why are you so nice to me?' he said.

After Wiremu had gone to work, locking the heavy deadlocks behind him, Maria lay on his low sofa playing nervously with her hands. It was Thursday night, which was pay night and benefit night, and therefore a big pub night along K. Road. She listened to the ragged sounds from the street below, the screech of tyres, snarl of engines, shrieks and shouts from the pub, smashing glass, the insinuating yowl of sirens.

Wiremu's room had become untidy again, the ashtrays were pungently full, the dresser crowded with half-drunk coffee mugs and greasy takeaway wrappers. She ignored the mess and looked away out the window to where the wrung-out evening sky sagged over the west, the long grey skeins of cloud tinged here and there with faded colour.

The nail of her index finger was loose. She had ripped it on the door chain a week ago. It had come partly away from the nail bed and was annoying her, catching on things, getting tangled in her hair. She lifted the nail away from the finger, feeling the painful tug on the stretched skin. She turned the radio on and sat listening, pulling on the nail occasionally, to make it hurt.

A magazine lay beside her on the sofa, literal-mindedly entitled *Woman's Monthly*. She began to read. My horror pregnancy. Sheree and Dwayne's crazy bungee wedding. Special family recipes with fun-loving Jude. Maria read through a recipe for Mum Dobson's Prune Surprise. Then flicked on. How brain-injured Leanne recovered from horror burns. How horror accident deprived bachelor Cory of his manhood. She inspected pale Sheree and wall-eyed

Dwayne done up in bridal gear, and shackled to a large rubber rope. Dwayne wanted this to be one special day. No way would game wee Sheree let him down. Nauseously Maria ploughed on. The happy pages. Family fun. Our tears of joy. Twins Jayden and Kyle ('Our precious wee angels'): these bubbly toddlers are just a wee bit special says Mum Gaylene, for they were born without arms or legs.

Look at it, Maria thought. The world turned to goblins and ghouls. *Woman's Monthly* was a horror comic, surreal with euphemisms, crowingly grotesque. She turned the pages with half-averted eyes. Look at fun-loving Jude. Gaunt, intent, sprout-haired and pale as a parsnip, fun-loving Jude was forcing baby carrots into a metal blender. Mum Gaylene was a smiling ogress. Game Sheree was practically blind with blubber and fear. And *Dwayne*, staring out of the grainy page, his face crooked eyed and moronically cruel: Dwayne had always wanted to be a serial killer, but torturing his new wife would do.

Playing with her hands Maria felt something give tinily, and looked down. In one hand she held the whole fingernail and on the other hand her index finger waved nakedly, as blind and featureless and disgusting as a worm. She stared at the wrecked finger, sick with horror. The room was dark and silent and cold, and outside in the street a woman was screaming.

Maria slept. She dreamed of knives and rakes. Metal kebab skewers. Drills, saws, nails and screws. She saw the cogs of a can opener, slowly grinding. Don't walk here, someone told her, the spikes will come up through your shoes. She heard voices howling indecipherable words. She was tired, but a voice screamed at her, don't lie there, the bed is full of knives. She dreamed that a metal spike was entering her urethra and a tin opener was clipped to her face. Then she was beating her own face, hitting it so hard that silver lights flashed in her eyes. She was walking along a close dark alley, feeling her way along the walls. A hoarse voice whispered in her ear, *Someone is in here. Get out.*

She reeled up into consciousness. Her head was full of pressure, her balance was strange and the shadows in the dark room pulsed and moved. She sat up and the room whirled vertiginously. Her eyes were fuzzy and blurred. Her face and hands felt bruised and sore. Her eye was swollen. Fear picked her up off the sofa, fear pushed her dizzily towards the door. She opened it a crack and saw a light under the bathroom door. From the bathroom now came a regular metallic scraping sound. She listened and realised it was the sound of a knife, being slowly and rhythmically sharpened.

Maria ran to the front door and clawed at the deadlocks, tearing her nails, feeling the numb dead end of her nail-less forefinger scraping uselessly on the metal. At the end of the corridor the bathroom door opened abruptly and yellow light flooded into the dingy hall. Wiremu stepped out and came towards her, blocking out the light so that the weak yellow beams from the bathroom shone around his bulk and his face was shadowed and monstrous. He looked up and saw her standing there and turned on the light.

'What's wrong?' he said as Maria ran frantically past him, switching on the lights as she went, and then rushed past him again, throwing herself down on the old couch in a shaking heap of shouting and gibberish.

'What's wrong?' he asked again, following her into the room.

'Keep the lights on,' she shouted.

'OK . . .'

'Keep them fucking *on*.'

'What's happened?' He crouched down.

She rubbed her face and stared at him, her eyes screwed up with terrible fear. Her face was red and swollen, as if she had been in a fight. 'I can't tell . . .' she whispered hoarsely, clutching him, 'I can't tell whether I'm *awake*.'

He stood up. 'You're awake,' he said calmly. 'It's 4 a.m.'

She felt the rough folds of his pungent bouncersuit. He lit a cigarette and squinted down, amused. 'Yeah, I'm real all right.'

'What were you doing in the bathroom?'

'Cleaning my teeth.'

'I thought you were sharpening a knife.'

He laughed toughly, shooting out a stream of smoke. 'You're a funny little person. Someone been over? Who give you the black eye?'

'Let's go down to the All Nite.'

'I was going to go to bed.'

'Please. Please.'

'Oh, all right then.'

In the All Nite diner they sat side by side over a steaming bowl of chips. She was still agitated, chain-smoking, tapping her feet on the floor. Talking non-stop. She'd had a terrible dream, she'd thought she'd woken up but she was still dreaming, there were sharp things, knives. She'd been beating her own face in her sleep, would you believe. She had gone mad, she was dying of fear . . .

Wiremu sat back and listened to her for a while. He nodded seriously and shot two long streams of smoke from his nose. You saw it all the time. Nightmares. Mental stress. Terms of Endearment. Vietnam. He cleared his throat majestically and leaned over. He touched the side of her face and said in a soft, rich, television voice, 'Look at me. *Look* at me.'

She looked at him.

'Easy there, *easy*,' he soothed, his eyes half closed, and in an instant her expression changed. Out of the blank, wide-eyed, panicking stare surfaced amusement, irony, derision. And gratitude, this time. He hesitated and coughed. He went to continue. Hold me. Let it all out. Our burden of pain. But she was laughing at him. A big jagged smile.

'You kill me. You break me up,' she said. She rested her cheek on his smoky bouncerlapel. 'I love you, Wi. You're my best friend.'

At five o'clock they picked themselves up and headed back. On the way along K. Road in the tired dawn light she took hold of his arm suddenly and said 'Everything's going to change.'

'What?'

'I can feel it.'

'So you're going to move in with me?' He put his arm contentedly over her shoulders.

'Everything's coming to an end.'

Wiremu sighed happily and lit a cigarette. There. Good as gold. She had calmed down. Everything was fine. Soon the sun would rise. It was still dark but the morning air was beautifully mild and still. She put her arm around his waist and they marched together along the road. He hugged her close. Right now there was nowhere else in the world he would rather be. He extracted his great bunch of keys, unlocked the metal door, took her by the elbow and escorted her tenderly up the narrow stairs.

14.

Marcus had never written so well or so easily. The ideas came fast. His head was clear. Sometimes he laughed at what he had written, sometimes his eyes filled with tears. He sat in his stripped and cleaned bedroom day after day, and the hard men tiptoed past the door, speaking in reverent whispers and occasionally bringing shy offerings of soup or grass.

Sometimes he went to the shops for smokes or baked beans and the world whirled brightly around him and seemed unreal. Only his novel was real to him now. Only *The Hard Men* was real. Once he looked up and saw the morning rain falling straight down through the windless air and the garden glowing under the dark grey cloud. For a moment he watched the water beating down the bowed ponga ferns. He looked up again and it was dusk, and all the lights were on in the houses opposite. The air was cold and the rain had gone.

Brendelia shouted and argued around the house and refused to be shushed, and he wrote on, hearing nothing. Or hearing her sometimes, listening and putting her down on the page. Some of the stuff he wrote and read later – he couldn't say whether he'd made it up or not. He lived among them, and they lived with him, in his head.

He banned all drugs. He needed a clear head. In the evenings after writing all day he walked down to the waterfront and bought fish and chips at the Fishpot and watched the cold grey light moving over the sea.

He spent all day talking to no one. One evening an old woman stopped him in the street and asked him the time and he felt as if he couldn't speak, his mouth had been closed and inactive for so long.

He croaked something at her and she looked at him doubtfully and hurried away.

His room at Connick Street remained stripped and bare. He liked the fact that it had become orderly and neat. He found himself picking things up off the floor, fussily, as if disorder and mess would threaten his train of thought. At night he lay in the silent cell with the Silken Annihilator curled at his feet and listened to the hard men bouncing against the walls.

One night Mike slipped drunkenly on the mossy steps outside and broke his arm, another night Branko was arrested in the city and arrived home with a platoon of cops who thundered through the house searching for drugs. They did Marcus's room over with the rest, while he stood about looking smug and long-suffering until a large policeman stood on the Annihilator's milk saucer and broke it, at which he protested furiously and an angry grey detective with thin wet lips came prancing in, rolling his neck and jogging on the spot and threatening to run Marcus in for giving him lip. Branko was led away into the night, his face set grimly. They'd met their match there, Marcus thought, looking on. Trying to get Branko to talk. They'd have to tear off his arms, just to get his date of birth.

He was running out of money, of course. Rapidly. Fish and chips became too expensive, and he lived on sardines and baked beans. Occasionally he stole something from Mrs Tiwari, although he swore to himself he'd pay her back when he could. But even that was getting fraught – the fragrant old woman grimly following him around the shop every time he came in. He couldn't face going on the dole again. Down at the Social Welfare with the terrible little cubicles, the pink carpet walls, the waiting-room banter, the cama-raderie of defiance and shame. The time was coming when it would have to be done: a close encounter, of the parental kind.

The time came. He couldn't pay his bills or his rent. His clothes were wearing out. He couldn't even pay for the bus. He rang his mother and arranged to meet her in a café in the city. He walked and got there on time to find that she wasn't there and he sat tensely waving away the waiters, not daring to order anything in case she didn't turn up to pay for it.

Dot Klein arrived, wearing one of her ankle-length blanket skirts and lace-up brown boots, her little hair-helmet slicked down over her small head. Around her neck she had slung a large box-shaped camera: one of her props. He asked her, smiling his pointy smile – and thinking of Klint Steel's aerial – whether the camera actually *worked*. Dot returned a fond glare of reproach before launching into an elaborate maternal pantomime.

'Darling,' she mimed, poking him in the ribs, holding him at arm's length to inspect him, shaking him as if he were a puppy. '*Darling. Look* at you. Come home. To be *fed*.' She beamed sternly through the thick specs.

He played with the menu. Oi. Enough small talk. 'Hungry?' he hinted. He knew now that it was going to be all right. It was going to be OK.

He enjoyed talking to her. He told her about his novel, how he was changing it around, reordering it, making it better and richer all the time. He was even – and here he paused and stared glazedly at his salad, entertaining the idea properly for the first time – he was even thinking about changing the title of his book. When he'd started out it had been *The Hard Men*, a vibrant, angrily honest, throbbing tale of the gutter (here Marcus impatiently pushed away a mental image of Maria, laughing), about Connick Street, about drugs, about Mike and Mike, about life in the tumbledown chaos of the squalid house. But the subject matter was getting away from him now, it had expanded like a colourful joke snake-on-a-spring and he grappled with it day after day, and couldn't stuff it back in its box. He grappled, he reordered, he added and deleted, he smoked and sighed and typed, and somehow the thing sprang away, and the more he couldn't force it to be what he'd set out to make it, the more he loved it, and thought of it as something mysterious and strange, something alive. The joke snake. Was it just that he no longer wanted the box? Maria Wallis. Wiremu Ihaka. Leon Pavel. They weren't at Connick Street. And neither was Chrissie. Marcus heaved a deep sigh and ate steadily on, consuming an indecent amount while the hyperactive Dot sat grandly ordering more food and pushing more wine at him and shouting on about the gallery and her camera work and your father, how I struggle to keep him in line, and him so secretive, never giving anything away. His ferocious, acidic little mother, talking non-stop, puffing energetically on her cigarette. She hadn't changed. Feeling a surge of gratitude and warmth towards his diminutive parent, Marcus suppressed it immediately and frowningly demanded more wine. Then, clearing his throat in a manly way, he brought the conversation, as subtly as he could, around to the delicate subject of money.

He came away with a cheque so large he felt shocked. Tearful even. Dot's family were wealthy. They owned property. And Uncle Friedrich had died recently, and Aunt Miriam the year before. Childlessly. His mother ran through the list of the family dead, smiling wryly, shooting cigarette smoke out of her mouth in short puffs.

'Fuck,' he said, when he saw the cheque she was writing out. 'Are you sure?'

'Of course. Hopeless darling boy. We want you to have it, your father and I. Finish your novel. Buy yourself some *shoes*.' She talked on, sentimentally.

He went on writing. He felt organised, coherent. He tidied and cleaned his room every day, and the bareness of it pleased him. He was venturing less and less into the kitchen and sitting room at Connick Street, preferring (like the deft and silent Annihilator) to come and go through the balcony window. Often he ate at the café down the road where Chrissie used to work, and after his meal he would sit there and remember her walking around the tables all serious-eyed, shaking her thin wrists above the order pad as if taking inept aim with the pen before putting it to paper, frowning and glaring at him, daring him to laugh. The current waitress was plump and red-haired and insinuating. She pretended to be made uneasy by his absent-minded staring, and when he realised that she thought he had been ogling her he was embarrassed and stayed away for a while.

One afternoon when he was in a frenzy of writing Mike and Brendelia started a low-level fight. Just bickering at first, and aggressive observations about each other's failings and omissions. I hate the way you, and do you really have to, and it's so disgusting when you. Marcus was writing about Chrissie. He closed his door and blocked his ears with rolled-up paper.

By five o'clock the hostilities had escalated into a screaming row and by nightfall Mike had thrown all Brendelia's possessions out the kitchen window into the gully and Brendelia had taken to Mike's car with a brick, and the neighbours finally lost patience and called the police.

Once again Marcus stood to attention at the door of his room while a squad of policemen marched through the house. After Mike had been bandaged up and taken away to the Refuge for safety and Brendelia had been thrown in the tank for the night to cool off the house settled down again for the evening. But Marcus couldn't concentrate. He'd got some material out of it. Some dialogue: Cunt. Fucking cunt. You're just a *cunt*. Etcetera. But he was impatient. He had to face it (face it! he told himself sternly): things had changed. He wanted more than the hard men in the novel now. Much more. Chrissie and Maria had got into it. He'd put himself in it, too. And even that wasn't enough. He would write about the three of them, and Leon. And Wiremu Ihaka too.

It's hard all over. One night when he was down at the wharf eating his takeaways the thought came to him. It wasn't only the Connick Streeters who led interesting lives. *Life* was occurring all over town. Pleased with the possibilities, the licence in this idea, impressed by the lack of resistance with which his writer-self absorbed it, he finished his chips, went home and experimentally crossed out the title on his manuscript. *The Hard Men* . . . After a while he wrote it in again. He doodled on the page. Under the scribblings and patterns he had drawn he wrote *Quays*. Then *Quay Street*. Then crossed it all out again, and so on.

Marcus walked warily out into the hallway on the morning after Mike and Brendelia's domestic and observed immediately that most of the sepia wallpaper had been pulled from the wall. By Mike, no doubt, clawing at the wall as Brendelia dragged him down the hall. In addition, the phone had been ripped out of the wall and thrown down into the gully. Now Marcus paused, lifted his feet and cautiously inspected his soles. Under his socks the carpet was saturated with a sticky and malodorous substance. Without inspecting any further he tiptoed back to his room, fed the Silken, changed his socks, picked up his jacket and exited through the bedroom window.

He went to buy a *Herald* from Mrs Tiwari, noticing how she sprang to attention when he came into the shop and how, as he browsed at the magazine stand, she seemed to exchange fierce nods and winks with an invisible person at the back of the shop. At the counter she snatched the money from him, glaring and bristling. He ignored her. Some people. (Clearly obsessed with money.) Rustling his paper he sauntered from the shop.

He found a park bench in the sun, lit a cigarette and turned to the property section. He had made a decision last night, looking on with the other residents as the titanic Brendelia was wrestled past them in a headlock and thrown bodily into the van. It was time to leave Connick Street. Finish the novel in peace, then think about leaving the country. London . . . He pursed his lips and ran his half-closed eyes down the column of ads, circling some with a red pen. Parnell, perhaps. A nice one-bedroom . . . Why not?

That afternoon he typed fast for an hour, until gradually the pace of his writing slowed. He stopped and read through what he had written. He drew heavily on his cigarette and stared fiercely out of the window. He read what he had written again. Yes, it was true. The time had come, the point had been reached. There was no going back on it now: he was going to have to get in contact with Maria.

Mike had retrieved the phone from the gully and reconnected it. To Marcus's surprise it worked. Watched closely by the Annihilator Marcus dragged out the phone book and looked up the number for Quinn St John.

He stroked the cat's arched back and stared at the damp ruin of the sepia wall. Welcome to Quinn St John Trisha speaking how can I help you? sang the operator, insinuatingly, as if he were ringing to order a pizza, or a masseuse. He asked for Maria Wallis. And got Clairene. Welcome to Commercial Property Clairene speaking how can I help you? He asked for Maria. And got a man. Flup Peeks-Berlyn? the voice announced, delicately, apologetically. Sighing, Marcus asked for Maria. The phone rang for a long time. And then she answered. Hurriedly, as if she'd snatched up the phone. As if he hadn't spent minutes waiting while the call was aimed at her and rebuffed, diverted, electronically fended off.

'Maria Wallis?'

'It's me,' he said.

'Oh?' she replied, without hesitating. He heard her sigh, a neutral sound. No indrawn breath. No faint shriek of pleasure and excitement. Surprised and disappointed, he pressed on. 'Can you talk?'

'Sure.'

'Do you want to meet me somewhere? Today? I . . .'

'Yeah. Why not.'

'After work?'

'Where?'

'My place,' he said. She hung up.

He went back into his room and tidied it, then sat down at his typewriter again. He stared at the keys, began to write, then changed his mind. He looked out the window and watched the sinewy Annihilator stalking a blackbird on the lawn. He turned back to the keys, lifted his hands and then sat back and shook his head. First things first. He put his manuscript away. Taking the property section of the *Herald* he went back to the phone and began ringing to inquire about one-bedroom flats.

At six thirty she knocked on the door. He was so pleased to see her it surprised him. He greeted her with a kiss on the cheek, noticing that she looked rather strange. She was pale and puffy and unhealthy, as if she had been indoors for a year.

'You're looking well.' He grinned slyly, before he could stop himself.

'I've been living on onion sea dogs and cigarettes.'

'That'll be it. I've been leading rather a healthy life myself. Long walks. Big meals. No drugs.'

'What's happened to your room?' She looked wonderingly around the pin-neat cell. 'Drug raid?'

'Yeah. Bastards. They took everything.'

He felt around under his bed and brought out a bottle of red wine. Then he ushered her into his chair, uncorked it and poured her out a glass. 'Did you miss me?' he asked.

'No.'

There was a dangerous note in her voice. He stared at her for a moment, feeling uncomfortable. Then he said quickly, 'I've missed you. And I've been so preoccupied. I had these problems, with Chrissie, with money. But that's all over now. And I wanted to see you. I wanted to talk.'

She sipped her wine and looked at him carefully. She lit a cigarette. She looked odd, brittle, intense. He carried on with difficulty. 'There are things you've never told me about.'

'About what?'

'What it was like. You know. When he got . . . um . . . run over.'

'Leon?' Her eyes were icy.

He pressed on. 'And what he was like. And afterwards, what happened. The police. And where you've been. What you've been doing. And Wiremu Ihaka. His flat . . .'

She narrowed her eyes, her wine glass poised at her lips, and he felt the force of her scrutiny.

'What do you want to know about Wiremu? That he's twenty stone? That his family are northern cannabis farmers. That he says *nuse* instead of *use* . . .'

'I just wanted to talk. I've been lonely. I've been wondering how you were getting on. All I want to do is talk.' Humbly he leaned his cold face against her cheek, and to his surprise he found that what he was saying was true. 'I talked to my mother recently,' he added.

'Oh?'

'It gave me a sort of appetite.'

'What for?' Maria inspected her fingernails with an air of faint contempt.

'For people who understand what I'm saying.'

He glanced sideways into her face and saw her smile quickly and unwillingly, with involuntary warmth. With amusement too. He poked her in the ribs, encouraged.

'More wine? Where are you living?'

'I spend a lot of time with Wiremu. In K. Road.'

'Jesus. That's so . . . seedy.'

She gave him a strange, unhappy look. 'Seedy but safe.'

'Safe? Living with that monster?'

'He's my monster.'

'You mean you can control him? Like you're some sort of *mahout*?'

She laughed angrily. 'I mean he's my friend. My *friend*.'

'But how can you stand it? Isn't it squalid up there? What are you doing to yourself?'

The Annihilator leapt in through the open window. Maria jumped. Wine slopped over her hand.

'What've you been doing to *your*self?' she retorted coldly. They sat silently for a second while the cat wove around the legs of the chairs, purring richly.

'Tell me what you do at Wiremu's.'

'We watch videos. We listen to music. We . . .' She broke off and stared at him. She looked stricken suddenly.

He said, 'Will you come with me tonight? I've got some money now. I thought we could go out for a curry or something.'

She accepted the invitation. Thoughtfully pushing the hair out of her eyes, leaning forward in her chair to run a hand over the cat's knobbly spine. Inwardly jubilant and relieved, Marcus tidied his room quickly and tipped cat biscuits into the saucer on the floor. But he could feel her watching him. The old challenging light in her eyes. He kept his back to her, busying himself for the moment with his few chores. After a while, she said in a voice laced with a certain intelligent menace, 'And how are you getting on with your *novel*, Marcus?'

He straightened up hurriedly. 'Oh, it's fine. Excellent. Littered with corpses . . .' He stopped himself. She was sitting forward in the chair looking at him as intently and beadily as a bird.

Then she smiled, and her expression was equal parts wicked understanding and grief. She held the wine glass in both hands and looked up at him, nodding slowly.

'Littered with our dead,' she said.

In the early hours of the morning in an expensive restaurant in Parnell Marcus sat in the yellow glow of the ornate lamp and studied Maria's face. Everything registered in it – she had no mask. Waiters splashed into the conversation, breaking her expression into ripples of awkward shyness. The wine and food coloured her cheeks and the company gave her a guilty, greedy look, as if she had broken into a cake shop and was bingeing on the spoils. She put her hand over her mouth and laughed, giving the impression of desperate fleeting glee. She had become even more nervous, more extreme, as if this meal were her last, as if she expected to be taken out afterwards and shot.

Watching her, the thought occurred to him, with a thrill of private adrenaline, that if he took her home and got her into bed she would behave as if the *sex* were her very last. Delirium. *Extravaganza*.

They had been talking for hours. She had talked and talked and so had he. Marcus felt the old luxurious sense of being understood. It was a dangerous, seductive luxury. He felt as if she could see right into his soul. He enjoyed the feeling, but it made him feel vulnerable, too. Exposed. But she was preoccupied now, talking about Leon and Quinn St John and Giles Speer and Wiremu Ihaka, and fear and grief (or non-grief, since she said she had never cried over her dead friend, she had gone very strange and mad instead). Grief (or non-grief and madness) had given her her new intensity, her air of last-fuck-on-earth desperation (she would fuck you like there was no tomorrow) and she had an aura of shame about her now, too, the shame of the guilty, the winged, the condemned, that made him feel as if she would be astonishingly dirty and lawless in bed.

She gazed around the tables. 'You said we were a folie à deux. Leon and I.'

'Did I?'

'I suppose we were, at first. For years. But I started to want something else too. I went looking for things. I wanted things . . .'

He stared at her, disconcerted. 'What things?'

'You. Sex. *Life*.'

Marcus studied the bill distractedly and took out his tattered cheque book. Look at that. One hundred and one fucking dollars, exactly. Carefully he wrote the amount on the cheque, *One hundred and one fucking dollars*. He showed her. She laughed and said, you're not going to give it to them like *that*, and put her nervous hand over her mouth again. He left the cheque on the table, got up, took her by the hand and towed her out into the warm black windy night.

They found a taxi, got in the back and he got half over the top of her and put his hands everywhere, practically clawing at her he wanted her so urgently, so much, and she began clawing and mauling him back so that by the time the taxi reached Connick Street they were breathless and scratched and half unbuttoned and the taxi driver, rigid with furious Moslem disapproval, threw the change at them and roared away into the night so as not to see them staggering and pawing and unzipping their way into the house.

While they were doing it on the bed and on the floor and up against the wall, while the bed squeaked and groaned and creaked and the workmen's orange lights flashed, and the stripes from the blinds fell in black bars across the floor, the Silken Annihilator, watching silently in the shadows, blinked his cold golden eyes and, with a dry tongue and a dry rasp, neatly licked one dainty delicate paw.

15.

Maria woke in the morning with no idea where she was, until a lithe shadow wriggled its way under the blind, slid front paws first down the wall and landed silently by the empty milk saucer. The Annihilator blinked at her accusingly, opened his mouth and gave a series of urgent feline croaks and chirps. His wiry tail thrashed.

Maria pulled up the blind and poured some cat food into the saucer. Then she tiptoed to the bathroom and stepped into the shower with its alternate trickles of scalding and freezing water.

Back in the bedroom the light was all dusty and golden with the morning sun and Marcus was sitting alertly up in bed. He smiled broadly, with all his pointy little teeth.

'Are you going to come back later?'

'I might.'

'Do you want to?'

She didn't answer. He pulled his clothes on, shivering, and went over to his typewriter. He inspected the page stuck in it. 'I hope you come back. I wish you would.'

He looked her straight in the eye humbly, beseechingly, and he was usually so effortlessly hard and ironic that vulnerability and sincerity, when they made an appearance in his face, had an extra-ordinarily touching effect.

Maria smiled around the sunny room. Then she looked at him steadily. 'I don't care,' she said.

'What?'

'I don't care.' She picked up her coat and went smoothly out of the room. He followed her to the front door. 'Wait a minute. Are you going? What don't you care about?'

'You.'

Maria was summoned to Giles Speer's office as soon as she arrived at work.

'Come in, Maria.' Ms Klara Leather delivered the most brief and vicious of smiles. Maria entered Giles Speer's office and sat down at a round table. Ms Leather opened a cardboard file. Maria waited. She caught sight of her reflection in the brown mirror glass, and automatically smoothed down a stray strand of hair. Outside the door the energetic Clairene wafted back and forth with a file in her hand, waiting.

The lift pinged and they heard the scrape and thump of Speerish footwear in the hall. Looking even more put-upon than usual, his fringe of hair hanging wispily over his eyes and his shoulders bowed, Giles Speer skated slowly into view, braked, sidled into the secretarial bay and spoke in a hushed monotone to Clairene. She nodded and stalked off along the hall, casting a spiteful glance over her shoulder.

Impatiently Ms Leather tapped her nails on the table but Giles Speer remained silently in the secretarial bay for some minutes, until Ms Leather tired of tapping and sighing and looking at her watch and put her head around the door. 'Giles? Are we . . .?' she hinted. He coughed and mumbled apologetically and rolled himself around the door frame. He gave Maria a ghostly look. Ms Leather smiled.

'Shall we begin?' she said. Giles Speer removed some files from his chair and sat down heavily. The adjustable seat-back readjusted itself with a crack and he lurched backwards, flinging his arm out and scattering a pile of files on to the floor. Scrabbling to right himself, he kicked the leg of his desk and pulled his telephone cord out of the wall. When he had untangled and replugged the phone, and pushed his chair upright, and picked the battered files up off the floor, Ms Leather gave him a frosty nod, took the cardboard folder in her hands and drily addressed Maria. We're here to discuss progress since our last meeting. *Your* progress. A quick perusal of your file tells us that progress per se has not been made. To go back.

And to be candid. Our last encounter was most unhelpful, was it not. Issues were addressed by ourselves, but the party was not come to by yourself. Your lack of attention confirmed most of our current concerns. You did not seem to appreciate or even take in the seriousness of the situation. Now here we find ourselves today in a similar position, although appreciably worse . . . *Giles*! The partner, who had twisted his arm behind his neck and was now unhappily massaging the top of his head from behind, jumped to and sat up, apologising. He picked an unrelated file off the desk and jiggled it. Papers spewed on to the desk. He nodded vigorously.

Klara Leather leaned on sharp elbows over the table. To continue. Enlighten us. How many fees do you expect to bill? Do you know the state of your budget? Let's approach it this way. How many files are you currently *working* on? Maria glanced out of the window. She saw a seagull hovering in an updraught, mutely calling. The sky was flat as metal. Blue light out there. Sea light. Four? Four files. She gestured vaguely. But possibly three.

Possibly *three*. Scandalised, Ms Leather repeated the words and slammed down the file, shaking her head, resting her case. Is there nothing you want to say? Giles Speer held his forehead with the tips of his fingers and sighed and looked down. Ms Leather resumed. We need hardly tell you where we have to go from here. The options have narrowed. There is only one course for you to follow: *find yourself another job*. Relishing this last line Ms Leather repeated it for emphasis, tapping the shiny table with her pen in time with the words.

Maria reeled. The words were expected – she had been waiting for them – but they were so brutal, heard aloud like that in the brightly humming office air. She realised now, suddenly, with absolute clarity, the scale and the seriousness of what had happened. She felt tears rush to her eyes and looked at Giles Speer, looking for something, some communication or clue. But he sat with his head in his hands.

So this is where it ends, Maria thought. I really *did* let go. I just didn't want to hang on to anything any more. Because things couldn't carry on as usual, the world couldn't remain unchanged. The dead are buried, the world marches on – I couldn't stomach it any more. So I stopped, and let the world go on.

No more Quinn St John, she thought. No more Giles Speer. Mr Giles Speer: I can still see you now, skiing away down the hall, hitching up the back of your trousers, rubbing cake crumbs into your hair.

Maria stood up and tossed the cardboard file down on the desk. She turned to Ms Klara Leather and said, 'Ms Leather, I've been sitting in that office for months. I don't know what took you so long. I can't imagine what took you so *long*.'

To lie back, and let it all slide away – there's nothing simpler. It just takes a bit of patience and perseverance, a bit of time. Some dead time, drawing doodles on the notepad, watching changes in the moving sky. Not coming in, coming in late, not bothering to answer the phone. Not even talking, after a while. A bit of time for people to notice and call you in and ask you to explain. How can you behave this way? Why don't you explain? Don't you know what will happen if you carry on this way?

You will be left with nothing. Your whole life will disappear. See how it happens, slowly, inexorably. Stopping in the great whirlwind of Quinn St John, with its deadlines and budgets and schedules and rules, just stopping in the middle of it all until everything falls away. All torn down. Torn down.

Maria, carrying a cardboard box of office things, walked for the last time through the bright mall. Past mirrors, past colourful awnings and pungent food stands, threading her way through the cordoned clusters of tables and chairs. Through coffee smell and burger smell, through bright neon light. Faint, blinking, papery, watched and watching in mirrors, Maria moved through the sharp and bright light. Goodbye Quinn St John. Her office was stripped, the name tag ripped brutally from the door. All her things – stationery, a coffee mug, some books – in the box in her hands.

And the crowds were thicker now, pushing around her, and she jostled and bumped and shouldered on, and came out on the open side of the mall high up, where the wind roared over the balcony rail, whipping and cracking the gaudy banners, and the streets were a wriggling mass far below. She leaned into the wind to reach the concrete rail.

High wind. High sky. Up here under the sky the city was land-scape, territory, nothing more. Cliffs, canyons, valleys, rifts. And all the animals down there, moving, scurrying, meeting and parting in lanes, fissures, tunnels and grooves. *I dreamed I flew over a red desert. Place of hard light, vast cliffs, the sand-sliding dunes. Everything gone, every person left behind.*

She leaned on the rail. High sky. She raised her face to the bright light. Look at it. Not a cloud up there in the chemical blue. The sky is a splashless pool. Dive in.

She put the box down on a bench. She closed her eyes. Life moved all around her. Noise. Sunlight. Footsteps, voices, traffic, the wind. The rushing roaring of the wind in her face. Air. Hot light. Noise.

Maria opened her eyes and smiled suddenly, with clear intensity. She looked out over the concrete canyon and saw on the great flat roof of the condemned building opposite the demolition men load-ing rubbish sacks at the edge of the roof, stacking them and then hurling them on to the building site below. Down curved the next sack, spinning, unravelling, slowly spewing its bright contents, until it juddered and opened up like a flower across the strewn clay floor of the site, the delayed sound reverberating up the mirrored walls, the white bombs raining down on the floor of the valley of glass. Down there in the dust, beyond the cordon, the white-faced ants scurried and scattered, parted and met.

Maria left the cardboard box where it was, on the wooden bench. She walked back into the mall and as she passed the foyer of Quinn St John she felt tiny, painful sensations prickling through her as if she'd tasted something sweet or sour or sharp, or thrown open a curtain to bright light, or jumped off after sitting on a wall, and felt the jolt, the brutal shock of blood in numbed feet. Walking along, she felt increasingly possessed of a strange, secret energy, as if a channel had been opened to a store of voltage she had always pos-sessed, but had been cut off from, and walking past shoppers and strollers she had to fight to keep her face straight, so crooked it was becoming with the strain of not contorting into a shape that would seem to the people in the mall to be odd or extreme. She felt as if her hair must be spiking up with electricity, she felt tears come into her eyes.

She breathed in fiercely, and was struck in an instant with a sense of exquisite comedy, the comedy of the mall, of her private self in relation to it, of her barely contained intensity, her heightened state. Possessed of the shocking secret (and now it seemed so shocking that it was comical) – that of having just been *fired*, she felt solid and compact and acutely aware as she looked into the unknowing face of each passer-by. The mall around her was only physical now, only terrain through which she moved, stripped of its abstracts and intangibles, deprived of its rigidly governing force.

Maria prickled all over, as if a new layer of her skin were forming. She was full of sensation, she was richly and privately *alive*. She walked quickly out of the crowded mall, into the bright street, and turned in the direction of Karangahape Road.

Destruction. Creation. Only when it's all gone can it all begin again. Maria hurried up the last stretch of Queen Street and turned left at the top. At the takeaway bar she went into the alley and took the four keys from behind the beer crate. She climbed the dark stairs and unlocked the four deadlocks of the metal door.

As soon as she had unlocked the door and pulled it open she screwed up her nose at the waft of dank and dust, the sour reek of the rooms that were never properly aired or cleaned, that were never rid of the greasily poisonous updraught through the lightwell from the takeaway bar below.

In the bedroom Wiremu was a great mound under the quilt, snoring, muttering, reeking of cigarettes and all the other smells he had brought back with him from his working night at Quays: blood and beer and cannabis, and the sweat of hundreds of dancing bodies packed in close. It was noon and pale beams of light from behind the blind shone in through the drifting air. He usually went to bed around five or six and slept until two, and his only daytime hours, his hours of light, were in the late afternoon and early evening, which was why he was such a curious colour – where he should have been dark brown, he was brown-grey – and why his eyeballs strained and boiled with their startling intensity of scarlet.

He had tidied the room. The carpet was vacuumed, the ashtrays were emptied, the furniture was dusted and neat. It was only the air itself that he couldn't purify, his work-related odours mingling with the cheap sad neglected odour of the tumbledown building.

He had added a book to his shelf: *The Exorcist*, the fat paperback carefully propped up with the other two, and his CDs were stacked in tidy piles. She saw his tax return, neatly filled in with blue biro, and a photo of his Aunty Mei standing with stiff pride beside her gleaming Road Warrior.

He had dusted and arranged his possessions: his plastic shaving things, a large turquoise bottle of Savershave, a cheap pair of cracked sunglasses, a garish weight-lifting magazine. A free double-movie voucher for *Korg 2: The Wrath of Onan*. Some notes to himself on a piece of exercise book, in blue biro – she bent closer to look – *One sea dog only per day. Don't take the lift – walk. One joint a night Mon, Weds and weekends. Don't hit too hard in skull.*

In a cream vase on the dressing-table he had arranged a bunch of pink and purple flowers, still in their polka-dot patterned cellophane and tied with a red ribbon, and a card next to them, with a picture of gambolling white kittens and a white horse. Maria opened the card. *For my dear Maria*, it said. *Love from Wi*.

He rolled over and propped himself up, blinking with the whole of his creased and fiery face, and the huge muscle on the inside of his arm twitched as he rested his cheek on his hand. He reached for his cigarettes and lit one, and rubbed his eyes and blew smoke out of the corner of his mouth. 'Where've you been?' he croaked. He cocked his head and squinted at her. The fine black hairs shone on his soft upper lip.

'At Marcus Klein's.'

He fell back and lay smoking and staring at the ceiling. '*That* nuseless fuck,' he said, rubbing his swollen hand. His eyelids were encrusted with scurf. A bad smell of flesh and damp sheets came out of the bed when he moved. He propped himself up again, the huge chest bulgingly rearranging itself under his T-shirt. He looked at her darkly and the blue tattoo stood out on his hand.

'Why've you been with *him*?'

'He's an old friend.'

'He's a cunt.'

'Well, it's my business. Isn't it.'

Wiremu glared at her for a moment, then shrugged. Sighing

heavily, he hauled himself out of bed, pulled his supersize sweat-pants over the great hammock of his underpants, and pushed his feet into a huge glowing pair of fluorescent trainers.

'Like my new shoes?' He put his hands together and looked side-ways at her. He wriggled his toes.

'They look . . . like life rafts.'

He laughed. 'I thought you'd like them.'

Then he shook his head and made a tsking noise. He sat down on the bed, and reached out and pulled her down to sit beside him. 'Maria. Look at me,' he said in a deep, soft voice, the voice so soothing it seemed to issue from the oleaginous depths of his bulk, so weighted with inertia that it only just made its way out through his big, soft lips into the air. She felt the rickety bed straining and sinking lower under their combined weight. She looked.

'I was worried when you didn't turn up last night. You've got to be careful. Look at me.' He squeezed her hand. Quickly she read-justed her gaze.

'I bought you some flowers,' he said in a humble voice, when she was staring into his streaked eyes with the required attention. 'I tidied the place, I polished it up. I was worried you mightn't come back. I want you to be happy here . . . I want you to move in.' He looked down.

'Something's happened,' Maria said. She looked at him carefully and cleared her throat.

'What?' He gripped her hand in alarm.

She stood up and went to the window. She could hardly say it. 'I've been . . . fired.'

He jerked his head with a high little laugh, shooting smoke out of his flared nostrils. 'Eh?'

'Yes. Today.' She closed her eyes. 'I knew it was coming. I . . .'

Wiremu relaxed and leaned back on the bed. He scratched his bristly head. He was silent for a moment. Then in a serious voice he said, 'Bummer. Rock bottom. Anyway. You can move in here, no worries. You can work if you want, or no need. I can get you a job at the club. Keep you busy. Bit of company . . .'

She turned back and said in a loud, excited, almost exalted voice, 'But don't you see? This is the *end*. Of everything. It's all over.'

Wiremu looked long and hard at her with compressed lips. Then he shook his head and began to laugh and snort and cough until the tears came to his eyes. 'I'm sorry, babe, your little face is just so serious. I thought it was going to be something really *bad*.'

Shaking his head and coughing and saying dear, oh dear under his ragged breath he lit another cigarette and then, with a clearing of the throat signifying that he was serious once more he went to the window, put his hand on the side of Maria's face, and looked deep into her eyes. 'You're a funny little person,' he said. 'Look at me. Maria. Look at me. Everyone gets fired *all the time*.'

She moved away from him. She put her hands up as if to ward him off. She spoke emphatically, energetically. Her face was glowing.

'Everything's going to change. Do you understand? This . . . this *time* is over.'

'This time?'

She regarded him for a moment, seemed about to say something and then changed her mind. She waved her hand impatiently. 'Things haven't been going very well, have they,' she muttered. She dismissed him with the flutter of her hand.

'But things've never been better. You and me. And look at my room. All our things. Remember what a dump it was?'

He stared at her, and she saw his face change as a flicker of doubt crossed it.

Maria turned away, opened the window. 'It stinks in here,' she said. Suddenly she sounded harassed, hounded. She glared out the window towards the west.

He came up behind her and put his arm gently around her shoulder. 'That's good. What you say. Change. Let the good times roll . . .'

He laughed lightly and passed his hand over his bristly head. But he could sense her moving further away with everything he said, he could feel irritation and impatience coming off her in waves. They stood silently for a moment, Wiremu sighing lugubriously and wondering how to continue, wriggling his feet in the luminous shoes and feeling her shifting from foot to foot under the weight of his arm. In a restrained voice she said, 'So . . .'

'So?'

'I have to go.'

He chuckled uneasily. 'What's the hurry? Where've you got to go? You've got no worries now. No more work. You can hang around with me now. We'll have much more fun . . .' He laughed again, falsely, and leaned on her heavier with his big arm.

'I've got a lot to do.' She pushed the arm off.

'Like what?'

'Like, everything. I mean,' and she faced him, her hands on her hips, 'I mean, for Christ's sake Wiremu, I've got nothing left. *Nothing*. I've lost everything, in quite a short space of time.' She began scrabbling round the room, picking her things up off the floor.

He was hurt, but he decided to take a stern tone with her. Calm her down. Pour the cold water. He said commandingly, 'Maria, you're just upset. You . . . you got fired. I'll make you a cup of tea. We'll watch a video . . .'

She straightened up and he was startled to see the patterns in her eyes rearrange themselves suddenly into hatred, rage, a real firestorm blazing up, just for a moment, so quickly that he thought afterwards that he must have been mistaken, because she had no reason to look at him like that, and he crossed his arms over his chest and stepped back one small step in consternation, the surprising thought coming to him that if there was one person in the world he *did* fear it was her, because she was unpredictable, because of the incomprehensible forces that flared in her eyes.

She said in a controlled voice, 'I'm going now but I'll come back later. OK?'

'Where are you going?'

She cleared her throat. Haughtily, 'I have to . . . there are formalities that you go through when you get fired. Loose ends to tie up.'

'Not where I come from. Swift kick in the arse and you're out the door.' He faked a jolly smile. 'You lawyers can't be that much different,' he added brutally.

He saw her wince, but she persisted, her voice patient and steady. 'I'll do a few administrative things and I'll see you later.'

He detected the patronising note and again he felt a shiver of fear, not of her this time, but of what was happening, of where he would be left if she didn't come back. He would be left here, and it would all become dirty again, because he would be alone. And all the things he had brought in to make the place homely for her, the pot plants, the books, the flowers, the linen, would become pointless, laughable, they would rot away. He saw himself a monster, living in the decayed debris of human things. Alone and imprisoned in the cartoon of his body. Avoided and feared. A fleeting vision, but painful enough to make her draw back at the way he was staring at her, at the way he was suddenly clenching his fists.

'Don't go yet, Maria,' he said hopelessly.

But she was backing away. He reached out, blindly, to catch hold of her, and she turned, her hands full of bits and pieces of clothing and hurried away down the hall. She faced him at the door for a moment and he thought that she had tears in her eyes. He reached out again and she shouted suddenly, agitatedly, 'Look, I can't . . . You must be joking. You must be *joking*.'

And then she turned and ran away from him down the stairs.

She hurried down the length of Queen Street, looking behind her to check that Wiremu wasn't following. At Queen Elizabeth Square she made a call from a phone booth. Then she found a taxi and gave the instruction, Seaview Road.

Leon's little house was unchanged except that there was a For Sale sign on the gate and the electronic sign with its rudely recurring instruction had been removed from the porch window. Maria sat down and waited in the afternoon sun on the rickety wooden porch.

Vic walked down the drive, pulling his reluctant dog on a leash. He said straightaway, 'I've been looking for you. To give you some of his things.'

She felt again the shock of recognition at the sight of his face, so similar to Leon's in shape and expression, and the voice that was Leon's too, despite the difference in weight and accent and age.

They opened the door to the old smells of spray paint and hairspray and glue. In the bedroom the dust lay thickly over the strewn dressing-table, over the wires and paints and circuit boards, over the pens and ashtrays and screwdrivers, and the painted television, and the telephone sculptures, and the stereo signed with Leon's signature: 'I'm not involved and I know absolutely NOTHING'.

Maria sat down on the bed and dust rose from the Hyatt quilt. The spray-painted pig smiled down from the door. Leon's colourful clothes hung from the wardrobe made of a broomstick strung on two chains.

The bright, silent room, in its unique detail, was so distinctly Leon's creation, so clearly an extension of himself, that Maria and Vic, as they cleared it, felt as if they were handling his corpse.

Maria took his bright red jacket. She took the painted stereo and the TV. She took some painted phones: the hundred-eyed phone, monster phones, hybrid phones, the phone with malevolent horns. She took one of the painted men too. The painted men were self-portraits, she could see that clearly now. They were shaped like men but they were really creatures – cartoonish, goblinish, garishly coloured. They lurched, they stared, they laughed. They were slim-waisted, shock-haired, alien.

As they were leaving Maria took a last look around the room. The colours – intense, weird and original – glowed at her. He was brilliant, hilarious, generous, wild, he was handsome, patrician and lawless. He was marked. Always marked. His treasures, stolen from the ordinary world and shaped into strange and wonderful things, would be packed into boxes and carried away. Then the house would be sold and painted white and the suburbs would close over it, leaving the street uniform again, the wooden houses ranged in silent rows across the bright lawns.

City of the dead.

On the driveway, Maria and Vic said good-bye.

'I'm going to go to Prague,' Vic said. 'I have family I can visit there . . . I think,' he added.

They embraced, and she looked for one last time into the face of her friend. And then he got into his car and waved once and drove away.

And everything was gone, then. Everything and everybody. Left behind.

16.

From his new kitchen window Marcus could see the mudflats, and at high tide on a bright day the bay was full and gorgeously blue, fringed with grey-green pohutukawas, water reflecting sky and sky reflecting water, all blue, blue, and at low tide and when it rained, the mudflats were melancholy grey, desolate, crossed by the driving squalls. He listened to the harsh cries of seagulls as they wheeled over the house.

Shallow water lay on the mud at low tide, and old tyres, under which the eels hid, and iron treasures – bicycle wheels, pipes, old drums caked with orange rust, and a broken signpost sticking out of the mud, drunkenly directing him out to sea. He could walk across the sewer pipe, all the way to Kepa Road. Where the pipe crossed the railway line he climbed on to the tracks, and walked along until he reached the tiny train station.

When it was hot the bank near where he walked on the pipe was jungly and steamy, and gave off a humid heat. When it rained the trees hung heavy over the clay banks, and there were slips where the cliffs were worn away by the running water.

He could watch the tide come in and go out, and it surprised him, the speed at which the water crossed the mud, quickly, busily, as if it were alive, nosing forward, filling the crab holes, carrying sticks and mangrove leaves with it, full of tiny bubbles and foam.

The view from his kitchen window changed every day – the endless combinations of water and weather. High tide, low tide, rain and sun, wind churning the water into muddy green, a morning when the bay was brimming with water, and made of glass.

He stood at the window making coffee, staring out. The kitchen, like the rest of the flat, was tiny but clean. His one-bedroom in Parnell. He lived at the top of a white stucco block. There was a large satellite dish on the roof, like an ear cocked up at space, he thought when he saw it, and a concrete courtyard full of wheelie bins and letterboxes and bits and pieces of detritus that other tenants had left behind. It was peeling and shabby, but charming, he thought.

The Annihilator had taken to the new flat after the initial shock of moving, after the necessary feline brawls that accompany the arrival of a new cat on the block, and had found that it could get out on to the roof and sleep up there in the sun, and that the strip of grass below was a good hunting ground, because the old lady below often threw her stale bread out the window, bringing hundreds of birds.

Marcus had a lucrative part-time job, with Shane Saloon.

One evening he sat over his typewriter with the Annihilator on his lap and typed into the night, effortfully through the dense, difficult hours of ten and eleven and twelve, over the threshold of midnight and down, coasting more freely, into the cool grey hours of one and two and three. On his lap the Annihilator twitched and chirped in feline dreams, of stalk and chase and kill.

When it was nearly four and the black night outside was fading to melancholy grey, Marcus paused to look out at the bay, and the light was grave grey-light, sad and stern. He watched the new day lighten the sky over the rooftops, then stretched his arms and cracked his fingers, and wrote on.

Dear Wiremu Ihaka, he typed (taking his tone from the solemn dawn). *One night I stood on Quay Street and saw the terrible blood on my hands. I wanted to die, I tried to die – and I thought you might kill me, at first. Instead you gave me everything you had. And in the end, when I had recovered myself, I went to your flat when you weren't there and removed all trace of myself from it, and walked out the metal door, and never returned. I cut you off (and you rang and wrote and shouted through the door, and I heard you, I heard all of it, and sent my silence back).*

And when I moved house (and you couldn't ring me at Quinn St John), I didn't hear from you any more. You could be dead now. Or in jail. In terrible Mount Eden, the great brown tattooed hands

reaching through the wooden slats. Or glaring down the queue out-
side some bad nightclub in the wasteland, squinting at the shrinking
punters with your terrifying pop-eyed glare. And you won't find me
in that part of the city, now that I'm doing all right again. Because
you don't hang around South Auckland, if all things in life are
going well.

The only story I heard about you was this, from Chrissie – I
met her walking in the street with her tanned car-salesman
boyfriend, and I didn't want to hear about you, I blocked my ears,
but she ignored my objections and chattered on – that after I left
you beat someone up very badly at Quays, and injured him seri-
ously, and that you were arrested for it, and lost your job.

I haven't forgotten, you see, even after all this time. I haven't
forgotten. But, in the end, the desire to live was hard to kill. I went
out looking for life, and found it, and everything began again.

It was half-past four. Marcus looked over what he'd written. He
made some quick changes, here and there. Maria, Leon, Wiremu,
Chrissie. And Marcus Klein.

He gathered the pages of his manuscript together, weighing the
solid block of them in his hands. Two hundred pages? Three? He
smoothed the stack of paper with his hand. Quay Street. *Quay*
Street. It was finished. It was over. It was done.

17.

He stood on the great open car park of the shopping mall, where the relentless sun had turned the asphalt sticky and the clear light shot painfully off the chrome of cars, and mothers struggling with shopping trolleys and pushchairs and baby seats talked loudly and laughed and flapped and strained as their intransigent offspring drifted and dispersed and absconded, or lay screamingly down, red-faced, nostrils streaming, small feet drumming on the scorching pavement, until they were peeled off and wrestled efficiently into the breathless oven of a waiting car. All hot, bright, teeming, loud, full of the sickly reek of fast food and ice cream, and the candyish colours of kiddy clothes, strollers, sweatclothes, trainers, all fluorescent and day-glo, and lines of plastic advertising banners smacking agitatedly in the hot wind. Across the steel hoarding high above him, against the intense blue, a giant man in a straw hat pushed a red wheelbarrow over a glowing lawn.

And in the dark brown glass tower (glass the colour of flat Coke) that rose out of the stacked blocks of the mall, somewhere inside the mass of steel struts and mirrored window that he stared up at now, shading his eyes against the harsh light and finding that the tower seemed to tilt forward, to fall towards him out of the waveless blue, inside the hushed corridors, in the whispering air, in the tinted light, Maria would be pausing, laying down her pen, and reaching for her phone.

'Timeless Furnishings,' she answered smartly. 'Maria speaking. How can I help?'

Marcus felt the greasy receiver sliding in his sweaty hand. 'When do you get off?' he said, exhaling noisily into the hot plastic.

*

They stood under the hoarding in the fierce afternoon light. She was gesturing, talking, he lounged against the hot concrete wall and eyed her with his usual insolent, half-smiling calm. Over the noise of the traffic she was saying, 'What a nerve. Putting us all in it.'

'I've put myself in it. My monstrous self.'

She handed him the block of pages in a plastic bag. *Quay Street*. She said, musing, 'It's a strange sort of conceit. I feel it sometimes too. Thinking that *you* make everything happen, that if you'd done things differently the whole world would be different. You think it was my fault that Leon died.'

'Isn't that what you thought? That it was your fault? And Wiremu . . .'

She said quickly, 'The file's closed. On Wiremu too.'

'And Chrissie. And . . . other things.'

'On all of them. I left everything. I left you. I left everything behind.'

'What about London? I want you to come.'

'Oh you *approve* of me now that I've been fired. Now that I'm as hopeless as you.'

'You'll get another job.'

She leaned against the wall and folded her arms. She closed her eyes against the lowering sun. 'The difference between you and I . . .' she began.

'Between you and me.'

'The difference between you and me . . .'

'Yes?'

'Is . . . Oh, forget it. I wanted ordinary things. I didn't want to cause any damage. And everything turned to horror.'

'You wanted an honest life.'

She smiled at him strangely. 'You make it sound stupid. You're a vampire. You use everything and convert it. Into something made up. By you.'

'A vampire?' He made a small gesture with his hand, of acceptance, complicity. He smiled with his pointy little teeth. 'But I haven't changed anything. I've just put down what happened.'

She said, 'Pretty unoriginal.' Then she said, 'I loved Leon . . .'

'I know.'

'But you. You *use* life. I don't think you love anyone.'

'I do. Come with me to London.'

'Don't be ridiculous. Leave me alone. You're turning into a stalker.'

'Come on. You can't go on working for *Timeless Furnishings*.'

She grinned quickly behind her hand – Maria's old involuntary spasm of amusement.

'It's only temporary, while I apply for jobs. I had to get *something* to pay the rent. I do the books. I get a sizeable discount on furniture and appliances.'

'Mmm. Terrific.' He watched her fight not to smile.

'Anyway,' and she pulled her bag up on to her shoulder, 'it's all over. Stop ringing me all the time. Good-bye.'

She walked quickly away through the crowds into the bright light of the street. She hesitated at the corner as if deciding which way to go, looked back briefly, then hitched up her bag and hurried on.

Marcus Klein waited, watching her for only a moment before following her, threading his way steadily through the bright mass, keeping pace with her, never losing her, never far behind.